VALENTINE TO FAITH

A Novel

by

Victoria Foyt

ISBN: 978-1-64786-455-2

Cover design by Carlos R. Segundo
Printed in the United States of America

www.SandDollarPress.com
www.ValentineToFaith.com

For my mother

and all the women who came before her

A FOOL'S PARADISE

Early communities were often established around a supply of Queen Conch shells, *Strombus gigas*, which provided meat, drinking cups, and, when modified, a trumpet with which to announce events. The wind instrument is made by cutting a hole in the spire and blowing the shell like a horn, adjusting pitch with the movement of one's hand in and out of the aperture; the deeper the hand, the lower the note. Because of its beauty, the conch has been valued as money, as well as for the rare pink pearls the mollusk produces and for the porcelain-like shell that can be carved into cameos.

SANIBEL ISLAND, FLORIDA

SPRING 1985

Angel was safe from the heart-wrenching reach of the sea. Why then did she have the feeling she was being watched?

Lacing her fingers around a steaming mug of coffee, she looked out the kitchen window to the yawning blue expanse of the Gulf of Mexico, which shimmered in the soft light of dawn. Along the shoreline a dozen or so shell collectors unknowingly stooped in homage to the Sea Goddess Yemayá. They had no idea, did they? Eager to possess precious shells to display in a clear glass lamp or curio cabinet, they were blithely ignorant of the dangers hidden in sea treasures. Angel was no landlubber; she knew better.

She had seen Yemayá make a grown man believe in mermaids and a righteous woman fall in love with the devil in disguise. Once the Sea Goddess entered your heart, you were doomed to suffer an endless cycle of love and longing, as predictable as the tide. Angel had banished her powerful influence long ago, lest she fall in love again. She might be lonely, but it was a bargain she could live with. *Forget it.*

She pushed a tray of cookies into the oven and set the timer. The wide overhang of the steep, hipped roof shaded her "Florida Cracker" bungalow and the air around it. Despite the baking oven, cool air entered through wide windows, carrying out the heat through a central cupola. Old-timey air conditioning, she called it.

The pink and aqua decor had yellowed with age over fourteen years, its spritely colors drained, like her, by rushed school mornings with her daughter, tedious homework projects, holiday pageants, menstrual cramps, and the annual spring search for the perfect party dress. On the kitchen bulletin board, littered with business cards, grocery lists, and coupons, hung a calendar with today's date circled and colored in a yellow smiley face: Friday, April 5th, the last day of school before the last spring break before Faith's high school graduation. Soon she would go to college—the first female in their line—and the pitiful cycle would end.

I did it. You and your lovesick spells couldn't stop me.

The Sea Goddess Yemayá paid her no mind. With sultry ease, soft rolling waves laid their frothy heads on the shore, startling a bind of sandpipers that scattered on spindly legs. The wide white stretch of sand lay still and waiting. In fact, the domed blue sky held nothing but the sun's proud crown and the promise of another picture-postcard spring day on the barrier island Angel called home.

And yet, experience had taught her it could all change in a minute. She worked hard to maintain a peaceful détente with the Sea Goddess, who held dominion over the dangerous watery expanse, while the cottage, however small, marked Angel's territory. A narrow strip of soft Florida sand skirted her home, providing the first line of defense. Bordering the beach, a wide, mucky tangle of low-lying tropical saw grass, sea grapes, and scattered palm trees created more distance. Set on pilings, the one-story house was built to weather hurricanes and the rising tide.

And yet, on a sudden breeze, came the seductive whisper she feared. *Come to me, my love.*

Wary, Angel stepped up to the mesh screen on the porch outside. The row of houses on either side sat quiet. A screech of gulls circled overhead on their morning hunt. Nothing unusual — until she caught sight of a pearly conch shell peeking from beneath a bright yellow hibiscus at the edge of her yard. Her body stiffened, numb as driftwood. *How in heaven's name?*

The intruder was no more than nine inches wide, maybe seven inches high, with a shiny rosy inner chamber and a ruffled lip like the flounce on a flamenco dancer's skirt. The Queen Conch that had dared venture onto Angel's side of the line was no ordinary shell but Yemayá's crown of the sea. *A very bad omen indeed.*

Oh, the Great Lady of the Sea had taunted her from time to time, sending the occasional salvo into her yard, nothing more threatening than a common Calico scallop or a delicate Paper Fig, in an obvious attempt to seduce her with the siren's song locked within every shell's chamber. Never had she dared to send such a formidable emissary.

Angel kicked off her slippers and slid into a worn pair of topsiders that sat by the screen door. Grabbing a gnarled garden rake, she tromped across the sand and hit the conch. *Whack!* It rolled halfway into the swamp and landed, not with its spire pointed at Angel, but with a flat accusing nub. She leaned in for a closer inspection, her heart beating high in her chest. For goodness sake, it was worse than she thought.

The spiral had been shorn; an inch-wide hole opened to the shell's inner channel. Someone had fashioned the shell into a trumpet, the kind Angel's people had used for generations to announce the news or suppertime, the kind with which Yemayá called to her beloved. *Come to me, my love.*

There had to be a rational explanation. Angel glanced two houses away to Maeapple's tidy back yard. Had her former neighbor left it behind as a remembrance? Angel dug into the spot where the conch had sat, searching for a note, to no avail.

The still, humid air seemed to mock her rising anxiety. Not a leaf fluttered; the gulf was as flat and shiny as glass. She gave the conch another sharp swat and it tipped into the muck behind a spray of red bromeliad cups. For good measure she began to smack it again, when a sharp voice stopped her mid-swing.

"Mom? What are you doing?"

Angel's breath caught, her pulse raced. A dozen explanations rose like a chaotic chorus in her head, none believable. She would have to lie; the truth was not an option.

She turned, perhaps too fast, and smiled, too enthusiastically. *A dead giveaway.* After all, she came from a family of liars and had decades of practice. And the lie flowed out of her mouth as easily as the beach rushing to meet the waves.

"I thought I saw a possum."

"Oh."

Her daughter stared past her, already uninterested, as she bit into a buttered bagel. The high-waisted, faded jeans emphasized her curvy figure while the white blouse set off her tawny skin. Dark curly hair, teased and sprayed, erupted around her oval face. The gleam of white teeth, a sparkle in her emerald eyes, and a dewy freshness gave the impression she was lit from within.

Angel gulped in the fresh briny air. "You better hurry."

As she followed Faith inside, she cast a backward glance at the hidden Conch and shivered. It may have only been a chance encounter with a wayward sea object, but Angel knew, as she had always suspected, that the Sea Queen was biding her time, her long cold wet dark salty arms beckoning. *Come to me, my love.*

Angel checked on the cookies, welcoming the sting of heat and the yeasty aroma of chocolate oatmeal. *I did what was best. Forget it.*

Faith's back brushed the rattan stool at the kitchen counter before she hopped up to pour coffee. She gave her mother a pained look. Finally, slumping on to the seat, she said, "I don't have a date for prom. Bonnie's bringing her cousin Larry. He's a freshman at UT, a total geek."

Since elementary school, Faith had adored Bonnie Jacobson and envied her big family, despite the insult to Larry. All she had was Angel. Not even a father. Even now, Angel detected the old sadness. Unbidden came a memory of the day her little girl had realized she was different from the others.

Why don't I have a daddy?

Because he was brave and died fighting for our freedom in the war.

He's dead?

Yes. He loved you very much, Kiddo. Don't forget that.

For God's sake, this was no time to allow in the creeping hand of the past.

Angel lifted a letter from a pile of papers. The university's fine watermarked stationery with its red and gold crest promised greatness.

"Hey, look, Kiddo. It's time to send in the deposit."

Faith spread her elbows on the counter like brackets that kept her from spooling onto the floor.

"It's a lot of money," she said. "Like, I could go to a community college."

"What?" Angel said. "No. You worked hard for this. We worked hard."

Faith toyed with the letter, shuffling it on the counter. "Yeah. But…"

With a flourish Angel set a written bank check in front of her. Her accountant had suggested she put the college funds in Faith's name for tax purposes, and after eighteen years of scrimping and saving, she relished the triumphant moment.

"Don't worry, I have it all figured out," she said, tapping the check. "Just sign."

"Seriously, Mom—"

"Where is this coming from?"

"Forget it," Faith said, signing with sudden intensity.

She shot up like a spring, bouncing to her mother's side. Wrapping her arms around her, she burrowed her head onto her shoulder. Angel sensed a storm of tears rising.

"It's normal to be scared," she said, patting her back. "Don't worry. It'll be wonderful, everything we've dreamed of, you'll see."

Faith stepped away, her face flush, and nodded, encouraging either her mother or herself. She slung her book bag over her shoulder and hurried to the door, with Angel in tow.

"Have a good day, Kiddo."

Faith started the ancient Volkswagen, the Red Bug, and waved goodbye. As its industrious putter echoed down the street, Angel told herself everything was fine. She had escaped the past and succeeded with nothing more than a high school education, three hundred dollars, a discovered talent for writing, and a Big Fat Lie. Like a sailor who sights land after an arduous crossing, she could finally let her guard down.

Angel cranked open the jalousie windows in her office, letting in the morning air laced with sea spray, blooming jasmine and a hint of coconut oil from eager sunbathers. When she bought the house, she converted a large storage room and installed the windows with a view of the beach. This was her sanctuary.

The old rolling leather chair squeaked as she twisted it to face the Underwood on her desk. For some time she had intended to oil the chair and clean the typewriter keys and organize her cluttered desk. Yet once she was "in," and had pulled the delicate gossamer thread that gave flight to her imagination, she forgot about the mess, and so it remained.

She rolled a crisp sheet of paper with a carbon copy into the typewriter then paused to re-read the last page she'd written. Several sentences along, she clicked "in," and the story sprang to life in her mind's eye, when the loud burr of the desk phone interrupted.

"Hello?" Angel said, breathlessly.

A brisk woman's voice replied. "Mrs. Rose? Hold for Ms. Feinman."

"Oh, Iris," Angel said to no one as Muzak flooded the line. Billy Joel's *A New York State of Mind.* She'd never been to that great city but imagined all its denizens were as brusque and competent as her editor, Abby Feinman, and her secretary, Iris.

She moved the typewriter aside and spread out the pages of proofs for her latest manuscript. The set was thin—after all, it was a children's book. The colorful cover depicted the whimsical protagonist, Stella the Starfish, dancing on a moonlit beach in the arms of a handsome merman. *Stella and the Merman*, the seventh book in the series.

And seven, she recollected, was Yemayá's lucky number. Angel shook her head. How many times had she watched the Captain count out seven pieces of bait or cast the fishing rods at precisely seven in the morning?

Abby boomed into the line. "Well, Angel? Don't you love it?"

"Yes, I like it very much. The pictures are charming, as usual; the art department outdid themselves this—"

"Any edits? I hope not. I've already mailed out advance copies."

Angel looked at the page where she had circled two words in red. Why did Abby bother to ask for notes at this stage when she rarely allowed them? She was another type of goddess, a literary one, whose whims moved the tides of publishing. By sheer luck, she had sold the first *Stella* thirteen years ago. If it hadn't been for her, Angel might still be selling cheesecake at Bailey's.

"I do have a few minor changes," Angel said.

"You authors would tinker endlessly," Abby said. "I have a schedule to keep. Initial reaction has never been better; it'll be a best seller. You approve the proofs then?"

Did it really matter if Angel wrote "a" instead of "the"?

"They're fine," she said.

"Good," Abby said. "Return a signed copy right away. Let us know when you've booked some local events. We'll consign as usual."

"Thank you, I'm thrilled really."

"Don't mention it. We love Stella. What's the next one called?"

"*Stella's Homecoming.* She discovers she's entitled to a rare coral reef and travels home to claim it."

"Naturally, she hits a snag or two along the way. I'll expect a draft by August."

"Well, the words don't always flow on schedule."

"Are you kidding me? You're my Swiss clock. Nice chatting with you."

Angel once more faced the blank page, inviting and terrorizing as a calm sea at dawn. This was how she had clawed her way out of the past, and she began again, to create the future, word by word.

The shrill cries of small children chasing after the waves floated into Angel's bedroom, a sound that somehow never changed, year after year. Those innocent hearts flirted with danger, while their parents sat nearby, dazed by the hot press of sun, unaware that the claw of the sea might at any moment snatch their young away. Angel shook her head. One unfortunate encounter with a majestic conch and, already, she was given to brooding thoughts of Yemayá. *Do not let* Her *in.*

Tugging the bodice of her crepe sundress, she squinted at herself in the dresser mirror with dissatisfaction. Time had rounded her figure. She could see the growth lines where additional layers had spread, just like a mature shell. What did it matter? At age thirty-seven she was not looking for love; one heartbreaking pummeling was enough to last a lifetime. Besides, love was for those who had nothing to hide.

At least the coral color, dulled from countless washings, still set off her pale green eyes and olive skin. She ran a comb through her auburn hair, dashed on *Long Distance Coral* Lip Polish and a spray of *Charlie Blue* cologne. It was the best she could do.

Her brown leather sandals slapped the pine floorboards like a salsa rhythm as she hurried past the cedar wall lined with pictures of her and Faith and mementos of school accomplishments. Hung low on the wall, in a cheap black frame, was a faded polaroid of Angel and Faith's father taken by a hawker on Duval Street in front of Sloppy Joe's: Angel at eighteen in shorts and blouse, Santiago in his Che Guevara beret and fatigues. Rebel outcasts in love.

Just the one photo existed—because her husband had died in Vietnam. That was the story she told: Santiago had left her a single mother with no family on her side and the paternal line lost to the Cuban embargo. Nearly two decades later, she still felt a twinge of guilt whenever she passed the photo.

She slung her purse over her shoulder and angled the tray of cookies out the door. Most of the homes boasted a white driveway of crushed clamshells that sounded crunchy when driven over, a sound Angel found as painful as the squeal of a stuck porpoise. At great and, in her opinion, necessary expense, she had removed the shells soon after she had sold her second book and replaced it with brick pavers. Vigilance against Yemayá's dark power was crucial to her survival.

Angel hurried to her trusty Town & Country wagon that sat baking in the afternoon sun. She entered Middle Gulf Drive, heading west onto Casa Ybel. Hot steamy air blew through the car window, tangling round her like a clinging vine. A light film of perspiration beaded her forehead.

She wondered if the chocolate cookies would melt, recalling in a vivid flash her mother's disappointment one summer day as the icing dripped off a Bundt cake intended for her prayer group.

For goodness sake. That was how it started. One lousy conch shell invaded your yard and then began the parade of regrets and longing.

The out-of-town cars clogged Periwinkle Way, the narrow road into the East Village. Every year the tourist crowd increased, even after the winter snowbirds had gone home, and Angel pined for quieter times. Despite endless dialogue about balancing development and preservation, more fancy new houses sprang up each year as predictable and awful as scourges of summer mosquitoes.

Angel could have driven blind to Seaside Books, her favorite store on the island. The original owner had championed authors and bookworms. Five years ago she had passed it down to her glamorous daughter, who might have been more at home in a beauty salon. Nevertheless, Angel reminded herself that she had built her modest career on the generous shoulders of small booksellers such as Libby Belle.

As she approached the store, a gust of wind rattled its robin's-egg-blue-and-white awning. In the short time since she had left home, the quixotic tropical weather had changed dramatically; a train of dark clouds cabled across the horizon, boxing in the sun.

A door chime announced Angel's entrance, and as her eyes adjusted to the cluttered shadows, she caught a sudden movement among the book stacks. As a flash of lightning illuminated the store, Libby stepped into the aisle. She bore down on Angel, her white platform sandals thumping the tile floor, the polka dot halter dress barely holding in her ample cleavage. Thunder rumbled in the skies, followed by heavy rain drumming on the roof.

Angel froze, one hand clenching a copy of manuscript proofs, the other reaching for the door. As usual, Libby made her feel like a fish dangling at the end of a hook, flapping in the air, desperate to return to her natural habitat.

"Look who's here," Libby said, giving Angel a smug once-over, which undermined the compliment that followed. "And don't you look nice today."

In comparison to the blonde beauty, Angel felt like a touristy shell figurine of a girl, each piece glued at an uncomfortable angle, a pale imitation of female attractiveness.

"I, uh, thought you'd like to read the new *Stella*," Angel said.

Libby snatched it from her. "*Stella*, baby! I hear the cash register ringing."

She glided towards the back of the store, where a sales counter built from Florida Pine faced an open reading area. Behind the counter a door led to the storage area. On the wall above hung a fishing net populated with Sand Dollar shells and fake lobsters.

As Angel approached the counter, someone startled her. She turned to find Greg Goodwin, a local construction worker. Years of manual labor had given him a boyish trim that suited his perpetually youthful personality, though he had to be near forty. Perhaps the lack of children kept him young? Did that explain Angel's weariness?

"Hey, there, Angel," he said, smiling shyly from under a wave of brown hair. He held up two cookbooks. "It's Kim's birthday. Which one you think she'd like?"

His wife owned The Pelican, a popular eatery, and the last thing Angel figured she needed was another cookbook. But he looked eager to please.

"You're asking a writer to pick just one?" Angel said.

He laughed good-naturedly as he set the books on the counter. "Hadn't thought of that. I can't afford both."

She sidled close to examine the books. *"Chef Paul Prudhomme's Louisiana Kitchen* or *Better Homes and Gardens New Cookbook?"*

Libby slapped her hand on the red and white checkered cover of Better Homes and said, "Go with the gold standard, Greg."

His soft brown eyes questioned Angel, who shrugged. "Kim probably has *Better Homes*. She might want to try something new."

"She might."

"She can always exchange," Libby said, dazzling him with the kind of smile that melted men like candles in the thick of summer.

"Okay, sure," he said. "Can you wrap it?"

"Anything for you, handsome."

What did Angel care if this man-eating barracuda twisted him around her little finger?

"Kim's a lucky woman," she said.

"I'll say." Libby snorted as she tore a length of seashell-patterned paper from the roller. An uncomfortable silence descended over the trio. Outside, the storm raged on. The proprietress flashed her hot blue eyes at them. "Well, she is, isn't she?"

Big brawny Greg looked like a boater who has sprung a leak. "Um, yeah," he muttered.

"Tell her I said happy birthday, will you?" Angel said.

"Will do."

She drifted to the children's section, thrilled, as always, by the prominent display of the *Stella* series. She fingered the gold-lettering of her name on the cover: *Angel Rose.* At least Rose was a part of her name. What did it matter when Angel Rose del Corazón no longer existed?

She heard Greg say, "See ya," and the doorbell clanged in a rush of wind. She turned the corner in time to see Libby's hungry stare following him.

"Nice bones on that one," Libby said. Then, without missing a beat, she flipped open her datebook and suggested a book signing on the third Friday afternoon in June.

"That's fine," Angel said. "By the way, I was thinking of an engraved pen for Faith's graduation."

"I've got the perfect thing." She pulled out a thick, expensive-looking catalog. "The Cross Classic Century ballpoint in sterling silver comes in a smart presentation box. Twenty-five dollars."

"With engraving?"

"Five dollars more for three initials." She began filling out an order form. "F, and R…what's the middle initial?"

Angel hesitated, overcome with confusion. She flashed on Faith's mile-wide grin when her first published article appeared in *The Island Reporter*. *Some day I'll win a Pulitzer!* Did she dare taint this instrument of her daughter's future success with false initials?

"Too expensive?" the shopkeeper said. "You can think about it."

"No," Angel insisted. For heaven's sake, there was no turning back. "A journalist needs a good pen. It's Matilda, Faith Matilda Rose."

"Matilda, cute. F, M, R." She turned the form around for Angel's approval. "Sign here." Angel obliged and laid down the pen with a sigh. Libby appraised her, one plucked eyebrow cocked. "You're a mystery, Angel."

"Excuse me?"

"You're good-enough-looking in a natural sort of way." She raked her red-painted nails over her blond bob. "Why you stay cooped up in your house like old Miss Havisham, I'll never understand."

Angel stared at her, unnerved by the unexpected compliment.

"Maybe it's on account of Stella," Libby went on. "You've got your books to keep you company, and Faith, of course. Me, I've got the store, people coming and going. Women like us don't need a man, not really. Maybe you've got to need one bad enough to settle. Until one day you realize something is missing. I just hope it's not too late."

"I'm sure you'll get whomever you set your sights on, Libby."

"Oh, honey, I was talking about you. You've got to make an effort." She fanned the air. "Me, I've got plenty of mileage left."

Angel mumbled a thank you for the booking and made a quick retreat. As a stiff wind pelted her with mean raindrops the size of jellybeans, she recalled the Captain's terrified pronouncement when once they hit a squall at sea. *La Sirena está enojada.* Well, maybe the Mermaid Goddess was angry, because this was one hell of a storm.

The wind buffeted the car as Angel doubled back along Periwinkle Way, pumping the brakes through deep puddles. Tall petticoat palms bowed over the road like lithe dancers. The windshield wipers raced to keep pace with the torrent, blurring her view of an ominous world cast into fairy tale shadows.

She wanted to go home to escape not only the storm but also a visit to Maeapple's store. After all these years, Angel had managed to avoid many invitations to the Fancy Shell Shoppe; single parenthood was a handy excuse. But if the storm kept everyone away, who would show up for her neighbor's going away party?

Turning onto Palm Street, she was glad to see a decent number of cars in front of the store. What harm could one visit do, anyway? Scrounging in the back for a jacket or umbrella, she came up empty-handed and grabbed a copy of *The Islander* from the car floor. Holding the newspaper over her head, the tray of cookies angled under her arm, she ran for the shop, her sandals flipping mud onto the backs of her legs.

When Angel opened the door, the wind caught a hooped shell chime that hung in the entryway and sent it crashing to the ground, its pretty tinkle silenced. She stepped inside and, with a sigh, took in the broken pieces and the trail of cookies she had left in her path. Turning to face the waiting crowd, she caught her reflection in a large shell-framed mirror: her dress was soaked and the paper drooped round her face like a scarf, smearing it with black ink. Everyone was staring at her.

And everywhere were shells, and more shells, display boxes and shelves and tasteful curio cabinets crammed with many species, common and exotic. There were shell-themed boxes, picture frames, beach signs, door chimes, even a miniature shell tea set. The overall effect felt claustrophobic; bile rose in the back of her throat. Well, if she threw up, wouldn't that just complete the picture?

She took a step back, when Maeapple called to her from a chair at the center of the room. "Angel, how kind of you to come."

Angel threaded through the crowd as the party chatter gradually resumed. The old woman reached towards her with a soft hand and an affable smile that sent her crow's feet into a row of white ringlets.

"I was hoping to see you before I leave," she said, her watery eyes intent.

"Of course," Angel said, ashamed of her misgivings. She squeezed her hand. "You're cold, Mae."

"Don't expect I'll survive winter in Chicago. My daughter says you get used to it. We're at the Holiday Inn till tomorrow. We shipped a few boxes; most went to charity. A lifetime of belongings cannot fit into one small bedroom." She adjusted her shawl as she surveyed her guests. "I do my best to put a good face on it, but you and I know this is my going-to-die party. We're not afraid of the truth, are we, dear?"

Angel shook her head. Her neighbor had no idea what a liar she was. Angel had fooled her, just like everyone else.

It took all of her courage to say, "If there's anything I can do to help close the store, please let me know."

"No need. Luckily, I sold it, lock, stock, and barrel." She winked. "I'm not supposed to tell until the paperwork is complete. You know how word travels."

"You'll be missed." Until this moment, Angel hadn't realized how true it was.

"I had a good run." Maeapple pulled a white linen handkerchief from the cuff of her sweater and dotted her teary eyes.

Angel followed the movement of the handkerchief as the sleeve swallowed it once more. "We'll keep in touch," she said. "I promise."

The same promise she had given to Tilly when Angel fled with her baby; she had sounded equally earnest then. *Liar, she was a big liar.*

Hiding her emotions, she offered the sparse cookie tray. "I'm sorry, most of them fell in the rain."

"Won't I miss your cookies." She pointed to the back room. "Why don't you put them on a plate? The server should have tea any minute."

Angel started toward the back room when Maeapple stopped her. "I almost forgot." She offered a Queen Conch carved with a woman's profile, her long locks trailing over the flared lip of the shell. "This is for you."

As she accepted the gift, a knowing feeling stole over Angel. A quiver in her gut. An inexplicable knowingness. The way the precise word moved through Angel, traveling down her arms and fingers onto the page. The way the Captain sensed a big catch right before the fishing reel went *Zing!* He claimed Yemayá had spoken to him, while her mother Mary insisted the Holy Ghost had visited. Wherever the information came from, it was always right, and Angel knew without a doubt that her life would experience an irrevocable sea change.

She held out the cameo shell, hoping the giver would reconsider. "Are you sure you can part with it?"

A bittersweet smile etched Maeapple's face. "It pleases me to know you have it."

"Yes, well. It's beautiful, thank you."

It was simple sadness at the final parting from a friend; that was all. Angel tucked the shell under her arm and stepped away, as others commanded the hostess's attention. She edged through a curtain of cowrie shells that separated the back room. As the shells brushed against her body, she recalled Tilly's irascible voice as clearly as if they'd spoken that morning. *You got seawater in your veins, Kiddo.*

Unnerved, Angel tripped and fell against the edge of a wooden table, rattling teacups on a silver tray. She dropped the cookies and shell at her feet, reaching for her wounded thigh with a groan. A red blotch began to bloom on her dress.

She had not registered the man's presence; his deep voice startled her. "You're hurt," he said.

Angel's head jerked up. The server grabbed a cloth and doused it with club soda.

Leaning towards the hem of her dress, he hesitated. "May I?"

"Oh, what a mess I've made," she said.

"Nothing so dramatic it cannot be fixed."

In a daze she watched the stranger bend over her, his strong hands on her clothes. The scratchy sound of the cloth against her dress loomed loud in her mind as he rubbed the stain. His musky scent of bay rum and lime hit her with dizzying effect. Her gaze trailed the crease along his neck, the short dark hair that begged her touch. He was handsome enough to be threatening, yet lacked the arrogance of such men.

Angel stepped away. "It's fine, really."

As the dress fell to her knee, the waiter rummaged through a cabinet. "A plaster? Yes, here it is." He handed her a box of bandages.

"Oh, thank you." She turned away to cover the cut. "You have an accent."

"I was born in Germany," he said, his inviting brown eyes studying her. "Max Sussmann. And you are?"

"Angel Rose." She picked up the cookie tray. "Do you work on the mainland?"

"I have often." She sensed a conflict. Perhaps the catering business wasn't going so well. "I'll concentrate here now," he added, as he helped her gather the cookies from the floor.

An unlikely request escaped her lips; she had never hired help. "Perhaps you could assist with my daughter's graduation party. Nothing too big or expensive."

Max grinned as they rose to their feet; the small lines under his eyes touching the gray along his temples. The warm color in his suntanned cheeks deepened. She guessed his was in his late forties, at least ten years older than she.

"I'd be honored," he said. "From the elementary school?"

"Flattery won't earn you a bigger tip," Angel said, trying to hide her pleasure. "High school graduation."

"Congratulations. And no tip required."

Suddenly self-conscious, she wiped her dirty face with a cloth. She had no business hiring or flirting with this man. An invisible weight pressed against her chest, and she began to cough.

Max turned on the tap and handed her a glass. "Water?"

In only a few minutes time he had ministered to her needs in ways both common and tender. She could not remember the last time anyone had tended to her. The walls felt too close, the room suffocating.

"Yes, well, thanks for your help, Mr. Sussmann."

"Please, call me Max. May I call you Angel?"

"Of course," she said, retrieving the Queen Conch. "I should get back to the party."

"Rub it with milk and salt."

"Excuse me?"

"Milk and salt will remove the stain of blood. An old peasant remedy."

A sweep of unmistakable sorrow passed behind his eyes, vanishing in an instant. She fought the strong desire to lay her hand against his broad chest, while their eyes locked on each other's, the whole world fading away.

Without another word, she left the store, welcoming the pelting rain and the urgent need to navigate puddles. Turning the corner, she tossed the cameo conch into a trash bin. She hated to do it, but she simply couldn't give quarter to Yemayá, not even for a sweet friend. For heaven's sake, dangerous proximity to shells had left her as wobbly as a jellyfish.

A clean sea breeze limped through the house as if exhausted from the storm. As the kitchen stove ticked nine o'clock, Angel poured a glass of Chablis, hoping to numb a gnawing worry that grew worse by the minute. Faith had missed dinner again.

Angel's preoccupation overshadowed everything else, like the eclipse they'd experienced last spring—flowers closed their petals, dogs and birds cowered in hiding, the temperature dropped sharply, as all but that burning intensity fell into darkness. Now that she paused to reflect, she noticed a disturbing pattern of inconsistencies: a missed dentist's appointment, the half-done grocery shopping, a brand-new blouse lost. To sum it up, Faith had been unusually distracted of late.

As if she's in love? But there was no boy in the picture. Most likely, it was pre-graduation jitters, nothing more. Angel was looking for problems. If only she could have a cigarette, she might relax.

She opened the pantry, her fingers playing an absent-minded tattoo on the door as she stared at a box of Virginia Slims Lights taped above the cans of tuna fish. She ran a finger along the green and blue-gray stripes at the edge of the elegant box. *You've come a long way, baby.*

This was her fail-safe emergency system: If she had to run to the store when the urge struck, her resolve would dissipate by the time she found a pack of smokes. However, a box-at-hand allowed her time to contemplate her promise to quit, and calmly weigh the consequences—namely, her daughter's fury.

Even now, Angel's chest tightened with the recall of the pungent aroma, the genie-out-of-the-bottle smoke, and the numbing nicotine buzz. She forced herself to slam shut the cabinet door. For ten solid years, Angel had kept her promise, and for heaven's sake, she couldn't break it. Maybe once Faith left for college, but not now. There must be no distractions, no upsets.

She sought relief in Faith's sunny yellow room. Sitting on the fluffy chenille bedcover, she studied her mementos—the school yearbook on which

Faith had been co-editor, the journalism class photo outside the boxy white building of the *Miami Herald*, the scarlet, black, and gold pennant of the University of Tampa, its tip pointing to a bright future, Faith's photo at the college dormitory, taken during their tour last fall. Her coltish laugh had floated in the air. *So you can picture me here!*

Angel read these signs, just as she had once learned to read sea shells: external conditions revealed age or exposure to rough waves; knobs or spines indicated the mollusk had lived on a hard surface; a smooth shell meant it had burrowed into sand or mud; telltale breaks revealed predator attacks. The signs in Faith's room pointed to a happy childhood, didn't they?

As she stood to leave, she noticed a partial map on the desk, unfolded from the pages of *National Geographic*. A cold, knowing feeling stole over her and, even as she flipped open the magazine, she knew it was a map of Vietnam. Angel recognized Faith's handwriting: dates and names of battles dotted the map.

Over the years, whenever her inquisitive child had posed questions about her father—where exactly did he die? was he a POW? did he send letters home?—Angel had deflected her curiosity with a standard response: *It makes me sad to think about it.* Which was true. A truth built on a lie, but true, nonetheless.

Eventually, the questions stopped, although Angel suspected that they still haunted Faith on those rare occasions when she grew quiet and tugged into herself like a mollusk burrowing into its shell. Angel had been a desperate twenty-year-old when she invented the lie. How could she have anticipated that one day her adult daughter might seek details about her father? When Faith was older, perhaps married with children, and understood the sacrifice a mother makes, Angel would confess all. For now, nothing must get in the way of her success.

The screech of car brakes startled Angel out of a deep sleep. *Faith was home.* Angel glanced at the illuminated hands of the bedside clock—nothing good happened at two in the morning. The engine quit, its metallic ping echoing in the night, while she waited for her daughter's safe entry. Minutes passed as the night settled into its quiet rhythm. *What was taking her so long?*

Against her better judgment, Angel slipped into her robe and rushed into the living room. *No more curfews now that she was eighteen. That was the deal, remember?*

Light footsteps, not the usual hurried clunk, landed on the porch. Faith crept inside, just as Angel flipped on the light.

"Faith?"

"Mom. What are you doing up?" There it was, the defensiveness of the guilty.

"I could say the same." Immediately, she wanted to take it back. Her daughter's eyes flashed, like an angry marlin caught on the hook. Angel softened. "Are you all right, Kiddo?"

"You promised you wouldn't do this."

"I'm sorry. It's late; I was worried."

The overhead light caught the sun-streaked tips of Faith's curls. She held her hands by her sides, rubbing her fingertips together like tiny kindling sticks. Her mother recognized the anxious behavior—she was weighing a decision.

Quickly now, with forced conviction, Faith said, "I'm going away tomorrow."

"What?" Angel said.

"I need a break, okay? I'm going to Fort Myers for the weekend."

"What about the scholarship essay? It's due soon."

"Like, don't I always make my deadlines?"

"When did this come about?"

"It'll be fun."

"You don't sound very happy about it."

"Because you're having a cow. I'm eighteen. I'm an adult."

Angel sighed. "So you don't want me to ask who you're going with, where you're staying? You want me to just say, fine, see you later?"

Faith shrugged. "Lots of parents do."

Lots of parents had other children or husbands. Faith was all she had.

"At least tell me Bonnie's going?" Surely, a girls' trip was acceptable.

Faith threw up her hands. "Can't you just chill? You act like I'm some juvenile delinquent. It's not like I'm going to Miami, I'm just going to the beach."

With that, she stalked off, slamming her bedroom door behind her. From habit, Angel began preparing tea, a ritual they often enjoyed. In a minute she would ask Faith to join her. They would entertain a calm discussion about expectations and responsibility.

However, her idea vanished when Faith reappeared with a duffle bag in her hand.

"You're going now?" Angel said. "What were you going to do, sneak out in the middle of the night and not tell me?"

Faith rolled her eyes. "I was going to leave a note. You know I'm not going to call you every day from college, right? Can't you think of this as a trial run? I'll be back Sunday night." A small pleading quality tinged her voice. "Two days, that's not asking a lot."

As usual, her daughter had employed formidable intelligence and logic to argue her point. Perhaps a trip would get her mind off the upcoming milestones she would have to navigate as a fatherless girl.

"Do you need money?" Angel asked.

Faith's shoulders relaxed; she had won. "I've got tip money. Quit worrying."

"But if something happens…who ya gonna call?"

"Ghostbusters!"

The popular movie had spawned their playful patter: they were a ghost-busting team. And wasn't that the point, Angel thought, banishing ghosts?

"Promise?" she said.

Faith leaned over to kiss her check. "I promise."

"I'll miss you, Kiddo."

"You'll be fine."

However, deep dread filled Angel, as she followed her into the moonless night.

How could she let Faith venture out into the world without a lifeline? Despite years of discipline, the barred door to the past swung open. She blurted out the same warning her father had given her long ago.

"*No olvides quien eres.*"

Faith looked up from the driver's seat in surprise. "Say what?"

"I said, never forget who you are, in Spanish. When I was young my father took me to the beach—"

"Spanish?" Faith shook her head. Over the sputtering engine, she added, "It doesn't matter if you say it in Chinese, Mom. I know who I am and I know what I want, so you better get used to it." Then she shifted into gear and soon the dark shadows swallowed her. For heaven's sake, what would the Captain have thought of Angel's broken promise? *No olvides quien eres. I won't, Papi.* How could she expect Faith to remember what she never knew?

As Angel turned back to the cottage, the memory deepened, rolling over her like a furious wave that knocked you under. She recalled the sweep of the sea air against her young skin, the bounce in her knees as she stood on the pilot's pulpit of their fishing vessel, riding the mild chop, up and over the waves.

It was a hot spring day, beads of sweat bubbling on her skin, her cotton shirt sticking to her back, the endless squint against the sunrays reflecting off the water, which gave her a dull headache. She never complained; at age ten she had earned a trial privilege and was determined to win her place in the crew.

La Libertad was a forty-four foot fishing boat with twin engines, polished teak deck and fittings, and a fully outfitted cockpit. Sleek and rakish like the Captain, she possessed a magical air, and his reputation for landing big fish was legendary. The Corazón family lived and died by the sea. And Angel lived for Papi's smile of approval, anticipating his commands: de-ice the bait and prep the lures, show the landlubbers how to hold the rod.

On that memorable day, she learned that she was not the only liar in the family. When three simultaneous strikes hit, the lines ran out and the Captain shouted praise. *Yemayá es buena!*

Angel froze on the spot in the cockpit and looked up to the flybridge where he stood beaming. *Yemayá is good?* So personal, so intimate, so love-struck was this call that Angel suspected she had discovered something important.

She bided her time until they docked at Garrison Bight Marina. The happy passengers debarked with an ice chest packed with fish, and the first mate Palo sauntered off for his fill of beer. At last she sat beside the Captain on the sun-bleached seawall, guzzling Coca-Cola, their shorts smelling of bait, worn docksiders keeping time to the lazy lap of water. As the setting sun drifted into the bay, folding vibrant layers of peach light into the blue horizon, Angel began her interrogation.

Papi. If I ask you something, will you tell me the truth?

Cómo no, Hijita? Of course, little daughter. Which, in retrospect, seemed ironic, considering the prevalence of lies in their household. She even had heard him swear to her mother that he only spoke to Angel in good English, and never in that crass Spanglish, a mixture many Cuban immigrants used.

'Cause I was wondering who's Yemayá?

His feet stopped; his jaw tensed. She was onto something big. Just as he had taught her to reel in a whopper, letting out the line, tugging and pulling at each lull, she had to land a confession from him.

It's all right, Papi. I can keep a secret, I won't tell Mother.

He brushed a lock from her forehead, studying her. Her auburn hair resembled his curly mop, and her eyebrows curved like his into perpetual question marks. When it came to her eyes, green as the rich sea, he always said the Corazóns had lost that fight to the Pinders, her Grandmother Willow's maternal family.

Eh, you want the truth, Angelita?

She crossed her arms over her flat chest. *Go ahead. I can take it.*

He laughed, his deep voice bouncing against the wet walls. *Fuerte como tu madre.*

Was she strong like her mother?

Her father turned once more towards the sunset, his profile set in concentration. Minutes passed while Angel considered other lines of inquiry. Soon he began a soft singsong lament that felt both foreign and familiar: *Ven a mí, mi amor. Tu eres mío, todo para mi. No luches mas. Ven.* She caught the words, though the meaning eluded her: *Come to me, my love. You're mine, all mine. Give up the fight. Come.*

Finally, he slapped his thigh and fixed her with a grin. *Yemayá says it's time.*

I didn't hear anything.

He held a finger up, advising patience. *Paciencia, Hijita.*

He jumped onto the gunwale of our ship and disappeared inside the cabin as a light shower began, a cool balm on her sunburned skin. The wind picked up, rocking the ship in its slip like a cradle. The Captain reappeared with a bulging canvas bag slung over one shoulder. He jerked his head—*Vamos*—and they walked to the old Chevy truck.

What's in the bag, Papi? He kept the answer to himself.

They drove across town to the eastern side of the island with the *plink, plink* of raindrops on the cab. Except for a few locals, Rest Beach was deserted. The rain turned the pristine sand the color of gray cement. Hard waves crashed with abandon against the shore. A soft crescent moon rose in the darkening eastern sky.

Without explanation, the Captain plucked a handful of papery bougainvillea petals and slipped them into his shirt pocket. He dared her with a mischievous smile before he took off running. Shrieking with laughter, she kicked off her shoes and gave pursuit.

Breathless and happy, she flopped beside him at the high-water mark, where the sand cooled her feet. She never had seen him look so serious, not even on those rare occasions when he accompanied Mother to church. He sounded as reverent as the preacher in the thrall of his sermon, as he told her to pay attention.

Escuchés bien, Angelita. He rose to his feet and opened his muscular arms wide to the sea. *La Señora Yemayá rules the sea. She's the mother of all—nuestra madre.*

What about Mother?

He shook his head. *We come from the sea, Angel. Yemayá is our true mother—a powerful mermaid.*

Angel laughed then, and now, as she pictured her father against the backdrop of the gathering storm, his serious expression at odds with the nonsense he espoused. Out loud, she repeated her stunned reaction on that long ago day.

"A mermaid? A real one, Papi?"

His eyes shone as he explained his belief: Yemayá was a powerful, beautiful mermaid. *Una sirena ponderosa y hermosa. Long ago, I saw her from my father's boat riding the waves with the dolphins. She wore a crown of seashells. Her long hair looked like seaweed, but hermosa, very beautiful, eh? It covered her naked body. If you are lucky, she appears to you, Angel. She brings you big love. El amor grande.*

Before breasts and hips had colonized her girlish freedom, Angel could have cared less about Big Love. Nevertheless, she tried to understand.

How can a mermaid make you fall in love?

She rules the moon, eh? La luna makes men and women crazy with love. He patted Angel's head. *Some day you'll understand.*

What she understood left her dejected: Poor Papi couldn't save her. He was an idolatrous heathen and, like her, damned to hell. At least, come Judgment Day, she would have company.

She kicked the sand, her eyes downcast. *Mermaids aren't real, Papi.*

Ah, Hijita, I waited too long. Now you will know La Señora. He took out a sheet of paper and pencil from the bag. *Write down your wish, an important wish. Don't worry; only La Señora will see it.*

I don't want to.

You don't have a wish, eh, spoiled princessa? He tickled her ribs until, overcome with giggles, she ceded to his absurd request.

Váyate. He nodded towards White St. Pier. *Make your wish.*

What did it matter? Perhaps they'd create some silly memories to share in hell.

She felt his eyes on her as she walked to the end of the pier in the drizzle. Leaning against the wooden railing, shielding the paper, she stared out at the choppy water. No one had ever asked her what she wanted. She had no idea how to name the restless feeling that burned within. She only knew she was sick and tired of her lies and the Bible verses she parroted to appease her mother.

On that blustery day Angel realized she wanted to be free. But supposing this Yemayá was real and took her wish at face value, she might kill her because what's freer than being dead? She remembered her satisfaction when she came upon the exact wording: *I wish to be free and happy.*

She folded the piece of paper in half and pressed it neatly in half again, guarding her wish within. She stuffed the paper in her pocket and ran to the shoreline where dark clouds advanced like a zealous army on the move.

The Captain hacked a hairy coconut in half with his machete. *Whack!* He lifted the two halves to his mouth and sucked out the sweet juice. With his head thrown back, strong legs braced for balance, he looked half his age. He handed her a piece of rubbery coconut meat, which she chewed with effort.

Remember, use only fresh coconut. And always leave a piece for La Señora.

Sure, Papi.

He cleaned out the remainder of the meat, placing a piece in each coconut half. Then he paced along the edge of the water, carefully holding them as if they were precious vessels. He turned, his excitement contagious.

Here, Hijita, está bueno. He pointed to the auspicious spot.

Caught up in the excitement, Angel joined him. He handed her one half. *Put your wish inside.* For extra measure, she tucked it under the loose fibers. Then he sprinkled a handful of the bougainvillea petals on top.

A gift for the Great Lady, eh? If she accepts it, she grants your wish.

He set his shell just below the high tide mark. Feeling ridiculous but oddly hopeful, she did the same. As a wave rolled in, she held her breath. Alas, the water swept the sand and receded, leaving her pitiful offering in place. At her dubious look, the Captain professed confidence.

We must call Yemayá.

As he lifted a sawn-off Queen Conch from the bag, he softly repeated the sad song. *Ven a mí, mi amor. Tu eres mío, todo para mi. No luches mas. Ven.* He raised the cut spire to his lips and blew hard. A rich, haunting sound like an ancient foghorn blasted the stormy air. *Buuoooaah!* When a few stragglers looked in their direction, the Captain shook his head.

No one talks to the sea anymore. In the old days many people call to La Señora. You hear it like a rooster in the morning, nothing strange.

Do it again, Papi.

With lovesick eyes he searched the granite-colored waves. Did he really expect to see a mermaid? Lifting the conch once more, he slid his fingers inside the lip of the shell, moving them deep or short or all the way to the tip, as if playing a trumpet. By turns, the sound rumbled with primal earthiness or soared like a heavenly choir. The music rose into the windstorm like a sea creature that grabbed Angel with its tentacles and left her dumbstruck.

As the last note lingered in the air, the Captain placed the conch in her hands. *You call, Angelita.*

How she wanted to please him. The shell was heavier than it looked, at least five pounds. Holding it with two hands, she blew as hard as she could into the spire but produced only a limp bleat, more like a cough, hardly enough to catch the attention of a goddess. She would never forget the disappointment in her father's eyes as he took the shell away.

A strong wave raked the shells, which bubbled with excitement, before its weight dropped with a crash. The water surfed onto the sand, shimming close to her small offering. The momentum halted a fraction of an inch from the gussied-up coconut.

The Captain told her to watch as he held the spire a few inches from his pursed lips. He made a spitting sound before he blew into the trumpet. Once more a woeful blast filled the air. He passed the conch back to her with an encouraging nod.

Raising the horn toward the ash-colored clouds, she made a few pathetic notes. She hung her head on her chest. *I'm sorry.*

It's not too late. Nunca olvides quien eres, eh? Never forget who you are.

Maybe that was the problem. *Who am I, Papi?*

I told you. Daughter of the Sea.

Was she *una Hija del Mar?* Like the bellow of the conch, the sea had always bewitched her, though she couldn't say why.

With his jaw jutted forward, he looked to the sea. *Don't worry. She hears you.*

The swells peaked higher; the watermark inched closer. Her bare feet sank into the wet sand; the cold knifed through her damp shirt. He took her hand as a brilliant flash of lightning exposed the phosphorescent underbelly of the clouds. Riotous thunder threatened to break the leaden sky. Hail-like rain slashed the air, pelting them.

She turned to run, but the Captain held tight, insisting she wait. *Espérate.*

Even more worrisome than the bone-chilling cold was his spiritual obsession—as fervent as Mother's belief in the Second Coming of Christ. Angel shivered with exaggeration, complaining of the cold, in Spanish, a childhood trick that carried more weigh*t. Tengo frio, Papí.*

He wrapped her under the wing of his burly arm. The musty smell of chum, sweat, and bay rum cologne, as familiar as the sea, comforted her.

Call with your heart, Hijita. She looked up at him, perplexed, as he pounded his broad chest. *She's inside of you—dentro.* He tapped her chest to make his point. *Dentro.*

She screamed as an electric crack zigzagged across the smoldering sky. From the opposite end, another bolt was hurled toward what seemed to be the competing side. And there, Angel stood in the middle of the celestial battle with no protection but a puny coconut boat. Clearly, Jesus would fight the Sea Goddess for the doubtful prize of her sinful soul.

For the first time, Angel prayed to no one and everyone, and maybe a little to herself. *I wish to be free and happy.* Her mother would never have considered it a bona fide prayer. To her, however, it felt as revolutionary as the Russian's Luna craft landing on the moon. She had traveled to unknown territory, the space beyond her fears, if only for a moment—and planted a small marker, *dentro.*

The captain's cry startled her. He pointed to the rocky waves. *¡Mira, mira! Look, look,* she *took it!*

Her prayer boat skated into the hollow of a wave, as if pulled by an invisible string, and disappeared behind a curtain of water. Of course, the storm would eventually sweep up anything in its path. But why nitpick when the Captain was so happy?

He hugged her tight. Then he held her by her shoulders and made her promise never to forget who she was. *Nunca olvides quien eres. You're the daughter of Yemayá. Prometémelo.*

I promise, Papi.

The dregs of the day simmered in the dwindling heat, as Angel rocked on the porch swing, watching the towering cumulous clouds cascade one to the next in a stairway to heaven. The rusty swing groaned under her weight; a bullfrog croaked from the swampy border. Shimmering sequins of sunlight fell between pots of waxy green bromeliads.

How could she be so miserable in paradise? She hadn't written a useable sentence all day, her concentration was shot. She took a drag on her cigarette and coughed as the smoke burned through her chest. Faith had been gone less than twenty-four hours and already Angel had smoked the entire emergency pack. Couldn't she keep a single promise?

She had taken up the vile habit soon after her escape to Sanibel Island in the spring of 1968. The click of the lighter, a tiny moment of stillness before the sucking intake—it had been a way to remember her lover, or perhaps to forget, she wasn't sure anymore. Even after she quit, the cough had dogged her—a persistent reminder of what she had left behind. At least the smoke numbed the pain, and the incessant question, which drilled in her head, then and now: *Had she done the right thing?*

She recalled the life-changing moment when she first invented the lie. She had dimmed the lights in their dingy apartment on Tarpon Bay Road. A Little Golden book wrapped in a grocery bag sat on the cardboard table. Faith, wide-eyed over a pink cupcake with two birthday candles that lit her sweet, innocent face, needed an answer.

Why don't I have a daddy?

Your daddy died in the war, Kiddo. It's just you and me now.

After she put Faith to bed, Angel had gathered up her new shell collection—a cluster of Queen Conchs by the front door, a driftwood mobile she'd made, pretty Sunrise Tellins taped in the shape of a heart to the bathroom mirror—and dumped them in the trash. That night she had shut the door on the past and her old ways. It was all or nothing—heaven or hell—she would never touch a shell or allow a smidgen of spiritual hocus pocus into their lives ever again. She and her daughter would be free and happy, no matter what.

Up until now Angel believed she had made the right choice. Why then had she poked a hole into their well-constructed lives with the Captain's warning? *No olivdes quien eres?* What the hell was she thinking? No, no, and no!

She stubbed the cigarette in the tray—the absolute last one ever—and hurried to the kitchen phone. Faith would be furious, but she simply had to know.

"Hello?" Bonnie's mother answered.

"Penny, it's Angel."

"Don't tell me you're calling to join the watch? With Maeapple gone, we could use your help. I'm hoping your new neighbors will take over her slot. Of course, they'll need an alternate, and everyone else is paired up."

Each year the local community came together to protect the ancient nesting site of loggerhead turtles from predators until the hatchlings made it safely to sea.

"When are the turtles coming?" Angel asked.

Penny chuckled. "Only Mother Nature knows the answer to that. We're usually ready by the middle of the month. What do you say?"

"Maybe next year when Faith is gone."

"If Jim didn't help out, I guess I couldn't keep watch, either. He's got the camper all ready, we're going to D.C. to see the monuments."

A terrible feeling stole over Angel. "Bonnie, too?" she asked.

"It was her idea," Penny said over the cry of her young son. "Look, the girls are practically out of the nest. Why don't I put you down for the sunset watch—that's the most popular time—six to ten in the evening?" As her son cried louder, she added, "I've got to run."

Angel slowly replaced the receiver. If Bonnie wasn't with Faith, then who was?

Angel waved the lingering stench of cigarette smoke out of her office window. A hazy gray twilight limped across the beach; the repellent scent of skunk drifted on a breeze, along with the algae stuff-of-life smell. She saw lights on in Maeapple's old place and made a mental note to drop off a welcome gift.

Another day had passed with little work completed. Needing a sense of accomplishment, she decided to clear her messy desk. With a flurry of energy she piled up the old drafts. She wedged open the closet, which was stuffed with manuscripts, carbon copies of correspondence, boxes of bank statements and school records. Standing on tiptoe, she pushed the pile onto the top shelf, past the braided spray of chinaberry leaves that deterred moths, and accidentally dislodged an old shoebox. It fell to the floor with a soft crash, spilling out dozens of old letters, written on Howard Johnson's stationery. The yellowed envelopes were addressed to Angel del Corazón at the old apartment.

Angel's breathing grew shallow, adrenaline pumped through her veins, as she stared at the mess—a stain upon her whitewashed life. She had forgotten Tilly's letters, just as she had forsaken her old friend. For heaven's sake, what if Faith had stumbled across the incriminating evidence?

She swept the letters into the wastebasket, when Tilly's words came back to her. *We're all lost at sea, Kiddo. All you can do is make the kindest choice possible when it's your turn at the wheel.*

Angel shook a handful of letters in the air and muttered. "You have no idea what you're talking about. I did the right thing, damn it."

Overcome, she dropped into her desk chair, while the sun passed the baton to the moon, opening the way to the nightly reign of the Sea Goddess. Angel tossed the letter in the trash, but the sight of those proud flourishes and bold exclamation marks claimed her. She could no more resist Tilly's power than the moon could refuse to rise.

February 20th, 1969

Hey, Kiddo,

Thanks for the birthday photo of Faith. I hung it up at the restaurant and you wouldn't believe how many compliments I get. Good thing she got your pretty eyes and Santiago's bee-stung lips. I see the Captain's jaunty smile, too.

I showed Faith's picture to your mother. Don't get upset! I ran into her on Duval and it nearly killed me to see her spirits so broken. She stared at the photograph for so long I thought she'd had a stroke.

Now, I know you're pining for Santiago. You can't fool me. You think things would have worked out if only you could have proved your love. It just ain't so. The shells say he'll see his daughter again one day. It won't be what you expect. Heck, it never is! Quit dreaming, Angel. Next time, I want to hear about a nice man you're seeing!

Your Old Friend,

Tilly

P.S. Thanks for the money order. It wasn't necessary, but I can always use the dough!

There had been no next time; Angel had never written to Tilly again. The words on the page blurred as her eyes misted with tears. *Forget it.* Faith would come home soon, everything would be fine.

According to Phoenician mythology, the god Melqart, protector of the city Tyre, and his mistress discovered their dog's mouth stained purple when it bit into a washed-up sea snail, *Murex brandaris*, Thereafter, they commissioned the production of the dye. Ten thousand shellfish produced one gram of dye, barely enough for a garment. A pound of pre-dyed wool equaled the value of a pound of gold, making Tyrian Purple a status symbol. Later known as Imperial Purple, it was reserved for the Roman emperor's togas. Cleopatra's ship in the doomed Battle of Actium famously boasted purple sails.

SANIBEL ISLAND, FLORIDA

SPRING 1985

Angel turned her grocery cart down the aisle at Bailey's and pulled a six-pack of soda off the shelf. Faith would be home soon, they would make root beer floats while they calmly discussed the future. Angel contemplated slipping in a few tiny details about the past— nothing major, simple thematic color.

She didn't notice the man coming in the opposite direction until their carts were side-by-side and he said, "Hello, Angel."

She was surprised to see Maeapple's caterer. "Oh, hi."

In his crisp white linen shirt and pressed khaki slacks, he looked like he had stepped out of a magazine ad for travel in the tropics. Angel swept back her hair, wishing she had on something nicer than her typical, rumpled uniform of button-down blouse and cotton skirt.

"Angel." He smiled warmly. "An unexpected pleasure."

Tongue-tied, she spit out his name. "Max."

"I'm pleased you remembered."

"It was a memorable day."

"Indeed, I have thought of it many times also."

Her eyes widened—had he thought of her? He mustn't believe the same of her.

"Yes, well," Angel said, attempting to correct the false impression. "It's natural to miss Maeapple. We were neighbors for a long time."

"Is that so?" Max said with odd enthusiasm. "Such a kind woman. I am honored she entrusted me with her customers."

"You certainly did a nice job."

He tilted his head with a curious expression. "Thank you, but you must come and see for yourself."

What kind of caterer invited you to the events he served?

"If I receive an invitation," she said, pointedly.

"Please consider it an open invitation. The store is open from nine to five. I am there most of the time, though I recently engaged a bright young woman to assist me."

It finally hit Angel. "You bought the Fancy Shell Shoppe?"

"Indeed." His face lit up. "For many years, I visited the island, always wanting to make it my home."

She felt the aisles shrink around them while Tina Turner's raunchy ode to love's secondhand status, *What's Love Got To Do With It*, blasted from the ceiling. She coughed into her sleeve, absorbing the fact that this handsome man would be a regular presence on the island.

"Are you all right?" Max unscrewed a bottle of Evian water and handed it to her. "Please, your face, it looks pale."

She accepted it, once again amazed to find him tending to her. "Sorry," she mumbled.

"Think nothing of it," he said. "I hope I won't remind you of your friend's absence."

She shook her head. "I thought you were the caterer." As he looked at her in surprise, she added, "You were in the back room, the tea cups and trays…"

They looked at each other blankly until laughter overcame them. The silly joyful feeling wended its way through her body, relaxing her chest, her mind. The door that shuttered her heart opened just a smidgen, nothing more, but it felt good all the same.

"Angel," he said. "Would you care to join me for dinner?"

She startled, like a flounder that digs deeper into the sand when disturbed.

"My daughter is coming home tonight," she said abruptly.

"Perhaps another night?"

"You're single?"

"I am. And you? Forgive me if I misunderstood the situation."

For heaven's sake, there was no situation. She had to set him right. And yet she hesitated, stunned to realize she might want to see him again.

"Thank you," she said, as her nerve failed. "But I'm very busy at the moment."

"I understand." Max gently took the water from her and placed it in his cart. "Nevertheless, I hope you will accept my invitation to the store. I shall look forward to seeing you again." He smiled as he took his leave. "Good day."

"You, too."

Angel continued down the aisle, her mind whirring in hot confusion. He was going to purchase the expensive water bottle when he could have left it with her. From the beginning, he'd been kind and attractive and inviting. Never mind, she had no business going on a date no matter how much she liked the way he looked at her.

She picked up a cheesecake for her new neighbors and hurried to the checkout line. On the way home, she stopped at Maeapple's old place and rang the bell. The house was quiet; she would return another time. She hoped the newcomers liked their privacy as much as she did.

Angel snapped a crisp white tablecloth over the dining table and it billowed like a sail catching the wind before making a soft landing. From a small credenza she took out her good china, the set she had splurged on at Burdine's after her third book. The pearly white plates with a silver filigree edge never failed to give her a happy taste of elegance and stability. In the middle of the table she set a vibrant arrangement of magenta bougainvillea leaves and yellow hibiscus that she had picked in her garden.

An electric fan rotated on the cocktail table, blowing the residue of cigarette smell out the side windows. The incessant reminder made Angel itch for a smoke—she mustn't, the fewer obstacles the better when Faith returned. She turned down the heat on the tuna casserole and took a glass of wine to the porch to wait for Faith.

The pleasant languor of dusk wrapped around her like an old, soft blanket. Her head fell back on the swing, heart and mind drawn to the dazzling display in the sky. Like a giant celestial daisy, leafy clouds clustered around the nucleus of the sun, which fanned its slender golden arms past them in a last-ditch effort to hold darkness at bay.

Midway between the sea brush and the shoreline, a line of "turtle stations" dotted the sand. There were poles and large rolls of black and yellow safety tape, along with beach chairs and first aid supplies. Soon the mother turtles would arrive to lay their eggs and local volunteers would guard their clutches day and night. The idea of being on Yemayá's turf for hours on end—in the moonlight, no less—scared Angel to death.

The ocean teased with small licks of waves that curled and swirled, drawing in the night. The dark current brought in the tide, carrying the Sea Goddess ever closer on the moonless night. Well, let her stir the deep blue depths where sailors slept; it had nothing to do with Angel.

The sudden rattle of the Red Bug sent her hurrying to the front door. She flung it open just as Faith pulled into the driveway. Beside her, a young man sat up and rubbed his eyes. Angel attempted to absorb this fact, but the idea that Faith had spent the weekend with this stranger sent her thoughts bouncing out of control like marbles across a polished floor.

The guy spoke to her daughter, who nodded several times, as if taking direction. She avoided looking at her mother. Afraid they might leave,

Angel turned on her heel, hoping they would follow inside. A nasty cough rattled her chest; her nerves were on edge. She leaned against the kitchen counter, downing the glass of wine. *Get to the finish line.*

She studied the guy as he sauntered into the living room. This was no high school romance—he was at least ten years older than Faith. Stubble dotted his bony, sunburned face. His thin and lanky frame looked in need of a hearty meal. Long dirty blond hair brushed against the collar of a worn denim shirt. His frayed bell-bottom jeans sported a patch that read, *Keep truckin'*. For heaven's sake, a realistic snake tattoo of slithered around his forearm. How appropriate.

Faith followed behind, shrunk into herself, like a mollusk peering out from its shell. What had happened to quell her bright spark and confident stride?

"Mom," Faith said in a warning tone. "This is Wayne Richardson." With a quick intake of breath, she added, "My boyfriend."

The boyfriend pulled out a pack of Marlboro cigarettes and, without asking permission, lit one. Faith offered no protest at all! Wayne clucked—that was the only way to describe it—in the general direction of Angel.

"Hello?" Angel said.

"Don't be rude," Faith said.

"Excuse me?"

Her daughter wanted to pick a fight, and it took all of Angel's will to deny her the easy way out. Instead, in her most civil tone, she said, "Would you like to join us for dinner, Wayne?"

"We, um—" Faith began when he cut her off.

"Man, I'm starving." He had a strong southern accent.

Angel quickly set out another place setting. "Where are you from?"

He tipped his cigarette ash in her best glassware. "Aiken, South Carolina."

"You're a long way from home."

"Wayne is a really good mechanic," Faith said, breathlessly. "He fixed the Red Bug the other day, saved us a fortune."

"Uh-huh."

Now he clucked at Faith, conveying disapproval. And Faith, rolling over like a trained pet, mumbled an apology. "Sorry." At Angel's look of annoyance, she said, "What?"

At least her daughter still had a bit of gumption. Angel bit her tongue and turning away, busied herself in the kitchen. Faith was inexperienced; when she met nice college boys, she would dump this loser.

Angel placed the casserole and salad on the table. "Please, help yourself."

Wayne sat back, while Faith served him. She waited to eat until he gave a go-ahead cluck. Who on earth was this sad, servile girl?

"Do you work on the mainland?" Angel asked him.

"Soon enough," he said, winking at Faith. "Won't we, baby?"

"We?" Angel said.

"When we buy the shop."

He dug into the food, using the knife more like a spear. "Beer?" he said to no one in particular, and Faith hurried to the fridge.

"Oh, what kind of shop?"

"Car repair, what else?"

He continued eating with remarkable concentration, slugging back the beer her daughter offered. He slammed down the bottle with a braying *aaah!* But where Angel observed an appalling lack of manners, Faith's admiring gaze lingered over his broad shoulder, the baby blue eyes.

"Bread," he demanded.

Again, her daughter complied, and this time, Angel cornered her in the kitchen. "What's going on?"

"We've got a plan," Faith said, as she placed bread rolls in a basket.

"Don't tell me you're going open a mechanic shop?"

"Fine, I won't tell you."

"With what money?"

A nervous smile slid across her daughter's face. "I have money."

"But, but…that's your college money." Angel had scrimped and saved for her future—not for this miscreant.

"Why go to college?" Faith said, picking at a roll. "So I can report on the hatred and greed and stupidity in the world? I just want a peaceful, happy life."

"For heaven's sake, what nonsense is this?"

"Bread," Wayne repeated.

When Faith moved to serve him, Angel blocked her. "Are you really going to throw your future away, everything you've worked for over some guy you hardly know?"

"Wayne loves me." Faith stared down, rolling a crust of bread between her fingers into a tiny doughy ball. "And I love him."

"Maybe he's after your money? Did you think of that?"

"You mean he wouldn't want me otherwise? Like I'm not worthy of love?"

"I never said that."

"What do you know about love, anyway?"

Pushing past her, Faith slammed the basket on the table. "Let's leave," she told Wayne. With a warning cluck, he grabbed her wrist. He never looked at her while he shoveled in food, holding her in place. "Please," she added.

"Is that how you let him treat you?" Angel said from behind the safety of the kitchen counter.

Still pinned to the table, her face tight with anger, Faith turned on her. "You have no faith in me."

"How can you say that? You're all I have."

"Get a life, Mom."

Wayne threw down his fork and announced they were leaving. "Let's get." He rolled out of the house without another word, not even a cluck of thanks, Faith hot on his heels.

Angel followed them outside. "Faith honey, where are you going?"

"To Wayne's."

"Where's that?"

"None of your business."

"When are you coming back?"

"When I feel like it." She slammed the car door.

Angel's words fell into the void. "But you're coming back, aren't you?"

As they shot out onto the road, a Great egret lifted off from a flaming Royal Poinciana, announcing its displeasure with a hoarse croak. She noticed a large nest built high up in the tree. Who could stop the forces of nature? No power on earth was able to keep Angel from loving Santiago; even the Good Lord's efforts had failed. If she had known then what she knew now, would she have given herself to him? But then, if she hadn't, there would be no wonderful daughter to love.

For five long days a boiling heat wave took up residence on the island. It hung from the rafters of Angel's childless, rudderless cottage, burrowing into her bed and into the cabinets, chasing away stubborn pockets of cool air, leaving her limp and listless. During this suffocating spell, she received no word from Faith. Each afternoon Angel drove aimlessly around the island, hoping to catch sight of her wayward daughter or the Red Bug. She thought of filing a missing persons report, but Faith was of legal age and didn't want to be found.

Work was stalled. She had even forgotten to mail the proofs until Abby's secretary called to remind her. For the first time in her career, Angel had writer's block. What was the point of working, if not for Faith's future? Had any of Angel's sacrifices mattered?

How had her daughter fallen in love with a guy cut from the same calamitous cloth as her father, when she had never known him? Despite Angel's vigilance, the past had scurried after them, like rats climbing along the ropes onto a ship, to infect her daughter with the same poisonous longing that Angel and her mother, and her grandmother, and probably all the women before them had suffered.

In despair, she lit a cigarette. As she sat back, she eyed the wastebasket with Tilly's old letters. Once more, her old friend's words demanded attention.

September 10th, 1969

Hey, Kiddo,

It's been six months since your last letter. If I don't hear from you soon I'm calling the cops! I fear you've forgotten old Tilly. Heck, I know it for a fact. I read it in the shells and took it pretty hard.

The wave you're riding stretches for an awful long time. You're stuck in the dark underside where shells tumble and swirl. Nobody can do a damn thing about it, either.

Just remember, you're a lot stronger than you think. You've got seawater in your veins, Kiddo!

Love,

Tilly

What did she know, anyway? Angel dropped the letter into the wastebasket and resumed her fruitless concentration on *Stella*. Her fingers hovered over the typewriter like birds leaning into a hurricane wind, when the doorbell rang. She sprang to her feet, energized by the possibility that Faith had returned.

Angel threw open the door, stunned to find Max on the porch, a rattan picnic basket in one hand. For heaven's sake, couldn't the man take no for an answer? And how on earth did he know where she lived?

"Hello," he said.

"What are you doing here?" she said.

"I believe it is six o'clock."

"Yes?"

Confusion colored his expression. "Penny told me I must arrive for the turtle watch."

"What? Penny Jacobsen said I'd help you?"

"I'm afraid so."

His charming smile made her forget her indignation, and she couldn't help but smile back.

"Well," she said, breaking the enchanting spell. "I'm afraid there's been a mistake. I told Penny I'd consider it next year when my daughter Faith goes to college."

He shifted his weight, switching the basket to the other hand. "Faith Rose is your daughter? Of course I should have made the connection."

"You know my Faith?"

"Only by acquaintance. She answered my advertisement for a shop assistant."

"My daughter, working at the shell shop?"

"She will begin next week when the school begins also. I hope you approve. She said she is eighteen and needed a job."

"When was that?"

He paused, remembering. "Approximately one week before the party for Maeapple. We were studying the books when she grew tired and departed right before your daughter arrived."

"Really?" *So Faith has been leading a double life for some time.*

The couple from Michigan with the small yappy dog walked past her house, glancing repeatedly at Angel and Max. The Parrot Line, that conflagration of gossipmongers, would soon be squawking all over the island about this unfortunate incident.

Angel stepped back. "Please, come in."

"Thank you." He regarded the living room. "Your home is warm as I expected."

"It's cozy; I like it."

"You've been here a long time?" He appeared puzzled as he looked round the room again.

"Is something wrong?"

"No, not at all." He dismissed the idea with a small wave. "Most of the islanders, they have so many shells, everywhere you can see."

"Hmmm." And look where it gets them, a broken heart or two.

"Have I upset you?" he asked.

"Of course not," Angel said. "It's just, as I said, I hadn't planned on the watch."

"Do you have plans? Perhaps you would accompany me." He tugged at the basket. "I have sandwiches and potato soup with hot chocolate and cookies. I promise it will be tasty."

"Is this your way of getting me to go out to dinner?" Angel said.

Max looked at her in surprise, recovering with a quick smile. "I'd be pleased if you consider it a date."

They were flirting, weren't they, and with surprising ease? Shyness overcame her. Studying the knots in the pine flooring, she muttered, "Yes, well."

"Excellent."

Her head shot up. "No, see, that's not what I meant."

"No?"

How could she resist his sweet regret? He held her gaze to the point of intimacy, long enough to soften her spine.

"Well," she said, "They say it's difficult to keep watch alone. At the very least, you need someone to spell you for bathroom breaks; four hours is a long time, don't you think?"

"I do."

"I suppose it's unfair to you and the turtles, simply because Penny made a mistake." She weighed the consequences of being a heartbeat away from Yemayá's watery reach against Max and his soft brown eyes. "I'll have to accompany you. Just this once."

"As you wish."

Angel led Max through the porch, suddenly shy as she changed into her beach shoes. Her slim feet had never felt so exposed or so in need of a man's touch. He turned to study the sea; his strong back all she could see.

They followed the beach path where a committee of seagulls huddled, like old women in an ancient whitewashed plaza with their hunched gray shoulders and bowed heads. As they approached, the birds scattered with indignant cries, a black specter rising to blot the crimson-streaked skies. She looked at the whirling feathered mass above, wondering when she had last stepped across the divide into the Sea Goddess's parlor?

Has it really been sixteen years since she walked on the beach? She came to a stop as an old memory surfaced of her young daughter's keen enthusiasm for sandcastles. Angel had managed to divert her interest with whatever it took—dance lessons, horseback riding, short trips along the coast—or she had abdicated to the protection of other mothers when a beach party loomed.

"Is something wrong?" Max asked.

She found herself inexplicably at ease, as she looked at him, waiting there, his strong shoulders kissed by the sunset. She knew she had to join him, no matter the risk.

"I was just thinking how lovely it is," she said.

"Paradise," he said.

They continued in companionable silence, passing under the black and yellow diagonal safety tape into the restricted area. The houses in proximity had dimmed their lights to prevent the loggerheads from mistaking the artificial glow for moonlight and head to their doom. If only it were that easy for Angel to avoid Yemayá's light.

Max guided her to their designated spot, directly in back of Maeapple's old place. A half dozen couples on patrol dotted the beach. Several yards away, Libby curled into a beach chair beside Greg Goodwin, so intent on him she wouldn't have seen a turtle if it crawled into her lap. Angel recalled that she served as an alternate, and his wife Kim worked long hours at the restaurant. She wondered if he ever bestowed the same goofy smile upon his betrothed.

Max set an elegant scene: low-lying folding teak chairs with nautical red-and-white striped canvas seats awaited them, the expensive kind that yacht people stored on board for beach excursions. A checked gray wool blanket looked enough for a bedspread. The sturdy picnic basket with leather straps contained real dishes, silverware and a thermos worthy of a climb in the Alps. On second look, she observed holes in the blanket, tarnish on the silver, a chip in one plate. Yet age did not undermine quality; the articles had weathered life well, like their owner.

He unwrapped a sandwich from the wax paper and handed it to her on a plate. Caught in the act of examining him, she noted the pleasure it gave him. Unlike some men who might have pressed her naked interest to their advantage, he appeared humbled.

As promised, the sandwich was uncommonly tasty. Clearly, his European background set him apart. She was not alone in her curiosity: several women on watch craned their necks to investigate the newcomer. Max seemed oblivious to the attention as he enjoyed his meal. He was watching the sun decamp across the sky like an empress trailing an exquisite blue coat embroidered with scarlet.

"*Sehr schön*," he said. "Very pretty, no?"

"Very," she agreed.

Like the others on patrol, they spoke in whispers, lest their voices frighten the mother turtles. The pleasant murmurs up and down the beach accented the rhythmic susurrus of the waves.

"When did you come to America?" Angel asked.

"In 1946, after the war." His voice dropped a notch, as sadness flickered there. "I was twelve years old, a 'kid with grit,' the G.I. Joe said. A kind older couple in Boston took me in. They lost their son, Roger, a sergeant at Hickham Field in Pearl Harbor." Max took in Angel's look, anticipating her question. "My family is Jewish, they also perished in the war."

"I'm so sorry."

A wistful smile shifted his expression. "John and Mary Sullivan built fine houses and taught me the trade after my schooling—they treated me like a son. When I was twenty-eight, a moving truck crashed into their car in a blinding snowstorm; they died instantly. Afterwards, I sold the business and took back my birth name. I moved to Miami for the sunshine and the shells. I never wanted to be again in the cold dark winter." Max scooped up a Sunrise

Tellin at the edge of the blanket. "For this I came, *Tellina Radiata*. As pretty as you."

Handing it to her, he clasped her hand in his. The electric connection stilled the evening sounds so that all Angel heard was the wild beating of her heart. Like an awkward teenager, she pulled away, and the shell fell between their chairs. He retrieved it, once more making an offering.

"You keep it, Max. It belongs in your store."

Did he really think she embodied the shell's happy rosy rays? Her life was dark and murky; he had no idea who she was. It was better that way.

He pocketed the shell and took out the thermos. "Sugar?" He rummaged through the basket. "*Ach!* But I have forgotten it. Excuse me."

As he hurried away, Angel turned to track his dark silhouette in the last rays of light. Why was he heading towards the nearby houses? She silently urged him to continue onto the path that led to the public parking lot, but he stayed the course—a beeline to Maeapple's former home. For heaven's sake, Max was her new neighbor.

She hunkered down in the chair, her mind racing like flying fish skittering over the ocean's surface. What was she doing here, open to the seductive moonlight? What had Papi said about his beloved mermaid? *She rules the moon, eh? La luna makes men and women crazy with love. El amor grande.*

And in the lapping of the waves, Angel heard the dreaded, sultry voice whisper. *Ven a mí, mi amor. Tu eres mío, todo para mi. No luches mas. Ven.*

"Get lost, you devil." Angel muttered. *"Vayáte, diabla."*

At dawn Angel awoke with a start, as if the pieces of a puzzle had clicked into place. What if Faith had been planning for some time to abscond with that rascal Wayne? Perhaps she used his address on a job application, which might explain why Max had assumed they weren't related.

A fit of coughing grew more agitated each time she recalled the previous night. If she had allowed it, she was sure Max would have kissed her when he walked her home. That's how it happened: a well-prepared picnic basket, a romantic night on the beach, and next thing you knew, a broken heart. She dressed quickly, resolved to put an end to his intentions.

Heading into town, she saw a smattering of rain clouds sulking in the north. And yet, near the lighthouse at Point Ybel, a sliver of light glimmered in the gloom. It could go either way, storm or sunshine. Just like her life.

Only minutes later, when she parked at Seaside Books, the angry sky had blotted out the light in preparation for an attack on the little island. The low-pressure system created an oppressive wave of humidity that the air conditioner could not defeat.

She wiped her brow, marveling at Libby's cool composure: the pressed, tight blue dress, her smooth blond bob. In contrast, Angel considered her unruly hair, the wrinkled khakis, the slightly stained shirt. How did she always manage to look askew?

Libby greeted her from behind the sales counter. "What brings you here?"

"I came for the pen," Angel said.

"Oh, yeah. Just a minute." She disappeared into the storage room. A moment later she handed Angel a refined blue presentation box.

"It's perfect," Angel said, eyeing the stylish silver pen. As she ran a fingertip over the engraved initials, however, a knowing tingle in her gut told her it was a mistake.

"Is something wrong?" Libby asked, checking the invoice. "Faith Matilda Rose, F.M.R., isn't that it?"

Angel drew back with a sigh. "I suppose it just hit me. My little girl is graduating."

"Heck." Libby flicked her bright red fingertips in the air. "You'll finally have your freedom. Get out of that damn house for a change. Date a nice guy."

A nice guy like Max?

Angel backpedaled from the subject she intended to discuss, turning instead to the stacks. "I'm interested in *Love and Shadows*, if you have the paperback?"

Libby pulled a copy from the Romance section. "People say it's not as romantic as *House of Spirits*, too political."

Did the proprietress ever read her wares?

"Well," Angel said. "She's such a good storyteller, I'm sure it's worth a read."

Libby shrugged. "If that's how you want to spend your time."

While gathering her things, Angel asked, ever so casually, "By the way, I was wondering if you'd like to team up on turtle watch with the man who bought Maeapple's store?"

Libby's eyebrows shot up. "Is he good looking?"

"He's very nice. He's a gentleman."

"You mean he's an overweight slob. That's why you're pawning him off?"

"Not at all. I thought you could talk shop. I'm on a deadline."

"Sure, I'll do it," Libby said. "I'm sick of waiting around for Greg and Kim. I never know if she's going to leave the restaurant. I need a committed situation."

In Angel's opinion, freewheeling Libby abhorred commitment, but why question her motives?

"His name is Max Sussmann," she said. "Perhaps you can go by the store—"

"Honey," Libby interjected. "I know how to wrangle a man."

Of course she did.

Something had to give. The mounting storm pressed the leaden sky over the town, sandwiching the broiling heat in between like a layer of melted cheese. No birds fanned high in the ash-colored sky, street traffic thinned; the world held its breath. A trickle of sweat dripped between Angel's breasts; the crease behind her knees felt sticky.

She parked beside the Fancy Shell Shoppe and checked her appearance in the rear view mirror. Rummaging in her purse for lipstick, she found none, and bit her lips for color. She must look self-assured when she explained that she preferred to be alone.

As shell chimes announced her arrival, Max peered round a pair of well-dressed customers at the counter. He smiled happily, his eyes quick with surprise. The women, a statuesque brunette in a cream linen suit and an older blonde in pink, turned to inspect her and, seemingly unimpressed, just as quickly forgot her.

"Hello, Mrs. Rose," he called out. "I'll be with you soon. Would you prefer to wait in the back?"

"No, thank you," she said. The back room where he had touched her skirt and looked deep into her eyes threatened intimacy.

Angel noted the pleasing new color on the walls, a soft blue-gray that set off the silver-toned exhibition cases and reminded her of first light on the sleeping sea. The many shells evoked unwanted memories—the Captain's canvas sack of sea tricks; summer days swimming in the ocean with her childhood friend Cathy; boxes upon boxes of shells in Tilly's workroom—it was like walking into a room full of old acquaintances of whom you were once fond but now found tiresome.

On the far wall, she saw a new display that sent her heart racing. She approached it as if walking through a door into the past—not only hers, but also many other's, because if anything ever captured a moment in time, it was a Sailors Valentine. More than eighteen years had passed since she had seen one, a surprising absence considering the island's shell mania—or perhaps a testament to her avoidance of shells. And yet, the absolute wonder she had first felt for the artistry of shell mosaics washed over her once more. *After all this time, you found me.*

Her fingertips itched with the memory of how difficult the handiwork could be. It might take several hours to fashion a single rosette out of False Red Strigilla shells, which were no more than three-quarters of an inch wide. The overwhelming variety of shells, the imaginative choice of designs, the symmetry of circles and geometric shapes that outlined sections, and the detailed images—flowers, boats, birds, an anchor, even figures—all made entirely of shells, was still hard to fathom.

As was customary, an octagonal shadow box framed each valentine. Angel recalled that they were usually made of mahogany or Spanish cedar. Dozens of examples formed a clock-like pattern on the wall, radiating along interior lines to the outside circle. At the center hung a rare double-sided piece. One side contained a sepia-toned photograph of a young sailor, his face full of yearning.

The majority of the Sailors Valentines included a sentimental phrase, made with tiny seed shells, such as *Love The Giver*, *Think Of Me When Far Away*, or *Ever Thine*. Often, the design and verse were complementary: *Love Points The Way*, encircling a compass.

Beneath each work, a neatly inscribed card gave the date or origin. Despite the romantic myth that sailors made these intricate works while pining at sea for their loved ones, in reality, cottage workers in Caribbean ports, such as Barbados, fabricated them in the 1800's, during the height of Victorian society's shell mania. Sailors purchased them as gifts for wives, lovers, mothers, innocently perpetuating Yemayá's dangerous spell of loss and longing.

From the "three o'clock" spot, a fragile Sailors Valentine with a missing cluster of Prickly Cockles called to Angel. Made in 1847, its simple message struck her: *Forget Me Not.* Once more, her father's urgent plea echoed from long ago. *Nunca olvides quien eres*. Never mind, she had no interest in remembering who she once was.

The classy brunette inquired in a Southern accent about the dimensions of a mirror, and Max replied, "We can make the mirror square, if you prefer."

Angel signaled him. *I'll come back.*

"Wait, please," he said, crossing the store. "Ladies, I apologize for the inconvenience, I'm afraid I must close. If you will return, I promise a ten percent discount." When the statuesque brunette started to protest, he added, "With free shipping." As she picked up her bag, her friend followed. "Good day, thank you for your visit," he said, flipping the sign on the door to *Closed.*

Before Angel could object, he hooked his arm through hers, sweeping her to the back of the store. "Please, join me for tea. This old soul is too thirsty to beg."

"I could have returned another time," she said.

While filling a brass teakettle, he peered at her over his shoulder like a fisherman focused on a slippery catch. "By the look on your face, I suspect I might have waited a long time."

She studied the old pine cabinets, unsure if she disliked being the object of such attention or was simply unaccustomed to it.

"You were examining the shell work on the wall," he went on. "They are called Sailors' Valentines. Are you acquainted with them?"

"Vaguely," she said.

Had she imagined his lips tighten? He had no reason to doubt her. She wished she could confide in him, but one thing might lead to another, until her ugly life's story was exposed.

He rooted through the shelves, muttering. "If I had known you were coming, blueberry strudel I would have bought. Now we shall have cookies in the box."

"Vanilla wafers are fine," Angel said.

"For you, perhaps," Max said with a shrug.

"Are you saying I have cheap taste?

"Ach!" He looked stricken. "That is not what I meant."

They looked at each other in confusion and began to laugh. She relaxed into a chair, but to her dismay, he continued talking about shells.

"Imagine, without telephones or television, how compelling were the messages in the Valentines. The frame often sat on a stand by the hearth, to remember the absent sailor, a brother, husband, or lover. Over months or years the sentimental message—*Home Again, Remember Me*—gave hope for their return. I suppose they bring me hope also."

The kettle whistled, saving her from a response. Max prepared the tea and soon the spicy fruity aroma of Earl Grey scented the small, overheated room.

As he sat beside her, she said, "Max, I need your help."

He leaned towards her, knocking the table. "I'm afraid I am a bumbler," he said, wiping up a spill of hot water.

She smiled, unable to deny his appeal.

Regaining his composure, he said, "Yes, Angel, you can tell me." His words reached so deep inside her that she feared she would tell him everything.

"Is the tea ready?" she said, breaking apart a cookie.

"Of course." He poured her a cup.

She peered at him over the steam, deciding whether to confide her problem. He sat back, waiting as if he had all the time in the world.

Finally, in fits and starts, Angel began. "Faith is going to the University of Tampa. At least, that was the plan. We worked hard for it, now there's this boyfriend. I never imagined she'd pick a guy like him. How can she throw away her future over someone so unsuitable?"

"Love makes the sane person act nonsense, no?"

"I suppose so." She studied her teacup, as images of making love with Santiago flashed before her. "Whatsoever a man soweth, that shall he also reap. That's what my mother would have said."

"Mine would say the apple does not roll far from the parents' tree."

"Fall," she corrected him.

"Ah, yes, fall far from the tree."

"Do you have children, Max?"

"I was not so lucky. I never married."

"I'll get to the point," she said, setting down her cup. "I'm wondering if Faith listed her current address on your job application. Of course, she's eighteen but, you see, she's left home and I must speak with her. You understand, don't you?"

"Just a moment." He pulled out a folder from a stack on the counter and wrote a note. "Perhaps I will lose my new employee," he said, handing it to her.

"Some day she'll understand, I hope." Angel hated to disappoint him, especially when he was so helpful, but it had to be done. "One more thing…."

"Yes?" he said.

"I have a tight deadline on my new book, you see. I don't want to leave you in a lurch. So," she drew in her breath. "I've arranged for an alternate, on the turtle watch."

"An alternate?"

"Libby Belle will take my place. She owns the bookstore and knows the ropes."

He paused to consider while she rose to leave. "I appreciate the thought," he said, following her into the gloomy store. The world had turned inside out; its dark lining blotted out the daylight.

He turned to her, his expression hopeful. "Perhaps it would be prudent to wait here until the storm has passed."

In another life Angel might have agreed, talking for hours in the back room, where he might once more put his hands on her and look at her that way.

Instead, she pushed through the door. "Thanks again, Max."

She reached her car just as the heavens opened, releasing a heavy deluge. Looking in the rear view mirror, she patted her face dry, but it was her mother she saw, stepping through the kitchen door in their home in Key West, her arms laded with oranges, dripping wet from the rain.

Heavens! She dried her face with a kitchen towel as she rambled on. *Mama adored the rain. She'd lie down on the front yard, happy as a clam, till the downpour ended. She had an unnerving pattern of speech, kind of like the high pitch of a dolphin. She'd say, 'Look Little One, see how my mermaid tail shines in the rain?'*

Angel sat back with a shiver as the memory deepened. Mother had looked at her aghast, suddenly aware she'd been speaking aloud.

Good Lord, forgive me! Your grandmother Willow tempted the devil, God Bless her soul. Best forget what I said, Angelica.

Until now, Angel had forgotten Willow The Mermaid. The poor woman must have been touched in the head. How had Mother, a devout Christian woman, tolerated her heathen ideas?

Finally, Angel noticed Max watching with concern from the store window, so she waved goodbye. As she drove home through puddles large enough to hold schools of small fish, other bits and pieces her mother had revealed began to surface, quilting together her story.

Angel pictured her mother, Mary Camela Porreca, at a young age. Even then, she probably looked uptight. At least her sparkling turquoise eyes lent her a lively air, the same eye color her mother Willow and all the women before her had possessed.

She pictured her mother's daily walk from Mary Immaculate Star of the Sea School to her home three blocks away on United. The rundown pink Victorian boasted unusual white wooden cutouts in an alternating pattern of liquor bottles and stars. Her father, Joe Porreca, a rumrunner, built the house for his bewitching bride, only to lose his life at sea soon after the birth of Mary.

Perhaps it was a chilly winter day when Mary paused in a shaft of sunlight that slanted through the large western window, warming her small body. Would Mama notice her, she hoped? Lost in another world, Willow was bent over the dining table; her long auburn hair cascaded around her bony shoulders, a flowing white dress engulfed her.

She glued a scallop onto a votive candle decorated with an eclectic mix of shells and Catholic imagery, which mirrored her odd mixture of beliefs. The high-pitched eerie tune she hummed repelled Mary; the boxes of shells piled high before her presented an impassable obstacle. The paltry income these handmade crafts brought at local gift shops barely supported them.

Mary turned a resentful eye on a Sailors' Valentine that hung above the rattan couch. Mama had toiled for years to make it, and each shell represented a moment of Mary's deprivation. How she hated the image: a rigged sailing vessel, its sails made of mother of pearl, under a spray of seagulls with three simple words in an ocean made of mussels, *Forget Me Not*.

If only Mama would not forget her. Why couldn't she give her the same lavish attention that she paid to the stupid sea?

Mary trudged to the kitchen at the back of the house and searched the bare cupboards, just in case a neighbor had dropped by with a homemade treat. But the neighbors avoided her odd mother, so she slapped a thin layer of peanut butter on a slice of old brown bread and poured a glass of milk, wincing at the sour smell. She ticked a check on the grocery list, which her natural sense of order compelled her to keep up-to-date.

With a heavy sigh, she took a seat across from her mother, who continued to ignore her. Mary began to play with a Jujube Top—one of her mother's favorite species. *Stupid shell.* Such sparkly things wouldn't fill Mary's tummy or buy her a new dress.

She spun the white shell like a toy top, which its shape resembled. Willow had removed the outer layer with acid to reveal its pearly essence. The low winter light caught the iridescent colors in a pretty arc as it sailed off the table and skittered across the floor.

At last, Willow turned her ethereal sea green eyes upon her child with the same detached wonderment she might view a mockingbird picking insects from the poinsettia tree outside the window. Mary's breath caught high in her chest. Such moments of connection were rare; she must make the most of it.

Hello, Mama.

Mary made a concentrated effort to smile, but unaccustomed to the effort, she offered only a grimace. Nevertheless, Willow rewarded her efforts with a welcoming smile, as warm as the Florida sun.

With a pale finger, she tapped a colorful image of Saint Barbara, who floated above the glossy sea with her shining halo and arms outstretched in a beatific pose. Around her head she wore a crown of shells. Her mermaid's bejeweled tail glistened in the sun.

Willow spoke in a soft singsong voice. *Mother Mermaid wears the jujube. She says we are like the pearl inside the shell. The waves will rub us clean and show our beauty.*

A small sigh of resentment escaped Mary's lips. Her hand twitched with the impulse to knock the whole stupid pile of shells to the floor.

Desperate for attention, she played along. *How does this mermaid talk to you?*

She tells me many things. She promised me you would be a good girl.

Mama, there is no such thing as a mermaid. It's a lie.

Willow insisted. *She's our mother.*

Mary stamped her foot. *How can your mother be a fish?*

Don't you see my tail, Little One?

To prove her point, Mary checked under the table, but as she met the sweet appeal in her mother's eyes, she swallowed her rebuke.

It's a pretty tail, Mama.

Willow's face brightened. Her hand undulated in the air, imitating the motion of the sea. *Mother Mermaid will call to you in the waves.*

Mary was terrified of the water and reminded her mother. *I can't swim.*

This disturbing fact often puzzled Willow, who swam like a fish. With a sad expression, she stared out the window in the direction of the sea.

Don't worry, Mama. I'll learn to swim, I promise.

Willow gave her a satisfied look before returning to her handiwork. Mary stared hard at her. Mama was strange, that was all there was to it. As this burden sank onto her young shoulders, she decided it was up to her to care for both of them.

Angel stayed snug in her car under the umbrella of an enormous banyan tree, while the storm raged around her. The huge prop roots, dripping with wet gray Spanish moss and covered with air plants, appeared like a hairy beast. A strangler fig had enveloped the tree and the screaming gusts dropped several of its large leathery glossy green leaves onto her windshield.

She peered through the blurry driver's window at a rundown white cottage, confirming the address Max had given. Trade Winds Drive was on the west side of the island, towards Captiva Island. She shivered to think of her daughter trapped forever in Wayne's lowlife world. When she was twenty-five he would be near forty!

Fifteen minutes later there was still no sign of Faith. A chill was creeping into Angel's bones. The hoped-for reunion would have to wait for clear skies. When she pulled into her driveway, she couldn't believe the Red Bug sat in its usual spot. Were the gloomy shadows playing tricks on her? Then a brilliant silver streak of lightning illuminated the front yard: Faith was home!

As quickly as the light vanished, Angel's glee hardened into purpose. Here was her chance, perhaps the last, to set her daughter on the straight and narrow. *Appeal to her innate logic. For God's sake, get rid of that guy.*

Pushing against the whipping wind, she stepped inside the silent cottage. As she headed towards Faith's room, the telltale squeak of Angel's office chair knifed through the cold silence. A cold sick feeling rode up the back of her throat.

Under the rumble in the skies, she reached the office just as Faith looked up, her bright green eyes fierce in the gray light. The lamp on the desk illuminated the letter in her hands. *Tilly's letter.*

Angel's voice compressed to a desperate plea. "Faith?"

As Faith shook the letter in the air, it rained dry blue ink powder onto her jeans. "What the hell is this, Mom?"

Angel's breath fanned like the gills on a dying fish. In anger, Faith resembled her father, as if he, too, reproached her.

"Answer me," Faith said.

The desk lamp flickered as a firebolt landed close to the house. Sheets of rain lashed the windows. How could Angel confess now? With sinking dread, she knew the truth would send Faith running to Wayne's arms, maybe forever. Just as Angel had fled home to be with Santiago. Oh, God, what had she done?

"It means I love you, Faith. That's all it ever meant."

"Wait," Faith said. "Tilly Kemble was my grandmother on your father's side." She screwed up her face as she scanned the letter, her index finger a missile that landed on the page. "But right here it says, 'your old friend Tilly.'"

"She raised me after a fashion. She taught me things I needed to know."

"I don't understand." She looked at Angel as if she were a thief caught in the act. "My father died before I was born. In Vietnam. This Tilly—your friend, not my great-grandmother—refers to him as if he was alive in 1969. I was two years old?"

"Yes," Angel said, matter-of-factly.

"Yes, what?" Faith rattled the letter again. "She says 'the shells say Santiago will see his daughter again one day.' What does that mean?" Her voice trembled as she zeroed in on Angel. "Did you lie to me? Did my father know me before he died?"

"You were just a baby," Angel said. "I tried to protect you."

"From my father?"

"From everything." With the lie exposed, Angel knew that whatever she said sounded suspect. One word fell from her lips. "Faith…." She had to believe she'd made the right choice.

"How could you?" her daughter said, jumping to her feet.

Angel took a step towards her. "I had to—"

"Lie to me?"

"Save you."

"You had no right. You lied about his death?" Faith paused and shook her head, as the enormity of the lie engulfed her. "Oh my God."

"Give me a chance to explain, Kiddo."

"Now you want to explain, now that you've ruined my life?" She waved an envelope in her mother's direction. "Explain this—who is Angel del Corazón?"

Angel's chest tightened. She sounded as if she were talking through a straw. "My family name."

"What?" Faith's knees buckled as she sank into the chair. "What the hell does that mean? Who is Angel Rose?"

“Rose is my middle name. Angel Rose del Corazón.” There, she had said it, though the relief she had always imagined her confession would bring never arrived.

Faith swayed back as if struck, the chair leaning with her weight. “You’re not Angel Rose. So…I’m not Faith Rose…and my dad wasn’t Robert Rose?” She slammed a fist on the desk. “Even the name on your books is a lie?”

“Children don’t care who wrote them.”

“For God’s sake!” She thrust Tilly’s letter at Angel. “Is Corazón your maiden name or your married name? Oh, my God, who am I? Is my name Faith del Corazón?”

“You’re Faith Rose,” Angel said, with a calmness that belied her panic.

“You’re lying!” Faith yelled over the booming thunder, her voice as electric as the storm. “My father. Is he still alive? Tell me.”

Deep down Angel had always known this moment would come. Now she stared at her daughter, speechless. She wanted to hug her and erase the pain etched on her face, but she had lost that right.

“I don’t know where he is,” she said. At least that was true.

Faith’s eyes welled with tears. “You mean somewhere out there I might have a father?”

The words spooled out of Angel like the line from a fishing rod. “You have to understand. You see, my father believed in the Sea Goddess Yemayá but my mother forbade it so he hid his—”

“I’m not interested in your stupid fish stories. Who was my father? What’s his name? What’s my name?”

If only Angel could breathe. “Faith Rose is your name,” she repeated.

“Tell me the truth, Mom. You owe it to me.”

Angel’s hand flew to her chest. “I can’t.”

"God, I hate you."

"Don't say that. I love you, Faith."

"You have a funny way of showing it." She grabbed a handful of Tilly's letters and pushed past her mother.

"Wait." Angel took the presentation box from her purse and thrust it at her. "Your graduation present—it's a Cross pen."

Faith snatched the gift from her mother's hand. Her exotic beauty, formed at the crossroads to many worlds, was even more dynamic in anger. The brilliant sea-green eye color of her maternal ancestors flashed like lightning on the battered sea.

"Wrong initials," she said, flinging the box to the ground.

"Are you going to Wayne?" Angel said.

"At least I can trust him." Then she hefted her duffle and left in the pouring rain.

After having carefully constructed their lives—yes, on top of a lie—how in heaven's name had Angel let the situation get out of control? Her chest screwed tight, like a collapsed sinkhole, leaving her gasping for breath. Listing like a ship off keel, she wove her way to the office and, with a violent swipe, swatted Tilly's remaining letters onto the floor.

She scowled at the raging sea, which heaved in irritated, brownish gray swells. A dark curtain of rain obliterated the horizon where lightning struck. In the luminous flash, nearly neon in contrast to the gloom, she swore she saw Yemayá riding the rollicking waves atop one of her handmaidens, a bottlenose dolphin. Long green hair flowed from underneath a glittering crown of shells, falling over her naked breast. Didn't she look pleased with herself?

Angel grunted. "You bitch, this is your fault."

Yemayá vanished in the trough of a wave, leaving Angel with an unexpected pang of hope. If the Captain had been right, if the Great Lady really was her mother, maybe, just maybe, she would come to her aid.

In clear capital letters, Angel jotted down her wish on a small piece of notepaper: *Give Faith a chance.* Clutching it in her hand, she raced through the house. Where had she seen a coconut shell? She would never keep one—but Faith might. There it was: a paperclip holder on her desk. She tipped out its contents, taping her plea into the hollow.

Angel slipped on her beach shoes, her mind filled with urgency that mirrored the terrible pounding in the skies. She was soaked to the skin as soon as she stepped off the back porch. Shouldering against the whistling wind, her hair whipping around her face, she plucked a handful of fluttering papery magenta bougainvillea leaves and laid them inside the coconut shell.

She scanned the edge of the marsh for the Queen Conch she had banished weeks ago. Its crenulated spire jutted from under the thrash of greenery. With a tug, she freed it. Tucking it under one arm, with the leaf-filled coconut shell held flat against her shirt, she made her way along the deserted footbridge.

At Point Ybel, the repeating beam of the old lighthouse pierced the darkness. A bad feeling gnawed at Angel, warning her to go home. She had no choice. Please, help me, she prayed, inside, *dentro*, to whoever would listen—Papi's Sea Goddess, Mother's Lord God Above—her freedom meant nothing now.

She screamed as an incandescent flash of light rent the turbulent sky. From the other side, another jagged thunderbolt was hurled in a dazzling display of celestial warfare. Spears of fire and the booming drum of sky-power dwarfed all below. Angel knew the heavenly fight for her immortal soul had only paused for eighteen years.

Each time she neared the shoreline, it moved out of reach. Her cold wet legs ached from the effort to cross the sand; twigs and debris whipped past. Powerful breakers roared onto the beach, competing with the din of thunder.

At last she wedged her offering into the wet sand at the high-water mark, just as Papi had taught her. Raising the conch, she blew hard with a deep painful breath. It emitted a puff of sound, swallowed in the storm. She never had done it well and this was no time to quibble. Dropping the trumpet, she yelled into the wind.

"Take it! Please, give Faith a chance."

Huge waves, fast and furious, swept in and out. Sea spray arched high. And yet the coconut shell remained. Lashed with cold wet foam, Angel dug her offering away from the wet sand and carried it closer to the sea. As she set it down, an angry wave slammed into her, buckling her knees. Arms splayed forward, she fell face down as the water retreated, tumbling her with it. Shells racked over her; seawater filled her mouth. Gasping for breath, she clawed in vain at the wet bottom, unable to find purchase.

The next surge rolled her like a child's hoop deep into the black belly of the sea. Angel lost her bearings as dark sky and churning water merged into one crushing mass. Water rushed into her lungs, her body turned numb and rubbery.

From nearby, the irresistible Song of the Fisherman, *La Canción del Pescador*, grew loud: *Ven a mí, mi amor. Tu eres mío, toda para mi. No luches mas. Ven.* Just like the Old Salt who woos his catch, Yemayá called to her, caressing her with icy arms: *Come to me, my love. You're mine, all mine. Give up the fight. Come.*

I'm coming.

CONFESSION

Seashells have been used as money on almost every continent, including by Muslim traders from Zanzibar, tribes in northern Australia, and the Chumash and Iroquois and Algonquian tribes in North America. Over three thousand years ago in China, the money cowry shell, *Cypraea moneta*, was used as currency. In fact, the classical Chinese character for currency originated as a pictograph of a cowrie shell. In Orissa, India, cowrie currency was in use until 1805, when the East India Company replaced it with the British pound sterling.

SANIBEL ISLAND, FLORIDA

SPRING 1985

A numb milky feeling cushioned Angel in her disoriented somnolent state, where disturbing fears of Yemayá pushed her deeper into confusion and solid reality lay just out of bounds. She pushed aside questions she could not or would not answer and focused instead on a deep voice that called to her with gentle regularity. Though she couldn't place the name, she found comfort in the concern and the warm touch.

"Angel? Can you hear me?"

As the hours flowed past like flotsam and jetsam, swirling on currents she could not control, officious strangers disturbed her, until their poking grew too bothersome to ignore, yanking her towards consciousness.

It was not the terrifying Sea Goddess she saw beside her but her neighbor Max. She gave him a blank stare as the realization dawned. His kind support had kept her from diving deeper into the morass of despair. And he was still holding her hand.

He leaned forward, his face lined with worry. *"Mein Gott!"* he exclaimed with a catch in his voice. "You are awake."

Like a dark rain funnel that swoops across the ocean surface, sucking up the water and spitting it out, the memory of recent events pummeled Angel. She recalled the cruel twist of fate that had left her life in tatters: the secret cache of Tilly's letters—a dark stain upon her whitewashed life—now in sweet Faith's hands. How in heaven's name could Angel have let it happen?

She took in the bright sterile room and clinical bed, the plastic tube that carried clear liquid into her vein. "Where am I?" she said.

"Healthpark Medical in Fort Meyers." His accent was thicker than usual. In fact he was a wreck: bloodshot eyes, rumpled and stained clothes. "I found you. In the sea. You were…" He shook his head. "Sinking."

Her tongue felt dry and swollen. "I'm sorry," she said, reaching for a pitcher of water.

He quickly poured a glass and placed it in her hands. "You must rest and you will be good as the new, the doctor says. That is all that matters."

She looked out the window at a smattering of stars etched against the opaque night. It was still light when she begged Yemayá for help. "How long have I been here?"

"Since late this afternoon. Six hours, more or less. They pumped the seawater from your stomach."

Angel reflected on the irony of Tilly's oft-repeated opinion. *You've got seawater in your veins, Kiddo.*

"Faith?" Angel asked. "Does she know?"

"I called her," Max said, his face darkening. "She is very inquisitive, she asked why you came to the store. You see, I told her the truth. She will not work at the shop, but no matter." Before Angel could comment, he rose to leave. "Excuse me, I am instructed to tell the nurse when you awaken. Is there anything you need?"

"I don't think so, thank you."

As she watched him leave, she wondered if in the last moments of consciousness, she had thought of him. The more she probed the vague memory, the more likely it seemed. But why? She hardly knew him. He had saved her—thank God—as any Good Samaritan might. No need to elevate him to yet another savior.

He soon returned, his exhaustion visible in the jerky stride and stooped shoulders.

"The doctor will be called," he said, taking his position and her hand once more. She did not protest; in fact, she wished he would climb into the bed and hold her.

"Max, how did you find me?"

"It is extraordinary." His handsome brow furrowed. "*Ach!* How can I explain? After you left, I went to check my house."

As he averted his eyes, she understood he had made sure she arrived home safely. A soft smile slid over her face as she squeezed his hand. He smiled back at her, and in the sweet lull, she once more discovered how easy it was to be with him.

"But why venture into that terrible storm?" she said.

With a quick nod, he continued. "Perhaps it is hard to understand when I say I heard you. As clearly as if you were in my house, you called." A faraway look crept behind his eyes. "This happened once before in my life when I was just a boy. During the war, *meine Mutti*—my mother—she took me to the train station for the *Kindertransport* to England. Many children were sent for safekeeping. I remember, in her gray gloves, five marks and a bread roll, she tucked into my coat. Then she kissed my head, the top, and put me onto the train. She left without a word. Like the heart of a sparrow, mine beat so fast. I pushed the other children from the window and in the crowd glimpsed her hat—her beautiful brown hair, all gray, it had turned."

He swept back a fallen lock from his forehead and sighed. "Forgive me, this is not the time for my stories."

"I want to know." *You*, Angel silently added. "Please, go on."

"Yes?" He rushed headlong into his tale as if it burst from within. "In Harwich a polite English couple accepted me. The Wrights, they were called. On an attic bed I slept with another boy, also Jewish. Perhaps a year I had been there because my pants grew small. One night there was such a wind like yesterday. And *Mutti* called to me. I could not say where she was but I heard her." He looked deep into Angel's eyes. "Perhaps I sound foolish, perhaps it was the wind, but I swear I heard my mother so clear I could not doubt it. In this way I heard also your call."

"What did your mother say?"

"Only my name, Maximilian. After the train I never saw her again. Many years later, at the Red Cross office, I learned that after we parted, one year later, in the Mauthausen concentration camp she was killed."

"I'm so sorry."

"So ist das Leben." At her quizzical look, he added, "It means 'such is life.' You see, without *Mutti's* mysterious call, perhaps I would not have recognized yours."

"What did you hear?"

As Max hesitated she wondered what, if anything, he might omit, possibly to save one of them from embarrassment. Finally, he told her, "I stood at the window watching the rain when I heard your cry. You said, *Help me*. I ran to the water and saw a trumpet conch and then a glimpse of you. In between the waves." He shut his eyes tight, as if warding off the memory. "I swam to you at once and when I reached you, somehow, I do not know how, I dragged you to the shore. A very kind man—the postal worker with the moustache—he helped me lift you onto the beach. I stayed with you while from my house he called the ambulance."

"My God. Max. I'm so grateful."

The timing of his aid, along with his unusual sensitivity, made her rescue all the more miraculous. Unnerved, she gulped the glass of water, fighting a raspy cough. As he waited, she sensed he was comfortable with the proximity to loss, perhaps too much so.

"Max?"

"Yes?" he straightened, color flooding his cheeks. "Something you need?"

"A cigarette, please?"

"No smoking," Dr. Nash said, as he swept into the room with his medical bag. His seersucker suit was rumpled, his white hair thick as cotton batting. Imperious yet kind-natured, he commanded respect. "You had quite a tumble there, Angel. They pumped half the bay out of you."

"Yes, well, thank you, Edgar. I'm fine now."

"I'll be in the hall, if you need me," Max said.

She couldn't resist watching him leave or the unsettling desire that welled up in her. After all, he had rescued her; it was natural to feel attached. The feeling would pass, just like her weakened state.

Nash placed a cold heavy stethoscope on her chest. "Breathe."

She studied his inscrutable face, wondering what he heard: a current breaking upon the wreckage of the past.

He moved the instrument to another spot. "Again." And once more, until he folded it into his kit and rubbed his glasses clean, avoiding her gaze. "I expect you'll have some blood from the irritation." Almost as an afterthought, he added, "We should take some X-rays."

We? That was how the saving started: *we're in this together*. Mother had used the same enticement when she first attempted to save Angel's soul. *You understand* we *must do this for your own good, don't you?* We *must be vigilant against evil.*

Time took on a strange quality in the hospital, an amorphous rhythm tied to the ever-present beat of mortality's drum. Her narrow brush with death opened the door to childhood fears she had long banished. Her old nemesis Lucifer danced into her dreams with a smarmy grin, his horns on fire. Was he hiding under the hospital bed, waiting to snatch her soul should she expire?

Each time she awoke, she found Max by her side, a safe harbor in the storm.

"Anything you need?" he asked.

"No, I'm fine, really. Just tired."

In the lee of sleep, Angel recalled her mother walking beside her after Sunday morning services. The brim of her straw hat shaded her delicate features. With ramrod posture, she carried an air of satisfaction that set her apart, as if she had accomplished a herculean task. Angel struggled to keep pace, her soft robin-egg-blue crepe dress brushing her bony young knees.

Where was Papi? Most likely he had a charter. During the fishing season, from October to May, his days were booked with clients. Mother worried over the damage to his soul, but they survived on the income.

And then, Angel remembered why she had tucked away this particular day into the recesses of memory for future excavation, perhaps when she might find herself in a hospital bed contemplating life.

There it was, a bump in the sidewalk. Angel squinted in the shimmering glare; human instinct told her it was no ordinary lump. As they drew closer, she realized it was a man lying on the ground, snoring. Mother yanked her to the other side of the street, her sea-green eyes full of scorn. *Drunk on Sunday. Another heathen sinner.*

Mother, what's a heathen?

Heathens aren't Christians like us, Angelica. They're going straight to hell.

As they approached the spruced up pink Victorian with the odd gingerbread trim of liquor bottles and stars, Angel recalled a world map she had seen in school. The enormity of millions of heathens hit her.

But Mother, how can they go to hell if they never even heard of Jesus?

It's our mission to share the Lord's saving grace. Without salvation, there can be no place in heaven.

Mother continued down the brick path across their lush yard while Angel lingered on the sidewalk. The bright sunlight glazed a profusion of pink hibiscus plants around the front porch. A large staghorn fern jutted from its helmet-like base under the canopy of the big oak. Several wooden baskets of white Moth orchids hung from the orange trees.

In this small slice of tropical paradise, she shivered at the hideous picture taking hold in her mind. Millions of Africans of all ages, male and female, lithe and stout, comely and homely, were writhing in the flames of hell, their dark faces contorted in agony, while Satan danced a gleeful jig over this huge crop of souls. Forever.

Mother beckoned. *Angelica, come.*

At the crisp snap of the screen door, the horrifying images shattered. Angel ran ahead. The wood slats of the front porch threatened to give way, spilling her into the yawning chasm of hell. She hurried inside, only to find a home that no longer offered comfort.

From the brick fireplace that occupied one wall of their living room, Lucifer oozed into form, his tail cracking the air like a lasso. He leaned against the chimney, leering at her. He wore a fine dark suit, the pressed pants draped over his hooved feet. A pair of glowing horns on his head lent him a dangerous, exciting air.

The handsome devil spoke to her with astonishing intimacy, his voice deep and silky. *Hey there, Angel Baby. Nice to meet you. You and me, see, we're gonna be real good friends. You can take it to the bank, we're gonna have a lot of fun.*

Angel wanted to scream when the clang of kitchen pots interrupted their meet and greet. Lucifer winked at her. *See you around, Angel Baby.* In a puff of smoke, he disappeared.

Again, Mother called. Angel found her bent over the kitchen table in her frilly apron with worn apple patch pockets, peeling a pile of potatoes for Sunday stew. A loaf of brown bread baked early that morning sat on top of the stove, scenting the air with yeasty warmth.

Angel was desperate to understand. *How about China? Are the Chinese going to hell, too?*

Of course. That is, except for those the Lord saves through missionaries.

What about Jewish people?

Mother brushed a tendril of auburn hair from her brow and sighed. *Angelica, the Hebrew people killed our Lord Jesus Christ. Naturally, they are doomed. Now, shuck the clams.*

Angel donned her daisy-patterned apron and dipped her hands into a bucket of clams that sat in the sink. She barely felt the icy water as her thoughts overheated with grotesque images. Millions of Chinese and Jews suffered along with the condemned Africans. The immense scale of carnage left her lightheaded. She leaned against the kitchen counter for support, as she raised her protest.

But, but…it doesn't seem fair to punish people for something they don't believe in when they don't even know about it. I don't think a good father would do that to his children.

Mother gasped. *Angelica Rose Porreca del Corazón. For goodness sake, what does the Good Lord tell us in John 3:16? 'For God so loved the world, that he gave his only begotten Son, that whosoever believeth in him should not perish, but have everlasting life.' Isn't that so?*

She nodded. That's what the Bible said.

Well, then you know no man enters the kingdom of God without the Lord Jesus Christ as his one and only savior.

Angel stared ahead while Mother's suspicions flared. It became apparent to both that Angel was not saved. Truth be told, she would have preferred salvation to the constant terror over the state of her soul. Who wouldn't prefer a first class ticket to eternal paradise to a cattle car in a pit of fire? Unfortunately, she didn't feel God's love, not in her soul, her bones, her head, nothing, *nada.*

Mother bit down on this revelation with the tenacity of a gator on fresh kill. *For heaven's sake, do you believe in Jesus Christ as your lord and savior?*

In those days the magical power of truth still held sway over Angel, and she freely spoke her mind. *I don't need a 'savior.' Besides, I don't think God will send me to hell if He loves me. Papi would never do that and the Heavenly Father shouldn't be so mean.*

Mother's cheeks flushed crimson. *Lord have mercy.* She grabbed the switching belt from a hook by the back door. At first, Angel puzzled over this because she hadn't been naughty. When her mother took her by the arm, however, she began to whimper.

Please, no.

Mother lit into the back of her bare legs. Over and over, Angel felt the sting of stiff leather. Time accelerated to the tempo of each lash. Her small body burned with fury and shame. As the final blow fell, her mother's exhortation rang out. *Flee, Satan, flee.*

At last she turned Angel to face her. Perspiration beaded her brow, her body hummed with determination.

Do you accept Jesus Chris into your heart, Angelica? Will you be saved for all eternity?

Angel hung her head and told her mother what she wanted to hear. They were only words; what did it matter?

I accept the Lord Jesus into my heart.

Praise the Lord.

Satisfied, Mother released her and took out a bottle of iodine. While she dabbed the red welts on Angel's legs, she sang. *Amazing Grace! How sweet the sound that saved a wretch like me. I once was lost, but now am found; was blind, but now I see.*

When she was done, she stood over Angel, her expression tinged with sorrow. *You understand we must do this for your own good, don't you? We must be vigilant against evil. Your grandmother Willow was too self-indulgent to be saved. Promise me you won't follow her misbegotten path.*

I promise, Mother.

I pray your name is written in God's Book of Life.

She returned to her peeler, and Angel to her shucking knife, the scrape and punch of their utensils creating a counter-rhythm that punctured the warm air, redolent of bacon and potatoes. The boisterous sounds of children whizzing by on bicycles floated in the open window; a driver leaned on his car horn and yelled—all blasphemous sinners disrespecting the day of worship.

In her heart, Angel knew she was damned like them. She simply had to find a way to be saved, no matter what it took. She would be on the lookout for a ticket to heaven.

One minor victory: she had not shed a single tear. Would she also find courage come Judgment Day when the Good Lord surely would question her salvation? She might have fooled Mother but you couldn't fool Jesus. He would see the stamp of a sinner on her soul as bright as a yellow sticker on a Chiquita banana.

As if to prove the point, her new friend Satan sang in her ear, inventing words to the popular banana jingle with a calypso beat. *I'm a condemned sinner and I've come to say, souls have to ripen in a certain way.*

Lost in her own thoughts, Mother mumbled a strange saying, *Whenever a star falls, a mermaid is born.*

Though Angel couldn't make sense of it, she filed it away as an important clue. On that day she became a spy in her own house. The beautiful efficiency of truth no longer served her; lying was an indispensable tool of the trade. Even then, she knew that, sooner or later, she would pay for her sinful lies.

A sheet of blinding sunshine beamed off the many rows of cars, blanketing the world. The intense glare dwarfed all other reality; only this parking lot seemed to exist. Angel squinted against the light, holding steady to Max's arm as they walked through the hospital doors. Twenty-four hours felt like an eternity, and she longed for her own perfectly imperfect bed.

He helped her into his old Mercedes Benz wagon, her cold tired bones welcoming the steamy heat of the leather seat. Max smiled at her as he started the car. To witness their easy companionability, the sweet smiles, as if they shared a deep secret, his clear concern and her easy acceptance, she thought they might be mistaken for a couple, lovers even. *Was it possible?*

"Do you mind?" she said, rolling down the window. "I miss the fresh air."

"It's a lovely day," he said.

"It's wonderful."

"Besides, the air conditioning works not so good."

"I've heard German cars are reliable."

"We have traveled many miles together." He affectionately patted the dash. "I call her my Shell-Mobile. There are several shell fairs along the Eastern seaboard and I have been always searching for the Sailors'

Valentines—this was the collection you saw on the wall in the shop, the shadow boxes with shell mosaics. Do you remember?"

"I do."

"I have placed small classified ads in towns where shipping ports once existed. It is surprising where I have found sellers, and also buyers; I have a number of collectors."

They drove in silence onto the causeway at Punta Rassa, past the thin stretch of sand and marl that stood between the bridge and San Carlos Bay. Small bands of fisherman dotted the narrow beach, their backs to the road, apart from the passing world.

The last subject Angel wished to discuss was Sailors' Valentines, but she felt she owed Max—and realized she wanted to please him. However, to speak of shell work without confessing her knowledge or the many afternoons under Tilly's tutelage was a lie of omission—just as grave in God's eyes as a bald-faced lie. She offered a general observation, a true one, since she had never finished a single Valentine.

"It must take a very long time to make one."

"Yes, depending, naturally, on the experience of the artist," he said. "When I began, what a bumbler I was, forever dropping the shells. My first example—*ach!*—it was for the rubbish."

"Where did you learn?"

"After my adopted parents died, I spent on Nantucket a summer. On a whim I joined a class. It was a pleasant distraction that became, I'm afraid, an obsession." Max laughed. "Not so bad a vice, no?"

She murmured encouragement, wondering if he understood the powerful realm of Yemayá in which he played.

"I find the work quite exciting," he went on. "So many subtleties to discover. Each Valentine tells a story, like so, the choice of shells, colors and shapes and yes, the design—this is not a coincidence. A careful, patient eye can read the artwork, perhaps like one of your books."

"It does seem complex."

"Precisely," Max said, with more appreciation than she deserved. "When the opportunity to purchase your friend's store arose, I could not resist. You see, I have the sickness of all collectors; my garage is full—I confess I prefer never to sell anything. But this is the game, no? Recently, I decided the shell work to teach, to keep alive the magic. The class will be in the workshop in my garage. Perhaps you would care to join us?"

Angel shifted her weight, angling herself away from him. See how romantic feelings bloomed like algae in August, clouding your good sense till you couldn't talk about anything but the damn shells. She never should have entered into the topic.

"I'm sorry, Max, but I'm on a deadline."

"Another time, I hope," he said, so plainly it saddened her.

"Would you like to come to dinner? It's the least I can do."

She could feel the smile that filled him. "Yes, I'd like that very much," he said. "When you are stronger."

"I'll be back on my feet in no time. How about Saturday?"

"I'd be delighted."

At last, as her cottage came into view, her body leaned forward of its own will.

"Tired?" Max asked.

"A little, yes," Angel replied.

"Would you care for the chicken soup? *Mutti* claimed it cured all."

"Please, don't bother. You've done more than enough."

He stationed the car near her door and laid a hand on her arm. "Angel," he said, "To care for you is no bother. I will bring the soup, no matter what you say."

Everything felt wrong when Angel awoke the next morning—the room seemed at a tilt, a sheen of sweat stuck to her skin. The bedside clock read nine, much later than she usually awoke. The pleasing, dappled light that fell from the window onto the bedcovers felt unjustified. Faith was gone—maybe forever. In a matter of days, their lives had changed with terrifying swiftness—just like eighteen years ago when they had fled from Key West. Cycles of love and loss repeating; for God's sake, when would it end?

Through the open door she heard sounds in the kitchen—the kettle whistling, a rusty hinge on the cupboard. She was glad she'd given in to Max's insistence to stay the night. She recalled how he had waited in the hallway while she changed, the dinner he'd brought, the small regret that had seized her as he left to sleep in the other room. Had she really wanted to cuddle with him?

A piece of paper on the bedstand caught her eye: Max had noted Faith's telephone number. Angel settled the white push-button phone in her lap. If she had known that she might be trapped in the future by decisions she had made long ago, would she have acted differently? Though it brought small comfort, she realized she would have done exactly the same thing.

After several rings her daughter answered the line. "Hello?"

"Faith."

A heavy silence hung between them. Her daughter had a right to be angry, but she was missing information, history, motives—for heaven's sake, context!

"I'm home," Angel said. "I thought you'd want to know."

"Max told me."

"Listen, I want to explain."

"I'm listening. Start with my father's name."

"For heaven's sake. One fact extracted from the whole won't give you a complete picture. Please, trust me."

"After you've lied to me, like my whole life?" Faith's voice rose louder. "I want my birth certificate."

A rush of energy—half uncomfortable laugh, half surprised gasp—escaped Angel's lips. "Your birth certificate?"

"Yeah, what?"

"Nothing." Like a thief who fears he's left a clue at the scene of the crime only to learn he's off the hook, a wave of relief washed over Angel. She hadn't filed a birth certificate until they arrived in Sanibel. "You don't need me for that; you can find it yourself at the courthouse in Fort Myers."

Faith hesitated. "Which means my father's name isn't listed." There was a sharp intake of breath. "My God, is my birthday correct?"

As an emotional screw tightened Angel's chest, her cough barked in protest.

"It wasn't all a lie, Kiddo. We've had a good life, you know that's true."

Like lightning zapped onto the sea, anger licked Faith's words. "I don't know what's true anymore. I have a right to know who I am."

"Why can't we just go on like before?" Angel said.

"It's none of your business," Faith replied. "But I'll tell you, anyway. I want my real name on my marriage license."

"What?" Angel jerked forward. "You can't marry him."

"You can't stop me."

"Well, I can't give you what you want."

"You can't or you won't?"

"It won't do you any good."

"I'm a reporter, remember?"

"What does that mean?"

"I've got your name, Corazón—maiden or married. Tilly's letters were postmarked in Key West—that's where I'll start my search. With two key facts I can track down my birth info and, maybe, even my father. I bet he'll explain it to me."

"Faith, you don't understand."

"No, Mom, you don't understand. I'm doing this with or without you. But if you refuse to help me, I'll never speak to you again."

Angel heard her daughter breathing into the line and pictured the hot glare in her eyes. She thought of the last time she had spoken to her mother eighteen years ago.

"Well?" Faith said.

"Oh, Kiddo, it's for your own good."

Click. The line went dead. Angel slumped in the bed as a hard cough racked her body. She spit up blood and pus into a tissue—nothing more than irritation, the doctor had said. *Forget it.*

At the sound of footsteps in the hall, she pulled on her robe, aware of how much energy the small effort cost her. A moment later Max appeared in the doorway with a food tray. The creamy orange sunlight softened the lines in his pressed linen shirt and tanned chiseled features. His warm, welcoming smile lifted her despair.

"May I come in?" he said.

Angel pulled the coverlet up over her. "What's this?" she said.

He set the tray on her lap. "Breakfast."

She took in the eggs and sausage, the crisp toast and steaming coffee, the bright yellow hibiscus in a silver vase. Her antibiotics and the daily papers, too—he had thought of everything.

"Goodness, I've never had breakfast in bed," she said. As he moved to leave, she added, "Please, stay, if you have time."

"Nothing is so pleasant as this," he said, sitting on a chair across from her.

"*Hmmm*," she murmured between bites. "Heaven."

"When there is time to prepare, I am not such a bumbler, as you suspect."

"I don't think you're a bumbler, Max. Maybe an idealist."

"Only a fool asks for perfection. To be happy I need so little but, yes, perhaps I seek the ideal. I believe all things are possible. This morning, the beach was inviting, gray and quiet, and I took a walk. So many shells after a storm, like a child in a candy store I was. I found this." He placed on the tray a brittle white bivalve shell with wing-like flanges. "*Cyrtopeura costata*. I wonder how it remained intact in such a storm? I have only ever found a single part."

Angel held her fork mid-air. "An angel wing," she said, running a finger across the brittle hinge as her thoughts turned to a long ago memory: she and Santiago wrapped in a lover's embrace, their bodies naturally connected.

The fork slipped from her grasp and clattered to the floor. Max was beside her at once.

"What is it, Angel?"

"I can't." Her hands flew to cover her face.

"Please, tell me. To me it will not matter. In this life difficult choices must be made. Often, for many years afterwards we suffer."

Touched by his compassion, she wondered what it would be like if he slipped into bed, his warm body next to hers, and held her tight? She would tuck under his arm, her head on his chest, and the spinning world at rest. She looked up at him, longing to confess everything that stood in her way. His patient expression invited, but the distance was too far and she was weary.

"I did my best, that's what matters," she said, picking up the cup of coffee.

"You must rest," he said, rising to his feet. "Please, call me if you need anything."

"Max?"

"Yes?"

"Thank you for everything. I don't know what I would have done without you."

"It's my pleasure."

Exhaustion or the steaming noonday heat, perhaps both, chained Angel to the bed. Each time she considered taking a stab at the day, she fell back into a troubled state, her legs restlessly swimming under the linen sheets in search of a kiss of cool air. She replayed the conversation with Faith over and over in her mind, gripped by the alarming possibility she might find her father.

Angel pushed herself up on the pillows and lit a cigarette, racking her brain for loopholes in the past through which the truth might slip. Thank God the birth certificate listed Angel Rose as mother; father unknown. No marriage certificate existed, either. Santiago had adhered to the Communist belief that marriage shackled lovers like beasts of burden, while Angel had believed they were already married in the eyes of God.

If, however, Faith went to Key West and spoke to Mary or Tilly, the trail might lead to Santiago. A cold sweat broke over Angel's brow. On impulse, she dialed her mother. Her heart jittered as she pictured the phone ringing in their old kitchen. What would she say? *Don't talk to your granddaughter?*

A recorded message announced the number was no longer in service. Had Mother moved? She called information, but the operator found no listing for Mary del Corazón. Angel replaced the receiver, afraid of what such a dead end might mean. *And what of Tilly?*

On shaky legs she rushed to her office. Tucked in a file, she found a dog-eared, green address book patterned with pink hibiscus flowers.

She dialed Tilly's home number.

"Digáme?" a woman answered.

Angel inquired if Tilly was home. *"Está en casa Tilly Kemble?"*

"No la conozco." She didn't know anyone by that name. "*Vivo aquí hace diez y seis años.*" Then she hung up.

If she had lived there for sixteen years, Tilly must have moved within two years of Angel's departure. Perhaps she had married Carlos? If only Angel could recall his last name. She dialed their former place of employment, Howard Johnson's on North Roosevelt, but reached the same impasse. How could someone as distinctive as Tilly disappear in a town that size?

Angel slumped in her desk chair, staring out to sea. A stifling haze had settled over the island, trapping time in the motionless mass of air and sea. The scalding sun hid behind the uninspiring gray curtain, like a dissipated rock star retiring off stage to recoup his energy for the next dazzling display.

There was only one way to show her daughter that lying had been the kindest choice: Angel would have to tell her story. What did she have to lose now that the can of worms had been opened? She rolled a clean sheet into the typewriter, pondering how to begin.

With your father's witchy nonsense, of course.

It was her mother's voice Angel heard, clear and strong. In her mind's eye, she saw her standing by the window with ramrod posture, her steely green eyes like beacons against the whitish blur outside.

Angel protested the lack of details; other than random facts, snatches of stories, her parents had not spoken often of the past. Mother dismissed her concerns with a stern shake of her head.

Faith never knew me, or even the real you, and yet, she's repeating our story, isn't she? For heaven's sake, you're a writer. Imagine each of our lives as an inevitable act in a long-running play.

The task was daunting. Even worse, Angel feared any liberties with the past might further alienate her daughter.

Angelica, when will you understand the invisible hand of God? If you allow the Holy Spirit to move through you, inspiration will come.

Even if Angel did not subscribe to her mother's beliefs, she had to admit she had a point—*let it come.* At that, she heard the sound of wild tribal drumming and a scene flashed before her with such fine detail that she could not resist writing it down.

* * * * *

A HOLY WAR

KEY WEST, FLORIDA

DECEMBER 4, 1935

Over one hundred miles from Key West, in a field outside Havana, destiny revealed itself to my father, Rafael del Corazón Ramos. In Cuba, December 4th is dedicated to St. Barbara, who led a double life—a custom my father and mother and I would later follow.

To those who adhered to the old ways of Santeria, a religion brought over from the Yoruba people of West Africa, St. Barbara was also known as Chongo, the patron of artillery, storms, and lightning. Santeria loosely translates as devotion to the saints or *santos*. Its practitioners saw no conflict in a saint's dual guise or gender, no matter how hard the Catholic Church tried to suppress their beliefs.

If you had been invited to the secret ceremony, or perhaps stumbled upon it in the countryside, lured by the loud beating of the drums, you would have witnessed an adherence to ritual as strict as a Catholic mass. The incessant drums that called to the *orishas*, or deities, would have horrified Rafael's devout Catholic mother, who believed her husband when he told her it was an auspicious day for fishing, a lie that his son would employ to his wife in the years to come.

Because my father was born on Chongo's day, he wore the warrior god's signature red and white colors on the day of his initiation, or *asentado*, into Santeria. At age fifteen he was handsome with olive skin and broad shoulders. In the shade of a pine grove, surrounded by his father, who sat in a trance, quivering like iron filing sucked into a magnetic field, his beloved godfather, a cage full of roosters, and a dozen priests, or *santeros*, he dreaded the farce at hand.

Rafael only believed in the miracle of pleasure, especially fishing and girls. Both his parents were crazy to believe in anything but warm sunlight on bare shoulders, the *zing* of a fishing reel, or the soft lips of a pretty girl. He shrugged off his irritation. After all, if the ceremony secured his privileges on *La Libertad,* his family's fishing vessel—also a convenient place for fucking—it was well worth it.

A dark-skinned curvaceous girl appeared in a shaft of sunlight that strafed the pine grove. Swaying to the beat of the drums, a basket on her hip, she walked through the grove towards a makeshift altar. Rafael had seen the doe-eyed beauty once before when he visited the *Iyalochoa*, or high priestess. This was her teenage daughter, Ines. *Qué guapa*. Stunning.

As she passed near, her bewitching scent of jasmine and cinnamon stirred him. From under thick dark lashes, Ines sent a coy look of invitation that hit him hard in the groin. He would initiate this bitch.

The diminutive high priestess, a revered witch, or *bruja*, did not miss the exchange. She banged her shaman's stick on the ground, which sent the dangling cowry shells twirling in the air. Ever since she had seen the mark of Chongo in the shape of a cross on his tongue, she had known he would favor the deity's devilish side.

Ines set the picture of St. Barbara upon the altar, as well as offerings to the *orishas*: corn meal and okra, apples, cactus fruit, and red wine. Young Rafael leered at the girl's backside. When the high priestess called his name, he barely registered her command, until a hand pushed him forward. She held a machete in one hand and gripped his arm with the other. Though he towered over her, he was powerless to move and swore she could read his deepest thoughts. He cringed as a *santero* handed the old witch a rooster.

Here we go—chicken shit.

The high priestess spoke in archaic Lucumi as she rubbed the squawking rooster on my father's hair and body so that his spirit, or *ashe*, would catch onto the sacrificial animal. As she repeated this ritual with yet another feathered offering, Rafael shared a bemused smile with Ines.

In a dark, guttural voice, the old witch cried out to Chongo. *Thwack! Thwack!* She cleaved the roosters upon the altar while a *santero* collected the sacrificial blood in a gourd. He offered it to Rafael, who winced as he swilled it down.

Eh, maybe the cock would increase his virility.

The high priestess poured water on the ground three times while she offered a prayer to Chongo. "*Omi tuto, ana tutu, tut laroye, ile tuto olodumare ayuba bo wo eve elese olodumare ayuba bai ye baye to nu.*"

As her eyes rolled back in her head, she began to jerk like a loose electric wire. Soon her movements calmed and she spoke in Chongo's deep masculine voice. She begged the deities to accept the young initiate when a psychedelic mushroom appeared around him with coded images that proclaimed his future: Rafael del Corazón's soul was cursed and he would bring ruin upon his family.

The *bruja* wailed at the bad news. "*Qué mala suerte.*"

The entire company held its breath. The drumming halted. Even Rafael took a step back; something he could not name disturbed him. Unbeknownst to him, centuries of beliefs—Canarian, African, and Catholic, which had washed upon these shores and worked their way into his genes—quickened from a dormant state to a full-blown understanding: a merciless death awaited those who failed to believe in the deities.

Resisting the overwhelming fear, my father forced a lustful glance at Ines. A cold hard dryness crept up the back of his throat, threatening to blot out even his desire for her. Holy shit, the crazy witch might shrink his balls.

He turned, ready to flee, when the Priestess stopped him with the point of her knife.

This is what she said: "*Lo te juro, si no te cases con una mujer de inestimable reputación, no vale nada tu vida.*" With a simple prophecy, she triggered his destiny, and therefore, mine, and yours, too, Faith. If Rafael didn't marry a righteous woman, his life would be worthless.

He looked the crazy hag in the eye and laughed. Like his great ancestor, Ponce de Leon, he was a conquistador of women. According to legend, the Spaniard had fathered a son with an Indian woman on his second trip to the Americas. When he left them behind, he broke the poor woman's heart. Thereafter, the little family was known as del Corazón, of the heart.

Rafael would never marry, either. "*Nunca me case.*"

The priestess quailed at such sacrilege, shaking her stick at him. No one escaped destiny, especially him. "*Nadie puede escapar el destino. Por lo menos tú.*"

My stubborn father took Inez by the hand—"*Vámanos*"—and the young lovers ran to a nearby field. There, under a moonlit sky, he washed away the bitter aftertaste of his failed initiation with the surefire salve of pleasure.

By the time my Mother graduated from Key West High in 1946, her frustration over her mother Willow's devotion to the Catholic saints had reached a tipping point. One fresh spring day in 1946, eighteen-year-old Mary quietly declared spiritual war.

It started out like every other Sunday morning, as she escorted her emaciated mother to St. Mary's By The Sea. Willow clutched Mary's arm, her swishy gait propelling her like a fish fanning its tail through the water. In the stiff westerly breeze her white caftan billowed around her bony body with a ghostly air. Her long hair hung as gray and brittle as Spanish moss.

As a well-dressed family of four passed them on the sidewalk, their questioning, superior looks passed judgment on Willow. Oblivious to their criticism, she simply smiled. The shame and defensiveness that Mary had harbored from a young age broke over her like a storm.

In a harping voice, she scolded her mother. "Why do we scrimp and save when you insist on starving yourself? Your Sea Goddess is a monster."

Caressing her arm, Willow responded in a singsong voice full of love. "The Great Mother feeds me, Little One."

"Humph." Surely, Christ, who had turned a single loaf of bread into food for the multitudes, did not approve of her mother's abusive fasts or wasteful indulgences to the church. "Remember how Jesus kicked the moneylenders out of the temple? He wouldn't want you to sacrifice your hard-earned wages to the priests' fancy robes."

Willow offered a radiant smile in reply. As they entered the tall Victorian edifice, Mary's back stiffened. The repellent scent of beeswax in the vestibule made her skin crawl like scorpions scratching to the surface in a rainstorm.

Her mother sighed like an ardent suitor, dropping her pitiful coins into the donation box to purchase yet another stupid candle that would not alleviate their day-to-day burdens.

They walked down the rich carpet along the center aisle, bathed in the pretty light that passed through arched windows of yellow and pink stained glass. The thick limestone walls offered a cool respite from the tropical heat. High arches supported a barrel-vaulted ceiling, compelling the eye toward the lace-covered altar and, above it, to the luminous stained glass image of Stella Maris, Mother Mary as Star of the Sea.

This absurd spectacle, with its outlandish fripperies and ostentatious adornments, was the root of all their troubles. Since this hypocrisy fooled her guileless mother, Mary decided to take matters into her own hands.

She helped Willow to her favorite spot in the front row and excused herself. A litany of justifications ran through her mind as she retraced her steps. Wasn't the collection intended for the poor, like them? Mama had given far more than her share. Why, if you added it all together, Mary could have gone to college instead of night school and avoided the daily drudgery of the factory, where she would spend the rest of her miserable life.

Alone near the collection box, she hesitated. She toyed with her hair, glancing side to side. No one was watching. She would take what Mother had given, not a cent more. Her hand shot forward—the deed was done.

With the stolen loot jammed into her skirt pocket, she slunk back to Willow's side. Oh, dear God, if she were sent to prison, who would care for

Mama? Of course Mary would not have to resort to such wicked behavior if not for the ridiculous excess of the Catholic Church. She must find a better way.

While Mary pondered a more efficient spiritual direction, Rafael del Corazón wondered why he hadn't caught a single fish since the season opened a week ago. He docked *La Libertad* in its slip at Garrison Bight, only a few miles from St. Mary's. Not a speck of trouble worried the clear azure skies, and the other ships in port boasted plentiful catch.

He slid down the ladder from the flybridge, landing with a thud in the cockpit, and cursed his bad luck. "*Qué mala suerte.*"

His first mate grunted. Eagle-eyed Palo, who had a reputation for spotting a sailfish leap over a hundred yards away, even on a choppy day, swore he'd seen fish turn away from their baited hooks.

The client that day, a salesman from New York, had lost stature in front of his trio of clients. "What the hell, Captain? You promised big game."

Rafael employed his charm on the infuriated Yankee. "Eh, *señor*, we ask the Lady of the Sea for her blessing, but she's fickle like all women. Next time, I give you a ten percent discount. But, if we catch a two hundred pounder—I done it before—you pay me ten percent extra."

The businessman weighed the risk. "What if there's no fish next time?"

My desperate father puffed out his broad chest, summoning his confidence, which was crumbling like the shoreline after a nasty hurricane. "The Corazón family has fished these waters for generations"—he started to tell the legend of Ponce de Leon but didn't have the heart for it—"and I swear, I never saw it before. The Great Lady of the Sea always takes pity on us. Unless…."

"Unless what?"

"Unless we don't deserve it." And here, Rafael cocked his eye at the client, implying it was his fault.

In fact, the New Yorker had lost a few deals. Damn, maybe he'd carried his streak of rotten luck south. Never mind, he still had the juice and he'd be back to prove it.

"Fifteen percent discount?" They shook on it and he slapped a hundred dollar bill into the Captain's palm. "The fish better be running next year!"

Alone with Palo, my father shot him a suspicious look. "You change the chum?"

The tight-lipped seadog shook his head. He never thought he'd see the fisherman's curse befall a Corazón.

Rafael examined the tackle, wondering if a new lure or the ugly whore he'd slept with or Palo's thinning hair was the cause of his troubles. In secret, he had resorted to dropping crushed Jamaican Dogwood overboard in order to stun the fish, something no fisherman worth his salt ever did. The fish still stayed away.

He shuddered to think of word spreading to Havana, and as his thoughts traveled homeward, he recalled the wild beating of the drums at his failed initiation, the old witch's whirling cowrie stick and her ridiculous pronouncement: His life would be worthless unless he married a righteous woman. *Could it be true?*

On the same day that the Captain's confidence hit bottom, Mary's life hit a crisis point. At eight in the morning, she punched the time clock at the Eduardo Hildalgo Gato's Cigar Factory near Mallory dock and walked through the huge, white, cake-box building with its dense aroma of tobacco, sea algae, and morning glories. When she arrived at her accounting office, she hung her linen jacket on the back of a chair and sharpened a No. 2 pencil with a sigh.

Her portly boss gave her a curt nod as he strode past her desk. "Good morning, Miss Porreca," That girl was the best number cruncher they ever had. Good thing, too, 'cause she wasn't much of a looker.

Mary knew what people thought. Neighbors no longer asked if she had a fella. As long as the bills were paid, and she could care for Mama, she accepted her lot.

At five o'clock on the dot, she gathered her things and headed to market. As she walked into the sunlit day, an inexplicable, gut-wrenching dread filled her. Though never one to indulge fanciful imaginings, Mary could not ignore an overwhelming presentiment: *Mama's in trouble.*

By the time she reached home, she was at a run. She threw open the front door and found poor Willow on the floor, her wan face twisted in pain.

Mary crouched beside her. "Mama! What's wrong?" As Willow's sides heaved like a beached fish, she made a sucking sound. "Don't leave me, Mama!" Mary ran to her neighbor's house to call an ambulance.

The nerve-wracking ride to Marathon took over four hours. Mary clung to her mother's side, fighting off grief with the same iron-willed formula that had ensured their daily survival. They arrived at Fishermen's Hospital in the still of night. The attendants who rushed Willow inside marveled at her ineffable glow. Even at death's door, this odd creature had uncommon grace.

The harried doctor offered Mary little hope. "Your mother had a debilitating stroke. It's in God's hands now."

Mary gently squeezed her mother's limp hand, longing to hear her singsong voice. Willow had barely belonged to this world, and now only a tenuous thread connected her. For the first time in her life, Mary wept for all the loving things she had never told her mother.

Early next Saturday morning she proceeded to Fort Zachary Taylor Beach, Willow's favorite spot for worship. The hot autumn sun lounged among a bevy of frothy white clouds. A mild salty breeze blew across the Atlantic, sending gentle waves to the feet of beachcombers stooped along the shore.

If my mother had looked towards the eastern end of the beach, she might have seen my father making a similar stab at faith. Destiny circled closer as my future parents begged for salvation—and I like to think I egged them on from a ringside seat in Baby Heaven.

Mary wrote a practical offer:

Dear Mother Mermaid,

Please save Mama. In exchange, I will owe you a lifetime of goodness.

Sincerely,

Mary Rose Porreca.

She tucked the note inside a coconut half-shell and covered it with bougainvillea petals. Setting the offering at the high-tide mark, she repeated her prayer, and sat nearby to wait for a miracle. To her dismay, an hour later, rolling sea and listless coconut never met. It was time to take the long bus ride to Marathon. Mary collected seawater into a Mason jar and sent the idolatrous coconut shell into the water with a swift kick.

That afternoon she decorated Willow's hospital room with her exotic votive candles. She sprinkled seawater on her fair brow, while she sang in pale imitation of her mother's high-pitched song to the Sea Goddess. And still Willow did not stir, not even a flick of her so-called mermaid's tail.

As a last resort, Mary took a shorn Queen Conch from her straw basket. She had often used it to call Willow when she tarried by the sea. Now she raised the trumpet shell to her lips and blew a short toot, followed by a long blast, filling the air with deep mournful sounds: *Buoo! Buuoooaah!* Come home!

A livid nurse charged into the room, but softened at the sight of Mary's grief-stricken face. The Bahamian woman gently loosened the shell from her grip.

"You can't blow de conch here, darlin'. I keep it at dem desk for you."

In the end, Mary's hard work and iron will had failed to save her mother. She buried her face in Willow's hand. *It was all for nothing.*

At first, she didn't hear the raspy sound Willow made. Perhaps the conch bellow had awakened my grandmother, or else, from her bird's-eye view in the nether regions of consciousness, she decided to have a hand in fate's plan.

Her eyes flew open. "Little one, buy a candle."

"Mama!" Mary edged closer. "Can you hear me?"

Again, Willow's voice squeaked. "Pray to St. Mary."

Her otherworldly luminosity spread through her feeble body, like channel lights illuminating the way, then faded once more as she fell back into her somnolent state before my poor mother could convey her love and regret.

* * * * *

SANIBEL ISLAND, FLORIDA

SUMMER 1985

Angel plugged in the twinkling lights on the porch and stood back to admire the pretty effect. The pinpoints of light against the dusky sky lent the cottage a festive air. The buttery aroma of baking fish, along with the music of Celia Cruz, the queen of salsa, wafted from the house. The music made Angel itch to dance. She had survived dark passage through an underwater grave and now a handsome man was coming to dinner—reasons enough to celebrate.

For three days Angel had been holed up in her office, communing with her mother and her mother's mother and her father and his people, and like the wave that sweeps clean the shore, their stories had eased her pain, if only a little. At the post office she had hugged an envelope like a life preserver before mailing it to Faith. Now, she looked past the end of the driveway, over the salmon-flared sunset, willing the pages of family lore to bring her daughter home.

Dear Faith,

Many times I was tempted to tell you the truth, especially when anger flashed in your eyes and you were the spitting image of your father. Fear silenced me, fear of losing your faith in me.

Now I've decided to write our story—it's yours, too. Please try to see beyond my role as your mother to the struggling young woman I once was. Think of my life as one part of a long-running play that led to your inevitable act.

Oh, I know you think you're nothing like me. True, the outer shell may be different, but the creature inside is similar.

The enclosed pages will introduce you to my parents. More will follow.

I miss you terribly,

Mom

Angel hurried to dress, hoping something would jump out of her closet and say, *wear me*, but nothing did. She searched Faith's closet, where a sunflower-colored sundress called to her. She slipped into the thigh-length dress, twisted the smocked bodice in place, and stood back to examine herself in the mirror. Oh, what did she care whether Max liked it or not? When the doorbell rang, she dashed on perfume and lipstick.

Overcome with shyness, Angel hesitated at the door. Why had she put herself in this uncomfortable position? Because she owed him her life, she reminded herself. After tonight, their relationship would return to minimal neighborly contact.

When she opened the door, however, and saw him standing on the porch in his pressed slacks and sky-blue linen shirt, his smile as inviting as the quiet dawn, with a bouquet of white roses in one hand and a bottle of champagne in the other, she thought, *how wonderful.*

"Oh, champagne," Angel said.

Max hesitated, taking her in with appreciative eyes. "You look beautiful," he said.

"Thank you." For goodness sake, she was giggling. "Please, come in." Then, remembering the fish, she exclaimed, "The dinner!" and hurried to the oven.

Returning to his side, she indicated the table set with nice linen and candles. "Silly, isn't it?" she said.

"When a beautiful woman has made such lovely preparations, silly is the word farthest from my thoughts. I am delighted." He offered the champagne. "Shall we?"

"Um, yes, I only have wine glasses."

"No matter." He twisted off the foil and wire hood, opening the bottle with a loud pop. The bubbly pour broke the moment of silence, along with the thudding of her heart in her ears.

"It's very fancy," she said. At his quizzical look, she added, "Special, I mean."

"Ah, yes." He set down the bottle and clinked his glass against hers.

She sipped appreciatively, eyeing the expensive import. "I've never had French champagne."

"Do you like it?"

"I do."

"Perhaps you will allow me to fix such crimes? What else have you missed?"

"Oh, everything." She giggled again. "This stuff is strong, isn't it?"

"It is best to sip it slowly," he said, repressing a grin.

"Too late." She held up her half-empty glass, which he filled again. "Do you dance, Max?"

"With pleasure."

The music had slowed to a slow haunting melody. He set their glasses down and, before she could protest, swept her into his arms. His arm was sure around her waist, his hand guided but never grabbed. They fit nicely and moved well, as if they had danced together many times. Their attraction was as natural and intoxicating as the soft sea breeze that drifted in through the windows.

When the song ended, he held on, looking into her eyes. She smiled with clear invitation. Her heart raced as he nuzzled her neck.

"Angel," he whispered.

Falling into a trance of desire, she pressed her cheek to his. When his lips sought hers, panic overtook her. Like a scallop that squeezes its bivalves shut to propel itself from a predator, she jerked away, too fast, and spun against the table with a little cry.

"Are you all right?" Max said, offering a steady hand.

"I guess the champagne got to me," she said.

Her hand rested in his, with Angel poised between desire and flight; she wanted to throw herself into his arms or else never see him again.

She moved towards the kitchen. "Shall we eat?"

He followed, his voice laced with regret. "As you wish."

ACCEPTANCE

With its grooves that join together at a single point, the fan-shaped scallop shell, *Argopecten irradians*, has been used as a metaphor for life's journey and the final stop before entering paradise. Legend has it that the apostle Saint James once rescued a knight covered in scallops. Or perhaps, while the saint's remains were being transported from Jerusalem to Spain, a knight's horse fell into the water and emerged covered in the shells. In medieval times pilgrims to the grave of St. James in Santiago de Compostela often wore a scallop on their hat or clothes. When presenting it at a church or castle, the weary travelers could expect as much sustenance as the shell could hold. By the thirteenth century, sales of scallops became regulated with over one hundred vendors in Santiago. Today you will find bronze street markers in the shape of a scallop.

SANIBEL ISLAND, FLORIDA

SUMMER 1985

Sweet, busy birdsong bussed the air outside the bedroom window, welcoming a sunny morning, while Angel lay tangled in her sheets, unable or unwilling to leave the dreamy hold of the previous night. She pictured Max across the table from her, his animated expression, as they spoke of his plans for the shop, Stella's progress through her book series, and the quirky ins and outs of island life.

Her body tingled with impressions his embrace had left on her body. She felt herself transported back in time to that moment when his eyes locked on hers and the scent of his bay rum enveloped her—nothing else had mattered but the two of them in a secret world in which anything was possible.

Admit it, she'd felt free and happy—more so than she could ever remember.

Angel's sexual experience was limited to Santiago and one other man whom she met soon after her arrival in Sanibel. That man, a manager at Bailey's, had dumped her when he realized she had a small child, and she hadn't tried again. After all these years of denial, she was hungry and wanting. She touched herself while she concentrated on the feel of Max. The iron grip of denial slipped and she found herself drowning in desire. Her body responded with a vengeance, bringing her to a powerful climax that left her shaken and confused.

Damn it, she had no business carrying on like a lovesick teenager. Hard work, not silly infatuation, had gotten her here.

Angel went to fetch yesterday's mail, forgotten in the rush of dinner preparations. As she stepped onto the porch, she caught sight of a shadow box—an empty frame for a Sailors' Valentine—perched on top of the old wicker table by the door. A white envelope was taped to the top of the frame, addressed to her in Max's distinctive script.

What was he thinking? This was worse than any sexual liberties he could have taken. And yet, the sweet memory of him standing on these steps with flowers and champagne moved her.

Dear Angel,

Thank you for a memorable night.

I would be honored to have you attend the shell class this coming Thursday evening at seven.

Yours truly,

Max

Ridiculous. Had a simple but wonderful dinner date suggested she would play shells? Max lived in the realm of Yemayá, and the more Angel unearthed the past, the deeper her resolve grew never to repeat its mistakes. The offensive frame simply had to go.

She picked it up, when the telephone rang. She shoved the frame into the front closet and hurried to her office.

"Hello," she answered, hoping it wasn't Max.

"It's Helen." Angel felt a rush of gratitude for Dr. Nash's no-nonsense nurse, who had guided her little family through a maze of colds and inoculations over the years. Helen went on in her usual brusque manner. "Doctor's ordered a set of X-rays. Next Tuesday, ten a.m. at Healthside, third floor, radiology."

"But what about the X-rays they took at the hospital?

"Tech must have been new. 'Jiggled the rig.' Or you moved. You gotta hold still."

"For heaven's sake. I'm much better. Will you please tell Edgar?"

"Tell him yourself. He gives the orders; I fill them. You know that. Did you write down the date?" She was growing exasperated. "Do I need to mail a card?"

"I've noted it, next Tuesday at ten. But I don't see the necessity—"

"When the film arrives, I'll call to schedule you."

"Fine," Angel said. The old codger probably thought he could scare her off smoking after the accident.

She lit a cigarette and, pulling the smoke into her lungs, read the signs of the day. To an untrained eye it looked like a picture-postcard day, but Angel noticed the ways in which the wind and currents had reshaped the shoreline since only yesterday. Over time, even small changes could amount to a major transformation.

A tight cough rubbed her chest like sandpaper, as she faced her typewriter. She scolded herself for abandoning *Stella's Homecoming*, but nothing was more important than writing her valentine to Faith.

* * * * *

Dear Faith,

I'm feeling better each day, but miss you more than ever. What did you think of the earlier pages? Are you ready to talk?

Love,

Mom

DESTINY STRIKES A BARGAIN

KEY WEST, FLORIDA

OCTOBER 1946

As word of Rafael del Corazón's bad luck spread around town, the local fishermen turned their backs on him to avoid contagion of the dreaded curse. Early one morning, he rampaged through the pantry at his family house in El Barrio de Gato; only a mile away from my mother's house, it was a world apart. There, he gathered seven empty bottles—seven was Yemayá's lucky number—twine, *petiveria alliacea*, a garlic herb, purple basil, mugwort, marjoram, and witch hazel into a large canvas sack. In the vegetable garden he hacked a ripe watermelon into pieces and picked out seven seeds.

Like a beggar with his sack slung over one shoulder, my father walked through the quiet grove of Casuarina pines at Fort Zachary Taylor Beach. Absorbed in his despair, he didn't notice the equally desperate young woman at the opposite end of the beach or he might have stopped to marvel at her good character.

With the precision of a surgeon, he laid out his purification tools on the sun-bleached sand. He filled each bottle halfway with seawater and added seven sprigs of the herbs along with one watermelon seed. During this process, he pictured the great beast that would land on his deck and change his fortune. Finally, he tied rocks to the bottles and let them sink to the bottom of the sea.

Throughout the long, lingering day, Rafael lay on the beach, the soft crooning of the waves at his feet. He begged the Great Mother to cleanse his rotten soul. In response, she paraded in the sky visions of dozens of beautiful women, whom he had loved and left. Eh, maybe the old *bruja* was right; only a fool believed he could cheat fate.

As a full moon sailed into the night sky, he slipped into the sea and poured the contents of the purified bottles over his head. It was not an exact ritual, but it had heart. With the last dose he vowed to marry a righteous woman if, in return, Yemayá would send the fish his way once again.

The next morning he donned his finest white *guayabera* shirt and, as he made his way to St. Mary's By The Sea, dropped a penny at each street corner. Inside the church, he took off his Panama hat, dipped a piece of white coral into the font of holy water, and tied it on a long string around his neck. Kneeling in the last row, he began to pray to St. Barbara, the Catholic alter ego of his appointed deity Chongo, when sorrowful sighs distracted him.

Across the aisle he spied a young woman, wrapped in devotion. Her somber suit and disciplined posture gave her a saintly air. She had slim ankles and a pleasant enough profile—maybe she'd look better when she wasn't sighing.

As Mary worked the rosary beads, Rafael angled to glimpse her left ring finger. When she set the rosary on the pew—an act of independence that would change both of their lives—he was delighted to learn she was single.

My mother must have felt his pointed gaze, for she looked in his direction just as a pinkish glow streaked through the stained glass and lit her face. The weary fight for her mother's life had softened her, and she had never looked more beautiful. Her compelling turquoise eyes, vulnerable with tears, briefly locked onto his.

A diamond in the rough, was Rafael's knowledgeable assessment. He would be the first—of this he was certain—to tame her. Perhaps he would even marry her. With his vast arsenal of amorous techniques, he never doubted he'd conquer her starved heart. He quickly gave thanks to Our Lady of the Sea/Yemayá, along with Saint Barbara/Chongo, and then hurried out to station himself near the entrance.

Mary dabbed her eyes with a dainty handkerchief, embarrassed by her weakness. *God helps those that help themselves.* Why depend on the inefficient, costly web of saints to intercede on her behalf? Where had that ever gotten her? At last she decided that nothing but a direct line to the Almighty would do.

At that, she set aside the rosary forever, threw back her shoulders, and knocked right on Heaven's door: *Dear Lord, please grant me a moment of peace with Mama, and in return, I will help someone of your choosing, any poor sinner you send my way. If you will answer my humble prayer, surely you will double the return on your investment.*

She stuffed the hankie in her purse and closed it with a snap. As she left, she gave the Virgin Mother a final curt nod, as if dismissing her services.

When she stepped into the bright daylight, a handsome, swarthy man slid in front of her and tipped his hat. "Excuse me, Miss."

She assessed the cocky grin and loose posture with the same objectiveness used to balance a ledger and come up with the bottom line: *A Conchy Joe after a good time*. Despite herself, she felt powerless to move past him.

A connoisseur of women, the Captain sensed the fleeting window of opportunity.

"My name is Captain Rafael del Corazón. Forgive me, but I noticed your distress. It would be an honor to assist you." He bowed his head; offering his hand would be too bold. Instinct, more than character, led him to be as guileless as possible.

Indeed, the sincerity of his offer touched Mary. "Thank you, Captain."

"May I give you a ride, perhaps?"

Captivated, she looked into his reassuring dark eyes. She couldn't afford another trip to Marathon until her next paycheck. However, she would be beholden to him for such a generous offer.

My father insisted. "Please allow me to assist you."

As his words hung in the air, my mother wondered if God had answered her prayer. The fella certainly had the air of a sinner.

"Would it be too much to ask for a ride to Marathon, Captain?"

Rafael could barely contain his glee. Marathon was hours away—plenty of time to work his magic on this poor woman. He swept his hat in a graceful arc.

"I'm at your service, *Señorita…?*"

"Porreca."

"Please, call me Rafael."

The Chevy rattled north along Highway One, as Rafael and Mary quietly considered one another. She held her headscarf while she leaned towards the open window to avoid the oddly appealing drift of bay rum and manly sweat. Unaccustomed to women of her ilk, he settled upon a tried and true strategy: throw the line out, reel it in slowly.

He cleared his throat. "Do you have family in Marathon, *señorita*?"

While my mother did not wish to appear rude or ungrateful, she preferred to keep the conversation to a minimum. "My mother is in the hospital."

"What a pity. I'll light a candle for her at church."

"Don't go to any trouble on my account."

"Please, count on me for a ride, anytime."

"That won't be necessary."

"I lost my sainted mother a few years ago." Here, Rafael crossed himself, which prompted a disapproving look from Mary.

The tension rose in her voice. "I'm sorry for your loss."

She stared out the window at the panning view of endless blue ocean against a never-ending blue sky. Why had she accepted this pesky man's help? She couldn't bear to add another debt to her bottom line. A weary sigh escaped her lips.

Like a hound dog on point, Rafael twitched his head in her direction, only to find the chink in her defense already closed. Rather than feel defeated, her resistance whetted his appetite.

They left Bahia Honda and climbed the sixty-five-foot, two-lane bridge, one of many that connect the Keys like a long knotted rope. The sun descended in the west, trailing a fiery glow across the bay. Mary studied the enchanting light, wishing Willow could enjoy the sunset, when she saw a large fish leap high several yards away. She caught her breath as it landed with a tremendous spray of water. "Oh, a sailfish."

"*Por Dios!* Where?"

She pointed towards the gathering darkness. "Over there."

The Captain's load was too big for him to disguise; his voice welled with despair. "The sea is unhappy with me, *señorita*. I haven't caught a single fish, *nada*, for many weeks. I am cursed."

"Nonsense." The man was as foolish as her mother. "Curses are for the weak-minded. Perhaps you need to try harder."

He gripped the wheel in confusion. What kind of woman would tease his cruel fate? If she were a man, he would have hit her.

"I swear the fish run away from me."

"Fish don't have feelings, Captain. They follow the laws of nature. It's your job to catch them. I suggest you do your job and forget such silly superstitions."

He jerked the truck to a stop on the narrow shoulder at the top of the bridge. It was a dangerous maneuver that placed the truck partially on the road, blocking traffic. Within minutes, cars piled up behind them, honking furiously. Mary shrunk back in her corner, frightened by his bizarre behavior.

With a wild look, Rafael seized her hand. "The Gods sent you to me. They told me to take good care of you. I promise you will be safe and I will tame the sea. You must marry me.

"Are you mad?"

"I love you."

"Stop this insanity or I'll call the police!"

All signs pointed to the truth. "You are the woman for me, *Señorita* Porreca."

The honking reached a crescendo. Frustrated drivers leaned out their car windows. Mary's blouse was damp with sweat, her cheeks flushed with anger.

"I insist we leave at once, sir. Please, drive on!"

Blood rushed to his groin. What a wild woman—*una mujer salvaje*. Without warning, he slid across the seat, took her in his arms and kissed her passionately. Despite Mary's struggle to free herself, it was a long kiss.

The Captain paused to stare into her dazed eyes. "Tell me you will be mine."

"No!" She tried to push him away, but he held on tight.

"Say you will be mine or we stay here all night."

"For heaven's sake, be reasonable. We don't even know each other."

"God knows us. The angels brought us together." With keen intuition honed over years of chasing big game at sea, he made a wild bet: "Didn't you pray for me, too?"

Mary gulped as she recalled her proposition to God. Surely the trade-off could not be marrying this crazy Cuban?

"But, but, but…" She elbowed him aside and crossed her arms over her chest. "If you must know, I asked God to send me someone worthy of my help. However, I did not specifically ask for you. Are you satisfied now? May we please go?"

The Captain smiled to himself. He was wearing her down, reeling her in. "On one condition: If God grants me a fish tomorrow, a big fish, you will accept my proposal."

Even if Mary escaped now, she feared the unbalanced fellow might pursue her.

What did she have to lose by agreeing to his absurd proposal when by his own admission he was a lousy fisherman?

"How big a fish?"

He considered what it would take to lift the curse. "A two hundred pounder."

Mary straightened her jacket. "Fine, I agree. Now, please drive."

"At your service."

An irate driver approached the Chevy. "Hey, what's the big idea, buddy?"

The Captain leaned out the window, alerting the line of travelers. "We're getting married!" His announcement was met with typical Key West Conch spirit of cheers and applause.

Late that afternoon, the Captain pulled into the hospital parking lot. Mary hurried away, muttered thanks, as she slammed the door shut. She hoped she never saw him again. When she exited three hours later in the dark night, exhausted and depressed from yet another lonely visit with her comatose mother, the Captain was waiting. Annoyed and yet relieved at the sight of him, she climbed once more into the truck's cab with a small sigh.

Sensing her mood, the Captain drove back to Key West in silence. Mary rested her head on the window frame, welcoming the fresh air on her face and, to her surprise, this strange man's company. For the first time in her life, she felt she wasn't alone.

When they arrived in town, Rafael spoke with gravity. "*Señorita*, tomorrow I must face my destiny. Your name on my lips will bring me courage."

Why did this irrational creature complicate matters, just like Mother? And yet, his earnestness moved her to respond. "Mary."

"Mary, a beautiful name. Thank you." His gentle appreciation seemed to belong to another man. Perhaps she had misjudged him.

She directed him towards her house and, in the last few minutes they shared, considered the man at her side. She recalled his strong arms around her and the thrill of his kiss. When he stopped in front of her house, she was sorry to leave. This time, she slowly gathered her things, allowing him to open the car door. As she stepped onto the curb, she lost her balance and fell into his arms.

"Are you all right?" The concern in his voice seemed at odds with the hot desire in his eyes.

Though her body burned with a dangerous longing, she pulled away.

"I'm fine, thank you. Goodnight, Captain."

"Goodnight, *mi amor.*"

My love? Good Lord, the man was deranged.

As my mother walked towards the shabby gingerbread house, a force stronger than her will made her turn. Like a cat ready to pounce, my father waited. For one long, confusing moment, she stared at him before she hurried inside. She had no business entertaining amorous thoughts of a capricious fool.

* * * * *

SANIBEL ISLAND, FLORIDA

SUMMER 1985

Bailey's asphalt parking lot radiated intense heat, making a trial of Angel's short walk from the grocery store to her car. The sun was a heavy iron weight on top of her head. She coughed in fits as she lifted the brown bags into the wagon. Wiping away the perspiration on her brow, she eyed the cart station near the entrance with dread. But if everyone left a cart willy-nilly, what a mess it would be. Her duties completed, she turned the car air conditioning on full blast. The immediate chill brought on a wave of nausea, and she shut off the air. It was all too much.

She drove towards the exit when she spotted the Red Bug tucked beside the Salvation Army bin. She hit the brakes—the tag was Faith's. Had she missed her inside the store? Then Angel spied Wayne sitting on the hood with his back to the parking lot. And he had someone cradled in his arms—Faith!

Swerving into the nearest spot, Angel told herself to stay calm. Any mother had the right to say hello. As she approached, she heard them laughing, but it wasn't right, the sound was off. Too late, she understood her error.

"Faith?"

The girl looked up from the shelter of Wayne's embrace with a cold stare, her dark brown eyes like velvet over stone. A thick gold chain with a cross dangled to her ample cleavage. With a flip of her long red hair, she adjusted her low-cut blouse.

"Who the hell is that?" she said, with a Southern accent born in the same place as Wayne's. Her possessive look at a red sedan parked in the next slot revealed plenty: the girl had driven here to rendezvous with him, but might cut and run at the slightest hint of trouble.

Oh, Angel wanted to strangle Wayne, and his angry glare matched her hate. His aquiline nostrils flared, his jaw hardened, as he made that offensive clucking sound.

"What do you want?" he said.

Her chest heaved with each word. "You're. A. Bastard."

Light-headed, she nearly fell as she spun around. Pushing the old wagon to the limit, she began to cough so hard she had to stop by the side of the road. She spit a blood clot into her hand and scrounged in her bag for a tissue. It didn't matter; nothing did, because she had the goods on that *cabrón.*

Angel parked in front of Fort Myers Senior High five minutes before the dismissal bell. She felt small and insignificant as she walked under dramatic towering white clouds that drifted across the cerulean expanse with regal authority. They dwarfed the miniature houses and tiny trees, as if the world was inverted and the real play above.

She positioned herself by the school entrance. The stifling heat pooled on the concrete, rising through her thin-soled sneakers, warming her bare legs, clinging to her linen skirt. In her hand, she clutched a manila envelope with the most recent pages she had written to Faith.

Maybe, just maybe, the Captain and Mother would talk some sense into their granddaughter, so to speak. Of course, they never succeeded in impressing their beliefs upon Angel, while Willow failed to instill in Little Mary a faith in her beloved mermaid. Perhaps the love that spurred each of them to convert their offspring to their particular religion was all that mattered in the end.

The bell split the air, followed by an exodus of kids. Before Angel laid eyes on Faith, she felt her presence, a tug at the invisible cord that bound them. She spotted a group of girls heading down the hallway with Faith's friend Bonnie leading the way. Wariness sprang into the girl's face. As she turned to look over her shoulder, Angel laid eyes on her daughter. A riot of reactions colored Faith's expression: surprise, anger, relief, and, at last, acceptance. She said something to her friends and hurried through the entrance.

"Not here," she hissed, walking past Angel, who followed her to a small grove of oaks at the far end of the parking lot.

"What do you want?" Faith said and, wrinkling her nose, added, "Oh my God, you stink. You've been smoking?"

"I'm sorry." Angel said. "I'll quit when you come home, I promise."

"Wow. That's manipulative. If I don't want you to die, I'll come home? How about you just quit because you want to do the right thing, for once?"

Angel took a deep raspy breath. There was only this sliver of time in which she might save Faith.

Offering the manila envelope, she said, "Did you get the pages I sent?"

Faith gave it a cursory once-over before she shoved it in her book bag. Angel studied her face for a sign she had read the story, and perhaps knowing this, her daughter maintained a cool blank expression.

"I can tell you more about your family, if you'd talk to me," Angel added.

"My father, too?" Faith said.

"Yes. Your father, too."

"Okay, what's his name?"

"I'll tell you everything, eventually. As the story unfolds."

Faith rolled her eyes. "That's what I thought." She turned to go.

"Wait." Angel grabbed her arm. "I saw Wayne earlier at Bailey's."

She jerked away from her mother's grip. "What did you do, throw a box of Rice Krispies at him?" Faith looked over her shoulder as a trio of high-spirited boys approached. The tallest one gave her a gleeful grin. She shrugged and turned a hard eye on her mother. "Well?"

"As a matter of fact," Angel said, summoning her courage. "I interrupted his rendezvous with a petite Southern girl. They were cuddled against your car like lovers."

She hated to see the pitiful mix of defiance and doubt that flooded her daughter's face. At least she had not walked off—yet.

"You're lying," Faith said, rubbing the strap on her book bag up and down.

"Listen, Kiddo. She has red hair and wears a gold cross necklace. Maybe you've seen her?"

"You're making it up. That's what you do, make up dumb stories."

"I thought you should know he's just another Johnny-Come-Lately."

"I trust him more than you. Even if you are telling the truth, which you're not, you saw it from some twisted perspective. I'm sure there's a good explanation—not that I owe it to you."

Angel shook her head. "If he really loves you, he'd want the best for you. He'd want you to go to college."

"I don't expect you to understand," Faith said, as she scanned the line of cars. "Wayne wants a traditional marriage. He's the man; I'm the woman."

"He just wants to control you. Is that the life you want?" The blank stony look on her daughter's face revealed how far apart they were. "How can throw away your future like it's a pair of old jeans you're giving to Goodwill?"

The sudden blare of a car horn startled them. They turned to see Wayne's angry stare behind the windshield of the Red Bug. Angel witnessed the nervous redistribution of Faith's energy. The brave but inexperienced girl was no match for the cunning predator.

Stepping away, Faith said, "Don't contact me anymore unless you're ready to talk about my dad."

"Wait, please," Angel called.

She watched her slide into the passenger seat and kiss Wayne on the cheek. The lying cheat accepted her affection as his due with none offered in return. As he took her away, the exhaust seemed to puff out the very word pounding in Angel's mind: *disaster!*

* * * * *

Dear Faith,

I'm sorry I upset you but I ask you: If Bonnie saw Wayne with another girl, wouldn't you want her to tell you?

Please, consider your future.

Love,

Mom

A CLEAN SLATE

KEY WEST, FLORIDA

OCTOBER 1946

Fishermen are a superstitious lot and my father was no exception. At dawn he motored out of the channel to fight for his future, while he calculated the portents in his favor: It was the seventh day of the seventh week in which he had begged for the Sea Goddess Yemayá's blessing; the seventh day he'd worn the blessed coral; seven hours since he'd seen his beloved fiancée Mary, and when he awoke the clock had read seven to five.

From the flybridge, the Captain surveyed the dark, glassy sea. The gentle swell wooed him like the curve of a beautiful woman's hips. A school of Yellowtail snapper skirted his boat, their bright stripes pointing like arrows out of the channel into deep water. Did he see a fish forming in the clouds? All signs pointed to an auspicious day.

He pictured Mary challenging him with her cold, beautiful eyes: *Do your job, Captain!* He would show her, he'd catch a monster that day, or else…the nagging doubt rattled him. What if he returned empty-handed once more? He'd be as useless as a stuffed fish on a wall. Even worse, he would lose Mary, whom he realized he loved. *Le amo?* Never had he felt love for any woman but his sainted mother.

Fingering the coral necklace, the Captain struck a final bargain: If Yemayá refused him today, it could only mean she wanted his soul. Like all true-blue fisherman, he believed he owed his life to the sea and there he would go, empty-handed and heartbroken. However, if he caught big game—at least two hundred pounds—he would marry his intended and lift the curse. By sunset, either the sacrificial blood of a great beast must stain his deck or he would tie the anchor around his feet and jump into the arms of the Great Lady.

Three nautical miles offshore, *La Libertad* reached the west wall of the Gulf Stream, the wide rapid current flowing northward along the eastern coast. The Captain slowed the twin diesel engines and set the wheel, letting the warm water carry him. He vaulted down the stairs to the cockpit, eager to begin a maritime ballet of precise steps, the reasons for which were long forgotten. His father and his grandfather and their fathers before them had practiced each nuanced step, guaranteeing an unbroken chain of luck, until now. And so he stripped away the unlucky touches he had added over the years—whistling American tunes, the fancy captain's cap, expensive feathered lures—and got back to basics.

He retrieved from the cabin a wide-brimmed straw hat, tattered from generations of use, and set it backwards on his head. He then selected two Spanish mackerel from the ice locker. By the feel of his hand, each weighed no more than two pounds; any extra would be unlucky. With his grandfather's fishing knife, he split their guts and sewed in a simple hook so the business end jutted like a lethal cock from the underside of the fish. Given his recent abysmal record, he would have preferred to use a heavier test line, but stuck to the rigor of the old ways.

The Captain admired his handiwork as he recited the Corazón pledge, "I'll have a big bitch today."

The sun climbed over the horizon, a glowing bird with rosy wings that sprinkled gold flecks across the dark sea, waking the watery underworld. Adrenaline filled his veins as he heard the rousing hum of the ocean, teeming with life. It was time to call the beast.

With a passion the women in his bed had known, he stroked his two favorite rods and the trusty Fin-Nor reels. He secured the sacrificial bait to the ends of his heaviest leaders. Before casting the lines, he spit portside, then crossed himself, asking for God's blessing.

"Qué Dios me lo bendiga."

Clink! The Captain locked the rods into the braces on his fishing chairs, which faced the ocean like sentinels on watch. There was no turning back now. His muscles rippled with tension as he climbed back up to the bridge. Twenty-three miles offshore from Marathon, he arrived at the West Hump, an underwater hill where fish are so plentiful, it's like dipping your hand in a candy bowl—unless you're cursed. Here, Mary had spotted the sailfish, and here would be his battlefield.

The Captain scanned the watery bowl for telltale signs of big game, but the sea mocked him with soft lazy undulations, not even a splash of contempt, as if he were already dead. A cold chill gripped him, despite tendrils of sunshine. So often, he'd gone into battle believing he was Lord and Master of the Sea. Alas, though the Corazón men might be sons of conquistadors, they ruled nothing without the grace of the deities. Oh, what a fool he'd been.

By the time the sun danced high into the cloudless sky, he knew himself to be nothing more than a beggar at Yemayá's table. He closed his eyes and, for the first time, prayed with an open heart. If the prize were given, he would receive it with gratitude and be a better man.

That day Fate rested its weary head on my father's desperate shoulders. Much more than his dignity was at stake; my own life hung in the balance. Perhaps my cries from the future—or even yours, dear Faith—reached him, spurring him to action: *Save us!*

Imagine, then, the Captain's experience, floating alone in the vast ocean, fighting against an implacable curse and lonely death. When he opens his eyes, he spots the roll of a fin, then several more just beyond the preacher's pulpit at the ship's bow. He jumps to his feet. *Dolphins! The Sea Goddess's escorts!*

Flying fish skitter like stones tossed across the water, escaping a school of hungry mackerels—the food of choice of still bigger game. Everyone is at the party, but where is the guest of honor?

Just then, the starboard reel sings out with an unmistakable, high-pitched whine. The line whirrs out to sea. *Zzzzing!* A strike! The Captain stares aft in disbelief, his nerves on fire. Not a single thought crowds his mind.

Then he sees it: a monster soars with gravity-defying power into the air, its silvery underside like a flash of lightning. The sword-like bill slits the skies. Its dark blue body thrashes before it lands in the sea with a volcanic spray.

A blue marlin—a big one, nearly ten feet long!

Heart pounding, the Captain slides down the stair rails, barely touching the cockpit as he pivots into the fishing chair. When he grabs the fishing rod from its holder, the blue marlin yanks him forward. He estimates its weight at three hundred pounds, probably a mature female, toughest of the species. *Por Dios!* The biggest catch he's ever had is two hundred, and no Palo to help now, either. It will take a miracle to land this beauty. *Do or die, Corazón!*

Gathering his strength, he braces his feet against the cockpit wall and leans the chair as far back as it will allow. He holds the rod tight between his thighs, one hand turning the reel, the other pulling the rod. As the great fish shoots forward like a torpedo, he lets out the line, patiently waiting for the turn. Inch by inch, he begins to rein in his prey.

For the next two hours, the Captain and the sea monster fight *mano á mano* in a dance to the death. Each struggles to reclaim his life. Back and forth, my father saws the breezy air, while the rod bends under the tremendous weight of his worthy opponent. Sweat pours down his arms onto bloody hands, rubbed raw by the twisting and turning of the rod. The great fish darts right, then left, while the Captain wills the rod and his aching body to surpass their strength, to save him.

No other sound but the slow turning of the reel's metal gears punctures his awareness. The pain in his back, ribs straining, the crushing tension in his legs—these belong to someone else, for he has become one with the creature. Rafael del Corazón is fighting for his life in the deep water, his beady black eyes blaze with resistance, his wild muscles pitted against the man who would suck him from the sea. With body and soul—*cuerpo y alma*—he loves the blue marlin; separation is unbearable. He licks his lips as the sleek glistening fish bulldozes the water. *I'll have this bitch today.*

Over and over, the Captain serenades the object of his desire with the stirring lament that a long line of Corazón men, all of them lovesick *pescadors*, have sung. He professes his love, begging the fish to give up the fight and come quickly.

"Ven a mí, mi amor. Tu eres mío, todo para mi. No luches mas. Ven."

At last, the marlin appears over the edge of the stern. Like a man on the precipice of orgasm, the Captain aches to claim her. One more struggle remains, the trickiest of all. Without his first mate to hold the gaff, he fears his beloved will slip from his grasp. Once more Mary's words come to him. *Do your job, Captain!*

He kicks the gaff free from the holding well and shuffles it within reach with his foot. In one desperate fluid motion, he locks the reel, drops the rod onto the deck and throws his weight on top of it, while he grabs the stick. Lunging over the stern, he hooks the fish in the side. A geyser of blood sprays his face. It fans over the water, mingling with blood from his torn hands—a joint offering to the Sea Goddess. The tired marlin thrashes in anger, clubbing the water with its stout pike. The Captain holds tight as the pole slips forward.

"Ven a mí, mi amor. Ven."

With superhuman effort, he hauls the beast onto the diving platform. As she gives up the fight, her skin color rapidly changes from black blue to gray. Hung over the stern, eye-to-eye with his conquest, fisherman and catch together heave a great sigh of gratitude. They are both free now.

"Gracias. Estamos los dos en casa ahora."

The Great Lady had shown the Captain her favor once more. Come hell or high water, his good luck charm, Mary, would be his wife.

Mary lay rigid as a tin soldier on her thin mattress, watching a thin ribbon of silvery moonlight waver on the ceiling, as she ruminated on her lot in life. Any day now, Mama would leave her alone, an unloved, penniless debtor, burdened by a mountain of medical expenses. Away from judging eyes, Mary released her tightly held burden in a river of tears. These were not the practiced tears of one accustomed to self-pity but the raw spurt of a fresh vein. Like a toddler learning to walk, she tumbled headlong into grief, oblivious to the knock at the door, until a commanding voice startled her.

"*Hola*, Maria. *Ven, mi amor,* come, please."

Mary's head shot up. Had someone heard her crying? She shuddered with embarrassment. Pulling on her robe, she peeked out the bedroom door and saw a man's face pushed against the front window.

It was that horrible Captain. For heaven's sake, drunk on her doorstep in the middle of the night. The neighbors began to shout. There was nothing to do but shoo him away.

Mary cracked open the front door and hissed. "Go away."

He proudly bellowed. "I brought you a prize, *mi amor.*"

"If you don't leave at once, Captain Corazón, I shall call the police."

"Please, Maria, open the door. Give me one minute, then I leave."

"My name is Mary, not Maria."

"Mary." The drunken slide of his accent turned it into yet a different name, so he called her darling in the sweetest voice she had ever heard. "Please, *querida*."

In her grief-stricken state, she imagined the small vulnerable boy he once was—like her, subject to the illogical whims of adults. His true innocent spirit was begging for help. A wild impulse to gather the defenseless boy in her arms and protect him from this brutish man seized her.

As she opened the door, the Captain swooped her into his arms and kicked the door shut. *"Gracias, mi amor."*

He devoured her with his eyes. Dazed by his ardor, Mary offered no resistance. Oh, how she longed to feel the thrill of his kiss once again. And yet, she despised him for the weakness he inspired.

"You are an honorable woman, *sí?"*

The question slapped her back to her senses. She pushed against his chest, but remained captive in his firm embrace.

"They say a promise is written in heaven." He pulled back the window curtain.

"Look."

As he tapped the glass, a handful of inebriated locals came to life on the lawn. Shouting and cajoling, several scrambled up a ladder that leaned beside a large cart. With thick ropes and heavy grunts they hauled the blue marlin by its tail into the air.

The Captain's chest puffed with pride. "Two hundred and twenty-eight pounds.

The curse is gone. I am a new man. You know why…?" He took off his lucky old hat, got down on one knee, and clasped her hand. "You bring me good luck, Mary. I cannot live without you. Will you marry me?"

She drew in a sharp breath. "Luck is hardly a suitable foundation for marriage."

A smile hid behind his eyes. At least she hadn't thrown him out. "I love you. *Te amo.* I never say this to a woman. I marry you for love." As he kissed her hand, he detected a slight tremor in her body. He looked up into her eyes with guileless devotion. "Do you feel nothing for me?"

He bowed his head with quiet calculation. He had tamed the fish, now he would tame his sweet Mary. Let the wild thing come. *Ven, mi amor, ven.*

My mother fingered the tips of his unruly mop, and as she breathed in his stirring scent of body heat, bay rum, and sea salt, her mission in life crystalized. This poor, superstitious creature needed her help, and whether or not God granted her request for a final reconciliation with her mother, Mary would save the Captain from his oppressive beliefs with a marriage based on the principles of direct faith.

Decided, she squeezed his hand. "I must marry in a Protestant church."

My father had anticipated requests for money, fidelity, social standards, but never such a crazy thing. The Corazóns had married their sons and daughters in the Catholic Church for centuries, with good results. If he married in a Protestant church, his family, Mother Mary, and St. Barbara would forsake him. Yet he could not lose Mary and face another dry fishing spell, perhaps a permanent one. Either way, he was sunk.

The Santeria priestess' warning tipped the balance: Unless he married a righteous woman, his life was worthless. Perhaps the good saints would forgive his betrayal. As the seconds ticked by, he felt his beloved stiffen. Fear of rejection overtook the Captain. In the end, he cared more about fishing than his soul.

"As you wish."

"We must attend church every Sunday."

He wiped his brow. Were all righteous women so difficult?

"No problem," he said. "Anything else?"

What else could Mary want? With admirable economy, God had provided a husband to save her from penury—a husband whom she, in turn, would free from the decadence that had engulfed her mother. To Mary's delight, her experiment with Puritanism had succeeded.

She smiled at her charge. "I'm satisfied."

He repeated the question. "Will you please marry me?"

"Yes, Captain."

A nervous blush stained Mary's cheeks as he rose to meet her. Released from a lifetime of misery, she poured her happiness into their passionate embrace. Rafael congratulated himself on his hunch; he had caught a wild woman.

He parted with a jaunty wave of his hat. "Good night, *querida.*"

Speechless, Mary watched him leave, following his silhouette until he and his cohorts blended into the dark shadows. As soon as he disappeared from view, my mother rampaged through the house, sweeping into the trash piles of votives and crosses, scraps of prayers, rosary beads, mermaid images, statues of the Virgin Mary, along with her grandmother's shell mosaic. *Forget me not, indeed.*

On her next visit to the hospital, Mary rid Willow's room of all signs of deviant worship. As she dumped the last relic into a bin, she turned to see Willow's eyes flutter open.

She rushed to her mother's side. "I love you, Mama."

With a soft sigh, Willow fell into an interminable slumber. A strong whiff of jasmine rose in the air, drifting towards the window that faced the sea. Mary heard her mother's reedy, singsong voice.

Forget me not, Little One.

Then she was gone.

Hoping to speed her mother's way into heaven, Mary arranged a spartan funeral at First Presbyterian Church, where she discovered the most direct line to God. As the handsome young Reverend Powell offered a simple, no-frills prayer for Willow's soul, my mother congratulated herself on her choice. My father sat beside her, their shoulders barely touching, his knees itching to fold under a Catholic pew. The thought of a plain Protestant wedding filled him with remorse. What kind of a bargain had he struck?

He escorted his fiancée home, gave her a respectful kiss on the cheek, promising to return the following Sunday morning. Alone in the silence of her home, Mary ached to hear Willow's singsong hum. She found herself digging through the trash to save a memento of her mother. Her heart leapt at the sight of the old Sailors' Valentine that had hung on their living room wall for as long as she could remember. She held the shell mosaic at arm's length, eyeing its primitive beauty as if for the first time: the old sailing rig, the flock of seagulls over the deep blue sea that seemed to move with power and majesty.

As Willow's reedy song came to her once more, Mary clasped the Valentine to her breast. Surely God would allow this one small measure of love. Besides, what harm could its simple message bring? *Forget Me Not.*

* * * * *

SANIBEL ISLAND, FLORIDA

SUMMER 1985

From her kitchen, Angel clocked the sound of Max's wagon heading home. She cleared her supper and went to the porch to wait until six p.m., the time she judged best to arrive on his doorstep. Any later would put her in the way of his class, any earlier gave them too much time alone together.

Pulling on her smoke, she surveyed the artistic display in the skies. God had dipped a paintbrush into buckets of rich red and peony pink and zesty orange, layering them onto the canvas, each folding into a kaleidoscope of indescribable beauty. One look reminded her that she was but a small cog in the wheel and her well-laid plans had failed.

What had Tilly said…*It won't be what you expect. Heck, it never is!*

Against the flare of sunset she saw the turtle guards packing up their stations as the evening shift entered the scene. Greg and Kim Goodwin shuffled across the flat plane of sand, like weary wanderers in search of an oasis, the petite wife ten paces behind her tall man, her shoulders bent under an invisible burden. She needed more than a cookbook from him—anyone could see that.

Someone else was staring at the pair: Libby, at the edge of Max's property. Perhaps Kim had forgotten to tell her she wasn't needed tonight. The blonde started towards them, when she came to a halt and, with a firm shake of her head, headed in the opposite direction.

Angel retrieved the wanted shadow box. *Time to end this silly charade.*

Max opened the door, his face awash in delight at the sight of her. "Angel."

Had her name ever sounded so good? She wished he'd say it again. Close in her ear. With the sexy accent that left her woozy.

"Please, come in," he added, taking the frame crooked over her arm.

She hesitated at the doorway, her will sinking like a foundering vessel. With a raspy cough she stepped into the simple living room—for just a minute, out of politeness—then she'd leave.

She noted the new paint of soft cream and white trim; Maeapple's clutter was gone. On the far wall a large window looked onto a back porch with white wicker furniture and blue-striped cushions. Overall, the dwelling and its furniture, including a sturdy old captain's desk, presented a clean view of the sea.

"The place looks nice," Angel said. "Much lighter."

"Thank you," Max said. "There is so much beauty outdoors, I think now the eye travels there."

"I see you have a knack for these things."

"I'm eager to show you the workshop."

How could she deny his sweet enthusiasm?

In startling contrast to the house's muted palette and minimal décor, the garage exploded with colors and shapes and a dazzling array of shells in clear plastic bins that filled the walls. Here was the beating heart of his abode. She recalled that Tilly's apartment had a similar feel and, with a guilty pang, once again wished she could share her experience with Max.

He placed the empty frame on one of two long tables that ran through the middle of the room. On the nearest table sat a pitcher of water and several glasses, beside a plate of cookies, as well as three more shadow boxes, each at different stages in the process of making a Sailors' Valentine.

Unlike the higgledy-piggledy mess of Tilly's craft materials, dozens of boxes catalogued in Max's bold script were arranged in alphabetical order, according to their common name, on metal shelves at one side of the garage. They seemed to glow with life—Glassy bubble, Calico clam, Baby's Ear, White Melampus, Lettered olive, Kitten's Paw, Wentletrap.

Several trays on the far table held a variety of simple tools—cotton batting, glue pots, paint and brushes, tweezers, push pins, pencil compass, and single edge razor blades, as well as some he had rigged for the unique purpose of shell work, such as a sea urchin spine snip for the tiniest shell placement.

Angel took in the room, full of admiration for its organization and precision, and also shame that she could not express the depth of her appreciation.

"It looks complicated," was the best she could do.

"Ah," he said, running his hand over a grid of squares inside a frame. "The steps are not so hard. Anyone can learn them, I believe. It is inspiration that is difficult, for myself, too." He picked up a small shell cluster that formed a white carnation type flower. "*Andodontia alba*, the Buttercup Lucine."

"Very pretty," she said, amazed that such a sturdy man could fashion the delicate handiwork. "I wonder how you became interested in shells."

An odd look, perhaps fear, flashed across his face. "I do not wish to bore you."

"I'd like to know."

Seeing her accepting smile, he visibly relaxed. As he spoke, a sense of longing crept into his voice. "In my house as a boy there was a tall wooden cabinet. My mother's mother, who was English, gifted it to her. I recall tracing my finger over beautiful shell designs inlaid with mother-of-pearl on the sides. *Mutti* kept a shell collection here. I must stand on my father's footstool to see inside; some species I never saw again. You see, partitions in the drawers created geometric shapes—I often wonder if this is how the idea of shell mosaics began."

His eyes drifted to the front wall where several Sailors' Valentines hung: a floral all-white motif with simple words: *Beloved Mother*; a rowboat in a calm lake, *Dear Father*; and *My Sweet Sister Klara*, a small girl and her poodle playing in a garden.

"These were my first," he went on. "*Ach!* They are not so good. I was happy, you see, to create the unique feelings I possessed for my family. I suppose the Valentines remind me of what was lost. Perhaps I am just a sentimental fool."

"They're lovely," Angel said. Though it wasn't a fair comparison, she realized they both had lost their families. "I can't imagine how you carried on."

"In every situation one has a choice. Compromise is not so bad, I think. Sometimes it is the best way." He adjusted his disappointment as if straightening his tie. *"So ist das leben."*

"That's life?"

"I'm afraid so."

He coughed to clear his throat and poured them each a glass of water. His tone grew more conversational. "You can imagine the fascination when trade ships brought colorful, exotic shells to England in the late eighteenth century. Charles Darwin also created an interest in natural studies. The shells exploded in popularity; especially women desired to collect.

"On my birthday each year, *Mutti* presented a beautiful shell to me and so, by the start of the war, I had a small collection. How often I wished I had taken it on the train. But she told me soon we all would be once again in the house in Leopoldstadt. I returned many years later, but the cabinet and the shells were no more."

He paused to study Angel, as if searching for an answer to an unspoken question. "I confess," he went on. "For some time I have not made a Valentine. I begin and then I stop. Many times." He indicated the far table where a linen cloth covered a frame. "I tried even weeks ago. Without the Shell Queen, it is pointless."

"The shell queen?" Angel said, unable to disguise her surprise.

"The shell that must the palette and design reveal," Max explained. "Otherwise—*ach!*—so many options, one grows weary." His gaze settled on her once more, as he added, "I am waiting for my Shell Queen."

Before she could refuse, he took her hand in his. "Angel," he began in earnest, when the doorbell rang. "Excuse me," he said.

She followed him, intending to leave, but found Libby blocking the doorway.

"Oh, hey, Angel," she said. "I didn't expect to see you." She winked at Max. "You've got the best single ladies in town."

A slash of color rose in his cheeks and he pointed the way to his studio. "Shall we?"

Libby swept past. "Believe me, I'm ready for something new."

As Angel stepped towards the door, Max took her arm. "But you're not leaving, are you?" he said.

"I can't, Max." She didn't deserve him or the shells.

"What can I do to persuade you?"

If only she could reveal her past, as he had done with openness and trust, but she couldn't bear for him to think of her as a liar.

"I'm sorry."

As she entered the street, a long shadow passed overhead—a siege of night herons sailing towards the ocean. From the swampy verge came a scratchy scampering that compelled her to walk across the footbridge. In the shimmering silver light of a full moon, she saw ghost crabs racing across the sand, following the same path as the birds—in search of fresh eggs.

The turtles are coming!

From the relaxed state of the groups on patrol, no one was the wiser. To Angel, it was as if a loud gong had rung. She retraced her steps to Max's doorstep.

"They're coming," she said, breathlessly. "The loggerheads."

"Just a moment, please wait," he said, turning towards the studio.

Through the living room window she saw Yemayá's pearlescent light draped over small ripples on the bay like icing on a cake. The Great Lady was calling to her. *Ven a mí, mi amor.*

A moment later Max returned with Libby. "Now?" she said. "You're sure? 'Cause I don't want to make a fool of myself out there."

He answered. "Already they are late, no? By the middle of May they are expected, and we are almost June."

He led them across the footbridge, and when they reached the dunes, Libby veered towards Greg and Kim. Her hushed call sent them to their feet. Soon an intermittent link of human protection formed in the nesting zone. Max took Angel's hand. She smiled, her heart bursting, as they ran to an unoccupied spot several yards from shore. He squeezed her hand, like opening a lock, and she moved under the wing of his arm. It wasn't so bad, after all, to love again.

Sea birds wheeled overhead, climbing the ladder of moonlight that stretched across the gulf, their cacophony of competing cries, like bets made at a sporting event, raining down on the beach. Angel sighted a dark, round shadow in the undertow. She nudged Max, pointing ahead, as another hump surfaced several feet away.

Up and down the shore, dozens of reddish brown loggerheads appeared, their jutting profiles like fierce figureheads on the prows of ships. They marched onto land, using their powerful pectoral muscles to heave their two-hundred-pound reptilian bodies across the sand. With scraping sounds, they pushed past surf zone. A high wave could swamp a low-lying clutch, while some would be lost to crabs and the rampant population of raccoons, despite the volunteers' vigilance.

A ponderous loggerhead moved doggedly toward Angel and Max, stopping mere yards away. She began to dig with her hind flippers, sending a flurry of sand into the air. Several minutes later, when she had finished her nest, she deposited several dozen slick, leathery, golf-ball-sized eggs from her ovipositor.

Hungry birds dove for errant eggs that missed the mark, their cacophonous cries in contrast to the silent guard. When a nest was complete, the loggerhead covered the eggs in another spray of sand. The uneven timing of the turtle march, with its inconsistent small sandstorms among the whirling and diving avian enemies, made for a riveting if haphazard natural ballet.

Angel's turtle—that was how she thought of it—turned seaward, obliterating evidence of the nest with a sweep of her fore flippers. The mother hesitated, perhaps to catch her breath or say a silent prayer for her young, before she moved forward, leaving a signature tractor-crawl in her wake. When she reached the moist line of crushed shells and seaweed, Yemayá drew her back into the belly of the sea.

Ven a mí, mi amor.

Would the mother forget her offspring as she swam deep into the blue? In two months, when the hatchlings arrived, would she wonder how many survived the perilous trek to sea?

As if on cue, the multitude of birds flew away into the night, the soft susurrus of surf resumed, while the moon glow waxed magical. The community waited in astonished silence for the spell to dissipate. After a moment, Max marked the clutch of eggs with a yellow flag.

"Our nest," he said.

He wrapped her in his arms, his body snug against hers, as she let loose the seams of desire. His lips found hers, and she received him like the shore to the sea, without hesitation or question. At last she had laid down the fight.

DEVILISH BAIT

Colonial traders in the eighteenth century carried shells to Europe, creating a mania for collecting, conchylomania, particularly for exotic rarities and newly discovered specimens. These "shell-lunatics" soon rivaled the obsession of the Dutch tulip mania, a frenzy for collecting tulip bulbs. At an auction in Amsterdam, the price of shells sold just below Johannes Vermeer's now-priceless *Woman in Blue Reading a Letter.* In 1840, a British magazine recommended shell collecting as "peculiarly suited to ladies" because "there is no cruelty in the pursuit" and the shells are "so brightly clean, so ornamental to a boudoir."

SANIBEL ISLAND, FLORIDA

SUMMER 1985

The memory of the moonlight kiss with Max floated in on a sea breeze as Angel crossed her front yard. Like an editor notating the pages of a romance novel, she underlined the way he made her feel: *excited yet relaxed*; *warm and safe*; *eager for his companionship.* But she reminded herself that she was a sinful liar like the rest of her family. Were her feelings for Max strong enough to risk the truth? Were his strong enough to accept her?

A sharp chest pain forced her to lean over the mailbox. She coughed violently until she spat onto the ground. For a moment she stared at the bloody plug of pus, wondering what, if anything, to do about it. *Forget it.*

Like a slumming dignitary, a fine white envelope with fancy red and gold crest was mixed in with a pile of junk mail. With gnawing dread Angel opened the letter from the University of Tampa. The balance of tuition was due in two weeks.

She hurried to the kitchen phone, hoping that Faith would listen to reason. Her daughter's angry response was as jarring as the sight of a shark fin in shallow waters.

"I told you I don't want to talk to you," she said. "Don't—"

"Wait!" Angel said. "I have news."

"What?"

"The rest of the tuition is due on June tenth."

"Forget it, Mom."

"But you'll lose your place, Kiddo."

"Look," Faith began in a familiar confessional tone. *I took an Easter egg from Bonnie's basket. I tried a cigarette after school.* "I already put a deposit on a brake shop in Fort Myers."

"You're kidding?" Angel said. *All that hard-earned money—gone?*

"I'm dead serious."

"But you can't even change a tire."

"Wayne's the mechanic; I'll manage the place. We're a team." Her exasperated exhale sent a crackle through the phone. "I don't know why I bother."

Like a drowning sailor flailing for a line, Angel grasped at her one chance for salvation. "At least tell me you're reading the stories I sent."

"More stories?" And with that, Faith hung up.

Unbidden, a memory surfaced of the Captain bent over in despair, his illusions shattered. All his efforts, his very life, had been in vain. *Fué todo para nada.* Was it true for Angel, too? Was it all for nothing?

* * * * *

Dear Faith,

As you will see, we all make mistakes. The key is to get back on your feet and set the right course before it's too late.

Love,

Mom

A SOUTHERN GODDESS ARRIVES

KEY WEST, FLORIDA

MARCH 1962

Dread churned in the pit of my stomach as I stood on the flybridge beside the Captain on a cloudless spring day. *La Libertad* cruised up the Gulf Stream, the scent of disaster as palpable as the Coppertone lotion I'd slathered on my skin. The sun hung well past noon and we hadn't had a single strike.

The quartet of well-paying passengers grew restless. A short wiry guy from Chicago bellowed from below. "Hey, *patrón*! Are the fish on vacation?"

"No, *señor*! They wait for you to catch them."

I'd never heard the Captain insult a client. He turned the wheel over to me and charged down to the cockpit. My anxiety ratcheted several notches as I leaned over the railing, watching him bark orders to no one in particular. He reeled in the line and, with manic energy, changed both tackle and bait, then instructed the men to use the fishing chair on the starboard side.

Chicago protested. "What about the rest of us?"

The Captain exploded. "Only here! This chair, *comprende?*"

At Palo's penetrating stare, the Captain rubbed his stomach, blamed his bad luck on a rotten meal. *"Mala cocina."*

The old Cuban looked at him with pity as he diagnosed his true malady. "*La maledición del pescador ha devuelta.*"

The curse of the fisherman had returned? How would we survive without his livelihood?

The color drained from my father's face. He crossed himself and spit over his shoulder. With his jaw set tight, he headed back to the wheel without a word. I drifted to the preacher's pulpit at the bow, a platform that extends beyond the ship. There I sat with my arms curled around its supports, my legs dangling over the sides, the water rushing beneath me. In desperation I prayed to the Captain's Sea Goddess. *Please send the fish our way.*

For several long hours we trolled back and forth in areas that usually netted some catch, while Yemayá continued to ignore us. The smell of diesel, a happy association of carefree days at sea, now made me nauseous.

Late afternoon, the sound of unfamiliar, unsteady steps on the metal ladder made me panic. I turned, shielding my eyes from the sun, aghast at the sight of Chicago on the flybridge, which was invitation-only. He stood angled to flee and spoke in a soft cadence, as if calming a rapid animal.

"What do you say we go back, *patrón*? My wife will be hopping mad if I'm late for her dinner party."

The Captain stared ahead at the sea. "I promised big fish or you don't pay!"

"Hey, you win some, you lose some. We'll recycle old fish stories."

"Today we win."

"Either way I got to be back by six o'clock."

"No problema."

As the client headed below, I scuttled across the deck to spy on the passengers who congregated at the stern, whispering in hushed tones. When they tossed furtive glances at the crew, I suspected we might have a mutiny on our hands.

When the skies began a Technicolor show, Palo climbed to the Captain's side. All hands watched from below, as a silent understanding passed between them. My father took off his old straw hat, his head sunk on his chest. In a single day he had become an old man.

In a feeble voice, he admitted his rotten luck. "*Sí, la maledición ha devuelta.*"

Palo decreed it to be Yemayá's will. "*Es la voluntad de La Señora.*"

Like taking candy from a baby, he commandeered the helm while the Captain rolled onto the bench with a soft moan.

I returned to the pulpit, where no one could see the tears I shed. I blamed our pagan worship of the Sea Goddess. Almighty God had caught us red-handed and there would be hell to pay.

That evening I trailed the Chevy on my yellow Schwinn to Rest Beach. From a distance I watched the Captain place yet another stupid coconut shell at the edge of the water. As twilight fell and the tide climbed higher onto the sand, his pathetic little offering never set sail. My poor, foolish father wept like a spurned lover over his rejected offering.

At last I tugged his arm. "Please, let's go home, Papi."

In a desolate voice he said it was all for nothing. "*Fué todo para nada.*"

Fishing, like gambling and salvation, is a confidence game and the Captain's tumbled like a house of cards. Within days, the charters trickled away, Palo stopped coming to work, and finally, my father gave up the fight.

Caught up in endless activities at church, Mother didn't notice the decline, until he refused to get out of bed. She stared into their bedroom from a safe distance in the hallway, blame percolating behind her eyes.

"What's wrong, Captain?"

He rubbed his belly, which growled on cue. "Upset stomach."

"Ginger dandelion tea will set you right." She hurried past me to the kitchen.

I peeped into the bedroom, but he took no notice of me, his expression detached.

Mother returned with a tray of tea and dry toast. "Let us pray for a speedy recovery." He nodded, but I noticed he kept his eyes open. "Dear Lord Jesus, please shower your loving kindness upon your humble servant

Rafael del Corazón. Heal him so that he might be a witness unto your goodness and mercy. Amen." She caught his irreverent stare. "Rafael?"

With a listless sigh, he closed his eyes. "Amen."

"I'll be at church if you need me," she said, as she departed.

I stood in the hallway for some time, silently urging him to reclaim his life. *Come on, get up. Fight back!* Instead, he fell into a frightening moral abyss. Over the next few days, his beard grew in, his stomach bloated from too many beers, while *La Libertad* rocked empty in its berth.

Mary established an emergency prayer circle for his recovery. Each morning a group of well-meaning women trotted into our living room to read God's word aloud and pray for the Captain. To my horror, he often took up the empty seat reserved for him.

The Good Lord had been biding his time, waiting for a chance to nab his soul and mine. If the Captain converted, my resistance would crumble—I'd be easy pickings. Things were looking dim when a real live goddess landed on our shores.

On the Rock, as the locals referred to Key West, news traveled quickly via the Parrot Line, a chattering tag game of gossip. The arrival of Miss Virginia Weathers was no exception.

My mother discouraged fraternizing with Catholics, but Catherine Daniels was my best friend. Like me, she was an only child, both of us budding into adolescence. Her family lived a few blocks away on White Street, in a two-story "eyebrow" house with a characteristic sloping roofline.

On that eventful spring day, Cathy stopped her bicycle on the sidewalk in front of our house and called out my name. Mother was busy with her prayer group, and I ran out before she could stop me.

A pale redhead of Irish stock, my friend's face glowed with excitement. "Wanna meet my aunt? She's real pretty. You've never seen anyone like her."

"Nah." Cathy was a big fat storyteller and I needed to keep an eye on the Captain's shaky soul.

"She's a stewardess. And…" She drew out the suspense with a smug smile. "She's got on her uniform. She even let me wear her cap."

I studied her pixie face for any hint of deception. In those days stewardesses were like rock stars. "That true?"

She crossed herself. "I swear on baby Jesus."

Glancing at the living room window, I saw Mother and the ladies in a huddle. The Captain's absence that day had added fervor to their prayers.

"C'mon, now, Angel," Cathy said. "Before she changes clothes. You might never get the chance again."

Giddiness overtook me. A real live stewardess...wings...freedom? The Captain would have to fend for himself.

"I'm coming!" I grabbed my bike and we sped away, bent over the handlebars, legs pumping fast.

At the sight of the willowy, pale blond standing on the front porch, I stopped short. Surrounded by a group of visiting neighbors, Cathy's aunt glowed like a delicate, translucent, rosy pink Sunrise Tellin in a patch of bland clamshells.

Oh, how I coveted her uniform. The Pan Am Blue suit with contrasting white starched collar and matching hat gave her an untouchable air. Her white gloves and black pumps were smarter than any you'd spot on Duval Street on Easter Sunday. Imagine if the golden wings on her jacket could fly me to faraway lands, just like the Chosen would ascend to heaven on Judgment Day.

A telltale piquant scent of bay leaves, sea salt, and fish interrupted my reverie. I turned to find the Captain climbing the veranda steps, a bucketful of fresh lobster tails in his hands. By some spiritual sleight of hand, like raising Lazarus from the dead, he was once more his mischievous self: the Jack of Hearts smile, the gold-braided captain's hat set at a jaunty angle, a sureness to his step.

The Captain offered the bucket to Cathy's mother. "A catch for you, *Señora* Daniels."

"Well, isn't that the sweetest thing." Mrs. Daniels said, signaling her maid, who took the bucket.

A catch? At that point, my father couldn't have trapped a mussel if it was barnacled to a pier. I searched his face for an explanation, but he ignored me, his attention riveted on the newcomer.

He drifted towards her, oblivious to our hostess, who said, "Allow me to introduce my baby sister, Miss Virginia Weathers."

When Miss Virginia's soft blue eyes landed on the Captain, she twinkled like the lights on the boats that paraded past Mallory Square on Christmas Eve.

"Well, hello there." The greeting hung from her red-coated lips like a juicy ripe mango. "Sister, dear, you didn't tell me the locals were so handsome or I would have visited sooner."

The Captain took her gloved hand in his large palm and bent to kiss it. The electricity between them energized the atmosphere, giving Cathy a fit of giggles that wouldn't quit until I elbowed her.

"The pleasure is all mine, *señorita.*" As a glint of light flashed in his dark eyes, I thought, *uh-oh*. It was the same hungry look of a fisherman who's spotted big game—the hunt was on.

Mrs. Daniels's high soprano crackled like a bell. "Mercy, it's hot out here! Y'all come to the parlor. I've made iced tea and shortbread cookies." She hurried away with the scandalized ladies in tow.

A Southerner from Georgia, she believed that strong black tea with a mountain of sugar cured any ill. In this case, she had sorely underestimated the powerful forces at work.

The Captain and Miss Virginia seemed unaware of the departing women, or anything else for that matter. Cathy and I drifted to the porch railing, standing between hanging orchid baskets and potted palms, to watch the show. Although I was acquainted with the mating dance of marine life, this was my first opportunity to observe it in mature humans.

The Captain released Miss Virginia's hand after what seemed an obscene amount of time. His voice had dropped a notch and sounded honey-baked. "How long will we have the pleasure of your company?"

Brushing the nape of her neck, she rocked on her heels. "That depends on how friendly the natives are."

They tilted towards each other, as if they had no will of their own. His shoulders had acquired additional heft, while her skin glowed with dewy, edible moistness. I wondered if Lucifer had worked his magic, perhaps in the form of the daddy-long-legs I saw high-stepping across their path.

"Miss Weathers—"

"Please, call me Virginia."

"Virginia." The name wobbled in his mouth like a raw oyster. "Us Conchs are friendly—"

"Conchs?"

He shrugged boyishly. "A local name."

"How charming." Her laugh was as playful as a dolphin's chirp.

"A sophisticated woman like you might find our ways strange."

"Oh, don't you worry, Captain." As she tucked her chin and batted his arm, the color rose in his face. "I'm just a little 'ole Southern gal. To tell you the truth, I've never been on a boat."

"In that case, please allow me the honor."

"I wouldn't want you to go to any trouble on my account, Captain."

"Please, call me Rafael."

Mother only called him by his Christian name on those rare occasions when one of them was ill or showed meager affection. How velvety his name sounded on Miss Virginia's pouty lips.

"I believe I'm free tomorrow afternoon, Rafael."

"Shall I pick you up at two o'clock for a personal tour of the islands?"

"That will be just perfect."

"Can we come, too?" Cathy said.

The pair shifted toward us, as if coming out of an enchanted dream. Miss Virginia produced two gray plastic replicas of her flight wings from her pocket.

"Would you girls like these?"

Was it a devilish bribe? Or a talisman that promised my future freedom?

We rushed to her side. As she bent to pin the coveted symbol on my blouse, the overpowering scent of rose perfume, flowers foreign to Key West's inhospitable rocky soil, made my head spin.

"Did I pinch you, honey?"

"No, ma'am."

She laughed easily. "Maybe you felt the liftoff."

I nodded, desperate to be in her good graces. She gave Cathy the other pair of wings, guaranteeing our complicity; at least that's how I saw it.

"If you two promise to be real good, perhaps one day I'll take you on a flight." Miss Virginia smiled at the Captain. "That is, of course, if your parents agree."

"Please, Papi!"

He looked doubtful. "That's a generous offer."

"No more so than a legendary Captain taking me on the high seas."

His hard suntanned face softened with bittersweet longing, the same look he wore when searching the seas for a sign of his beloved Sea Goddess. I guess he thought Miss Virginia would save him now.

Mrs. Daniels appeared at the front door, wagging in her hand a glass of chilled tea. "Y'all coming in?"

"I apologize, *señora*. I must prepare for an important voyage." The Captain gave Miss Virginia a conspiratorial wink. He threw my bike in the back of the Chevy, and we rode across town while he whistled a happy tune.

"Today we make *La Libertad* shine, *Hijita*."

I suppose, for him, swabbing the deck constituted male preening. In my bones, I felt a sea change coming. What could I do but stay alert and pray to Jesus and Yemayá, too, for sweet deliverance?

* * * * *

SANIBEL ISLAND, FLORIDA

SUMMER 1985

A sweltering slab of summer heat boxed in the island, impeding an ocean breeze. The day flattened into a one-dimensional frying pan. As Angel drove through the baking streets, she fiddled with the car air conditioning. But it was no match for the steamy humidity. The backs of her legs stuck to the seat; her underwear clung to her skin.

Parking in front of the Island Bookstore, she anticipated the fresh cold air inside like a lover's kiss. The heat had rubberized her limbs; moving was a chore. With great effort, she hefted two cartons of books from her trunk.

Stella and the Merman. The seventh book in the series, she realized. Papi believed it was Yemayá's lucky number. *Nonsense.*

To Angel's dismay, the front door was propped open, and the store a claustrophobic soupy mess. As she angled the boxes inside, she accidentally knocked the kickstand and the door swung closed. A metal fan sat on the front counter, blowing hot air on the proprietress, who looked no cooler for its efforts, and cross as a lizard that has lost its tail.

"Good Lord!" Libby shot past her and propped the door open again. "AC is broken, if you can't tell."

Angel pushed the books onto the counter, counting the minutes until she could leave. Libby resumed her spot in front of the fan with a desultory glance at the boxes.

"I'm expecting a good crowd," she said. "Max will have shells for sale. Cross promotion, they call it." Libby winked. "What's good for him is good for me."

An alarm went off in Angel's head. Why had she ever put him in the hands of this man-eater?

Libby's head jerked up, as a truck entered the parking lot. Expectation turned to fury at the sight of a gardening van.

"Where the hell is Bill?" she said. "He said he'd be here an hour ago. No A.C., no customers." She turned the full force of her frustration on Angel. "You know it's not easy running a bookstore. Margins are thin."

"I know your time is valuable," Angel said. "You'll be happy to know I can finally accompany Max on patrol."

"What?"

"It was kind of you to take my place, but there's no need now."

"Honey, you're mistaken. I wasn't doing you a favor, you did me one, and there's no taking it back."

"But it's our nest."

Libby shook her head. "If you think I care about the turtles, or that you should, for that matter, you have a lot to learn about men, Angel Rose. Max is a perfectly suitable bachelor. You said it yourself: we have a lot in common. Beside, he's cute, him and his silly obsession with shells, don't you think?"

"Cute?"

Libby began writing out a receipt. "Don't worry, he's not your type. Those Europeans respond to feminine glamour. It's in their blood—the flirting, the perfume, the chase, all that good stuff."

Was Max chasing after Libby? Angel felt like sinking under the floor.

"I didn't say he's my type," she said.

Libby snorted derisively. "Well, who is?"

"It's my civic duty, that's all."

"Uh-huh." Libby handed her the receipt. "Maybe you can partner with someone else—I think Greg and Kim are looking for an alternate."

The arrival of Island Air Conditioning's truck sent Libby out the door, shouting to the driver. Angel followed her into the blaze of wet heat, wondering what had just happened.

There in Max's studio, surrounded by a world of shells, Angel questioned the wisdom of her decision. Did she really want to engage in shell work or was she simply here for Max? Standing in the middle of the room, he presented an old double-sided Sailors' Valentine to her and the only other classmate, Libby, who sat at the opposite table.

"Often," Max said, turning it to reveal the clasp, "you will find a heart-shaped lock." Bent over her day planner, Libby stifled a yawn. "How romantic," she said.

If she was so interested in Max, why didn't she show more enthusiasm for his work? Angel detected no particular spark between them, but what did she know about romance? Perhaps underneath their placid demeanors raged boiling lust. Certainly, with her low-cut, swishy dress and high-heeled sandals, Libby was dressed to seduce.

Max unfolded the frames to reveal a maritime theme, which extended across both sides. A beguiling green-haired mermaid clad only in pearls sat perched on a cliff, tempting sailors aboard a clipper ship, behind which a pod of dolphins trailed under an azure sky dotted with white seagulls. Embedded within the sea was the legend: *Without You I Am Lost At Sea.*

Angel leaned forward, surprised to see Yemayá depicted as she always had imagined her.

Max looked at her, and said, "Have you seen such a design?"

"No, why would I?" she answered, fiddling with a random shell.

"It's not a crime," Libby interjected.

"I just meant it's unusual."

"It's beautiful, no?" he said.

Angel adopted a more supportive tone. "Yes, very."

He ran a finger over the design, from one side to the other. "Imagine a lonely woman hundreds of years ago in the soot-filled city of London, dreaming of the sea while on a Sailors' Valentine she works. A *Geukensia demissa* she chooses." He pointed to the row of smoky blue Atlantic Ribbed mussels that formed the wavy sea. "And then, like the sun that appears from behind the clouds, a mermaid with green hair and pearl necklace appears in her mind. You see how the Shell Queen carries the vision? It guides you to create the most beneficial picture for your healing. At least, that is what I believe."

"That's weird," Libby said.

"Yes, I suppose it is. I prefer to think of it as Shell Talk."

"Shell Talk?" Angel repeated.

She had never heard anyone but Tilly use that phrase. *Let the shells talk to you, Kiddo. Just like we're doing—Shell Talk.*

"Indeed." Max gave her a quizzical look. "It is an unusual but true expression, as I hope you will discover." Pointing to the boxes that lined the wall, he added, "And so, Ladies, this evening I hope you will find your Shell Queen. Please feel free to explore and ask questions."

Libby stretched her buxom figure as she rose to her feet. "Mine's going to have a picture of a rooster and two hens with the caption: *Not Just Any Cock Will Do*." Her laughter rained down in the silent room.

Oblivious to the others' embarrassment, she held up a small white clam, no larger than a penny, with tight concentric ridges and irregular tan markings, and with delight remarked, "Perfect for hen feathers, don't you think?"

"*Puberella intapurpurea*," Max said. "The Lady-in-waiting Venus has inspired many. I suggest you begin with a sketch."

"I can't draw more than a stick figure."

"For later reference it's best to capture the image. No great detail is required."

Angel rubbed the purple-brown zigzag ridges of a Turkey Wing. It was bold like her daughter. Funny, how a shell could bring someone to mind. Perhaps Angel was like an Emerald Nerite. It hid within the shelter of marine grasses, while she cowered behind a mantle of secrets. Libby, with her curvy figure and man-eating smile, was a carnivorous, Banded Tulip. And Max? Angel had yet to figure him out.

In her youth, she had heard the Song of the Sea and longed to hear it once more. Was it too late to love again? From long ago Tilly's answer came back to her. *Anything is possible with Shell Work.*

Feeling as hopeful as a sailor who spies land through the eye of a hurricane, Angel swam her fingers through a box of Rough scallops. After nearly two decades of denial, she prayed within, *dentro*, to all of them: the Captain, Mary, Tilly, Yemayá, and the Good Lord Above, because love, she decided, knew no boundaries. *Please, help me.*

Each Valentine had a particular tune, unmistakable though new, like a cherished piece of music heard for the first time. It was impossible to miss, like a whisper in a crowd or a raindrop on your cheek on a sunny day. *Ven a mí, mi amor.*

Giddy, Angel seized one particular shell. For a moment, the world stood still. Always, without exception, the exact message was intended for the handiworker, and Angel shuddered with recognition. *Love Is All There Is.*

With quiet excitement she placed the bright orange Shell Queen inside the frame. Only a fool would resist its power.

Max came beside her. *"Hmmm. Aequipecten muscosus*. Passionate and brave—it exists in Winston Churchill's coat of arms. Used well in a Sailors' Valentine, they say the Rough scallop signals a sea change."

Angel looked up into his soft dark eyes, remembering the sea change that had left the Captain castrated and her without an ally.

* * * * *

Dear Faith,

You might be surprised to know I've joined Max's shell handicraft class. By now, you may understand my insistence on keeping shells out of the house. Regrets weigh heavy on me now, particularly time we might have spent at the beach together.

Love,

Mom

KEY LIME PIE FOR SALVATION

KEY WEST, FLORIDA

AUGUST 1962

It was clear sailing at the Corazón household the summer Miss Virginia spent on the Rock—unless, like the young, vigilant spy, you noted the daily skirmishes in the battle for our souls.

The Captain began taking overnight fishing trips without his first mate. And guess who took a leave of absence from Pan Am and rented a second-story balcony apartment on Rose Street? Miss Virginia even sewed yellow gingham curtains for her new place. I know because Cathy and I spied on her when she bought the fabric and later, too, when she hung them in place.

I understood exactly which engines the Captain was running and why Miss Virginia went to such extravagance. If Mother hadn't had her nose stuck in the Bible, she might have seen Lucifer gloating at the living room hearth, his horned head feverishly aglow.

Hey, Angel Baby, why the worry? The fish are jumping for your Pa's charters. Your Ma's got plenty of dough to pay the bills. Hell, it's a miracle. Everybody's happy so quit your bellyaching. R-e-l-a-x. *I'm running the show now.*

He disappeared with a lewd wink, in a cloud of smoke that left me chilled to the bone. It was true: things were good. The Captain had stopped the drink and even attended church once a month—to give thanks for Miss Virginia, I suspected. I had to admit she was the best thing ever to happen to us.

You might wonder why the Almighty God doesn't do away with Lucifer, his sole competitor. But see, He's a jealous God who allows the devil to test His children in order to prove their love to Him. To even the odds, the Good Lord gave the Captain an impressive handicap: free will. My father might have resisted Miss Virginia; however, as these things often play out, the temptation was tailored to his weakness. And I imagine he was her cup of tea, too. There's one other hitch—let's face it; the game was rigged from the start. If the Captain's name wasn't written in the Book of Life, he wasn't destined to choose God, anyway. But then, no one knows What Is Written. If this seems complicated, trust me, it is.

The suspense kept me up many long nights. I lay in my small bed, a gentle breeze stirring the white lace curtains, sweat on my brow, as I anticipated various endgames. By late August I was exhausted from worry and lack of sleep and, frankly, sick and tired of being played like a pawn in the Spiritual Game of Chess. Then the Lord revealed Himself as one hell of a prankster.

Cathy and I were playing Gin Rummy on her hemp hammock under the shade of Royal palms when Mrs. Daniels appeared on the back porch with a key lime pie tied up in brown paper.

"Cathy-honey, take this pie over t'aunt Ginny."

Eager for Conch acceptance, she had perfected the local treat: frothy white waves rippled over a sea of buttercups. She used real Key limes from a grove on Matecumbe Key, and it sure was tasty. She placed the prized pastry in Cathy's bike basket and told us to "get going *toot sweet*."

We sped off, dying for an invitation to Miss Virginia's love nest. Racing along Flagler Avenue, the wind bubbled our shirts away from our sweaty skin. As we turned the corner, their laughter hit me like a sock in the stomach. I slammed on the brake.

Cathy stopped next to me and whispered, "Holy Moley."

Several yards ahead, in plain sight, the Captain carried Miss Virginia in his arms up her apartment staircase like a bride to the nuptial threshold.

With her head thrown back, her bright blond mane was a beacon of light, her pretty pale legs swinging free.

For a moment I forgot I was witnessing forbidden love and enjoyed a look-see at the good times the devil offered. As the lovers disappeared inside, the door slammed shut, shaking me from my sinful reverie.

Cathy blew out a hot breath. “You think they’re in love?”

I shrugged. “They’re sinners is what they are.”

“The nuns say adultery is a cardinal sin, only murder is worse.”

Catholics could measure the damage done to their souls with the number of Hail Mary’s. Of course, it didn’t matter because they were all going to hell, anyway.

I parroted what Mother would have said. “All sins are equal in Jesus’ eyes.” Though I suspected the Captain’s affair might outweigh a drunken night on the town.

“Well….” Cathy chewed on her lip. “How about we pretend we didn’t see anything t’all? I won’t tell, if you won’t.”

“What’ll happen to Miss Virginia if word gets out?”

“My Mama’s gonna kill her.”

Having spent years in the spy trade, I understood the trap into which we had fallen. “You’re forgetting one thing.” I pointed to her basket and the unwitting instrument of chaos. *The pie!*

Cathy’s freckles knitted into dark clusters. “Oh, boy.”

“I got to think. C’mon.”

We cycled round the Rock, cruising along the Atlantic to Highway One at our northern tip, then down Roosevelt along the Gulf, past Garrison Bight where *La Libertad* awaited its philandering master, zigzagging down Duval, until we landed at Smathers Beach.

My exhausted friend plopped down in the sand. “Well?”

“We’re trapped.” No matter how many scenarios I’d run through my mind, I saw no way out of this mess. In the end, we stretched under a large coconut palm and ate the whole damn pie.

As the sun arched over the island, as graceful as a limbo dancer bending to the pole, we headed back to Cathy’s house. We entered the hot kitchen, our bellies aching from pie, our hearts full of terror.

Mrs. Daniels cradled the phone receiver against her shoulder while she stirred a mixing bowl. She nodded towards the table laid with fresh conch fritters and slaw. We sat there, staring glumly at the food. Of course the devil had seen to it that Miss Virginia was on the line. Cathy’s poor mother was oblivious to her part in the spiritual drama.

“Nothing cools the blood like sugar, Ginny. Try my key lime pie. What? Why, I sent it over…I thought you said you’d be home this afternoon. Is that so? *Ta*.”

She turned towards us, her lazy tone as deceptive as a sunbathing gator. “Cathy-honey, where’s my pie?”

“We dropped it, I’m sorry, Mama, it was an accident.” She rushed—a dead giveaway.

Her mother stared to the side. Something held her attention, probably the sum of many inconsistencies that fateful summer.

“Well, did you stop by Aunt Ginny’s?”

“Uh, sort of. I guess not really.”

“Which is it? Did you or did you not see her?” Cathy shook her head; she just wasn’t up to it. “Well, did you drop the pie before or after you stopped by her place?” My accomplice kicked me under the table. Her mother’s voice snapped in the air. “Cathy?”

Fourteen years old, and already I was weary of all the lies, the Captain’s and mine. Funny how, in that moment, I recalled the little coconut boat carrying my plea out to sea. *I wish to be free and happy.* Perhaps the

Captain's mermaid answered me that day because I found the strength to tell the truth, even if it gave Jesus the upper hand.

I looked Mrs. Daniels straight in the eye. "We saw Miss Virginia, but we couldn't speak to her, and we sure couldn't give her the pie."

Mrs. Daniels raised her arms akimbo, her nostrils flared wide. "And why is that?'

"Because she was busy, ma'am."

"Heavens. How busy could she be?"

Like an angel of mercy, I delivered the coup de grâce. "Miss Virginia was busy with the Captain. They were occupied. Together, ma'am."

"I don't see…." The picture clicked into place. Mrs. Daniels' hand flew to her mouth. "Lord have mercy."

Mother often said God moves in mysterious ways. Well, I bet His clever ploy with the key lime pie became legendary in heaven even as its fame grew on the Rock.

That evening after supper, Mrs. Daniels paid us a visit and brought one of her famous pies. The knowing smirk on her face suggested my worst nightmare had come true. I eavesdropped from the kitchen, while Mother received our guest in the living room. When a sudden lull in the conversation occurred, I peered around the doorway and in the dusky light saw Mother's shocked reaction, her jaw slack, hands clenched tight.

Lucifer hoofed into view on the hearth and bowed with effusive grace. He spoke to me in a stage whisper.

What can I say, Angel, Baby? I gave it my best shot. The Captain had his fun, but all good things must come to an end. The Big Guy Upstairs is taking charge now. Don't worry, I'll be back when you least expect it. As he disappeared into the underworld, his parting words promised more chaos: *I've planned a hell of a ride for you, Angel Baby!*

The closing of the front door brought me down to earth. Mother stood alone in a vortex of fury and shame. I considered begging the Captain to flee on *La Libertad* with Miss Virginia and me. A vagabond trio, we would start anew, free of this maddening spiritual contest.

Mother beat me to him. From the hallway I caught the salient points of her heated condemnation: hussy, harlot, Jezebel, along with plenty of hellfire and damnation sprinkled in.

The Captain left in a frantic hurry, while Mother went to the kitchen to call our preacher, Reverend Powell. In hushed, desperate tones, with gospel verses raining like cats and dogs, she begged for Papi's redemption. An hour later my father returned with the slack-eyed, dead look of a gutted fish.

Our house had survived the elements for decades, but a different kind of tempest descended upon us that night. It began around eleven o'clock, with repeated blows against the board and batten walls. I feared that Mother's recent invocation of biblical righteousness had set the Second Coming into motion.

Then I heard a woman's angry voice. "Rafael del Corazón! You come here!"

Racing to the living room, I jumped behind the Victorian divan as a rock came sailing into the front window, smashing it to bits. A roundelay of noises pierced the night—neighbors yelled; windows and doors slammed shut; dogs barked; a rooster crowed off schedule. Oddly enough, the Corazón house remained quiet.

Peering over the furniture, I saw Miss Virginia standing in the front yard. A full moon lent the night a surreal stark glow. She was a tragic heroine on center stage—her hair askew, breasts heaving in a low-cut blouse, raw pain exaggerating her beauty. All eyes in the neighborhood were pinned on her.

Another rock came sailing through the smashed window and rolled across the needlepoint rug. My father's mistress shook a letter in her hand and cried out. "Come out, you coward! Tell me to my face you don't love me anymore."

Still not a peep from our camp.

Miss Virginia wound up her arm and let it rip. *Crash!* Now she broke the kitchen window. For a little Southern gal, she had remarkable aim.

The Captain barreled through the house and threw open the front door. I heard the pump of a rifle. A single gunshot cleaved the air. A swath of stunned silence settled over the spectators.

Poor Miss Virginia softened as tears streamed down her delicate face. "Oh, Rafi. How can you say you don't love me? You know it isn't true."

The Captain stepped into the front yard, his shoulders hunched, his jaw hard as an anvil, legs braced like twin anchors—maybe to stop himself from running to her side. Mother appeared in the middle of the room, watching through the smashed window.

"Go away." He called Miss Virginia a she-devil. "*¡Diabla!*"

At that, she faltered towards him. "Please, Rafi."

"It's no good." He spoke low, his conviction wavering

I almost cheered when the pitiful pair shared a tender look. Perhaps Mother also felt the tide turning, because she commanded my father in a firm voice.

"Come inside, Captain."

He stood rock still, his body tilting towards Miss Virginia, whose sad eyes enticed.

"I love you, Rafael."

He echoed the sentiment. "*Te amo,* Virginia."

I swear I would have traded a spot in heaven just to see him sweep her into his arms. Of course, I felt sorry for Mother, too. But had you stepped inside the fast-beating chambers of my heart, you would have understood: If love could set the Captain free, maybe it could happen to anyone, even me.

He took a step towards Miss Virginia, when Mother laid an iron hand on his shoulder. It was as if she had the strength of Goliath, and to my despair, the Captain was no rock-slinging David. With a heavy sigh, he turned his back on his dejected lover and followed his wife inside. The door closed shut with quiet authority—the Almighty didn't need to slam it shut.

Poor Miss Virginia. With a look of wild despair, she lurched towards our house, then stopped as a small anguished cry rose from her lips. Finally, the Southern Goddess turned and disappeared into the night, never to be seen again.

I stood at the window for some time, my face wet with tears. My parents' bedroom was as quiet as a tomb while the neighborhood settled back to sleep. For me, there would be no rest. The Good Lord was closing in.

With no goddess to worship, of either the Southern variety or one with a mermaid's tail, the Captain's luck dried up once again. A few times I saw his lovesick eyes scout the seas while he mumbled something about an old witch's curse.

After another fruitless day at sea, I begged him to send a coconut boat to Yemayá. "Make a wish, Papi." I beat my chest. *"Dentro."* He just gave me that glassy fish look.

Soon afterwards, on a still moonless September night, I watched through our new picture window as seven reverent men entered the garden, their black suits blending into darkness. I scurried out of the way, stationing myself in the back hallway where I could spy on the proceedings. That night our home was transformed into a temporary way station for the express train to the Promised Land.

The company gathered in a circle of chairs; one chair—the hot spot—remained empty. Mother kept to a corner of the room, the thick tatty family Bible in her lap. She had abdicated her authority to Reverend Powell, a good-looking, charismatic man. He nodded to an earnest young deacon, who led the Captain in from the kitchen.

Once master of the Sea, my father shuffled like a chained inmate to the focal chair. The slick surgeons of the soul stared at him, their expressions as impenetrable as the coral rock beneath our house. An inquisition was about to begin.

Reverend Powell read from the Bible in a booming voice, as brassy and persuasive as a carnival barker. "The Lord tells us in the Book of James, chapter four, verse four, 'ye adulterers and adulteresses, know ye not that the friendship of the world is enmity with God? Whosoever will be a friend of the world is the enemy of God.'" He regarded the Captain. "God has sent us here this evening as his emissaries. Tell me, Rafael del Corazón, are you a friend of the world?"

A reedy film of fear muffled the Captain's voice. "I am."

"In your heart of hearts, do you wish to be a friend to God and renounce your friendship with the world?"

"Yes."

"And Jesus answered and said unto him, 'Get thee behind me, Satan: for it is written, Thou shalt worship the Lord thy God, and him only shalt thou serve.'"

As he stood, the elders followed, engulfing the penitent in a sea of black cloth. Through a small gap, I saw them lay hands on his head or shoulders, my father bowing from the weight.

The preacher held the Good Book aloft like a divining rod, his voice flogging like a whip. "Rafael del Corazón, do you believe that the Father sent his only begotten Son to die on the cross to save you from your sins?"

I imagined God above pulling the strings as my father nodded like marionette.

"I believe."

"Our father which art in heaven, deliver this soul from evil that he might know your perfect goodness and mercy."

An unearthly wailing tore through the air; the men caterwauled and swayed, speaking in unknown tongues. The arrival of the Holy Ghost sent Mother into a paroxysm of ecstasy. Beside her, watching from the firebox, the devil shivered.

The preacher's dramatic plea rose above the din. "I beseech you, Rafael del Corazón, accept the Lord Jesus Christ as your Lord and personal savior!"

Tears streamed down the Captain's weathered face as he became born again. "I accept *Jesús Cristo*."

The men rejoiced. "Praise The Lord!"

I wondered what my father truly thought of salvation. To me, he looked like a dazed child whose raffle ticket has won a shiny toaster.

After the debacle of Miss Virginia, Mother redoubled her efforts to save our souls. She marched Papi and me to church for Sunday service, morning and night, and on Wednesday night, too, least we lapse midweek. Despite my hope that the Captain's conversion would be as fleeting as a run of amberjack, his buccaneer swagger softened and he rolled like a spineless sea cucumber. Sensing how little fight he had to offer, big game snubbed him. We barely subsisted on his reduced charters.

The Good Lord was breathing down my back. I swore I would not go easy like the Captain. One autumn day God decided to scare the hell out of me.

I was busy with schoolwork at the kitchen table when an eerie quiet descended. The usual clatter of neighborhood sounds—radio music, arguments, ringing telephones—vanished while an ominous whistling wind filled the vacuum. Our household sat still as a flounder hiding under a blanket of sand. With alarm, I noted the half-prepared tuna casserole on the counter.

"Mother?" No answer.

A clap of thunder sent me running through the house, where I found further evidence of life interrupted: the living room radio emitted static; a light burned bright in my parents' empty bedroom; Mother's purse yawned on the vanity. Again, I called but only heard the agitated wind.

Oh, God, what if she's been taken in the Rapture?

I knew there would be a signal, an angel's trumpet or tidal eruption—something dramatic would announce the Second Coming of Christ. He wasn't going to sneak by like a thief in the night. However, only the Chosen would be warned while sinners like me would be left behind in stunned surprise to suffer hell on earth. Sweat pooled under my arms while darkness shrouded the world. I'd been a fool to gamble with eternity.

As I threw open the front door, lightning flashed against the roiling skies, releasing a torrent of rain. I stepped off the porch to search for a sign of Mother making her way to heaven. Standing there in rain-soaked jeans and blouse, I swore I glimpsed the edge of her yellow dress before she disappeared from view forever.

The Good Lord was coming and I was in hot water. Legs pumping fast, I ran towards the ocean, where perhaps Yemayá would give me shelter. Hurricane shutters banged shut, debris floated past. A drunk staggered on the sidewalk where I spied not a single Good Christian. In the whole world, only us sinners roamed.

Perhaps there was still time to get saved if…praise the Lord: the sea had not yet turned to blood. Several yards off shore, an empty skiff bobbed in the choppy waves. It belonged to the preacher's model son who must have ascended, body and soul.

I expected to see "the Son of Man coming in the clouds of heaven with power and great glory." Indeed, the gray-black clouds formed a celestial throne for the coming prince. One possibility remained: any Doubting Thomas could slide under the wire to win a last-minute ticket to heaven. Who knew if my name was written in the Book of Life?

On bended knee I fell to the wet sand and, bowing my head in the pouring rain, prayed my heart out. *Lord, if you still want me, you can have me. I accept you as my personal savior. Amen.*

Time crawled past as I waited for my fate to be revealed: would Jesus lift me into his arms or would I receive the mark of the Antichrist on my forehead? I gave it fifty-fifty odds.

I don't know how long I waited there, cold and scared, my heart hammering like a two hundred horsepower engine. When the thunderheads parted to make way for a brilliantly hued rainbow, I got the joke. In His infinite love, the Heavenly Father had granted me a trial run. Like the fat kid released from schoolyard bullies, relief washed over me.

*****

SANIBEL ISLAND, FLORIDA

SUMMER 1985

Hot white spangles of sunlight glittered in triangles on the bay, winking at the passing parade of dancing clouds above. If the weather served as a barometer of happiness here on the island, summer solstice, the longest day of the year, promised to be wonderful. For Angel, too, the biannual ritual of offering a new book at the Island Bookstore filled her with hope.

The magical process of converting her daydreams into a book with glossy coated paper, blue-colored endpapers, and a charming cover jacket with anthropomorphic depiction of Stella the Starfish, not to mention with the author photo and bio on the back flap, never failed to amaze her. Her childhood reading material had been restricted to classics that enforced spiritual values, such as *Little Women* or *Great Expectations*, along with a healthy weekly allotment of the New Testament. Though she had enjoyed the classic tomes, the curiosity she witnessed in her young readers inspired her and, by magical osmosis, bit by bit removed the invisible bars of her lonely frightened youth.

She dressed in a white linen shirt and tan skirt, collected her marked copy of *Stella and The Merman* and, with a feeling of deep gratitude, headed to the store. When she arrived, vehicles already filled the parking lot; excited children, sloppy with sweat, spilled out of overheated cars, racing into the air-conditioned interior.

Angel scanned the area for a sign of Faith's Red Bug, but knew she wouldn't come. She had never missed one of her mother's readings here; the event seemed pointless without her. Why had Angel clawed her way to success if not for her daughter?

And yet, as soon as she saw the tower of *Stella* books on the sales counter and the eager children gathering in front of the author's blue and white upholstered chair, her misgivings vanished. Didn't she also have a right to claim her success?

"You deserve to be proud."

Angel turned to find Max smiling beside her. He drew her hand to his lips with a kiss, his gaze a soft caress. The memory of their moonlit kiss flooded into her mind, the buzz of chatter around them fell away. An overwhelming urge pressed on her like sticky summer heat that pervaded every inch of the body, until it forced you to quit your busyness and lie down and submit to its staggering power.

Then Libby interrupted. "I'll introduce you in ten minutes—give them more time to shop."

"I, um…" Angel appeared flustered.

Before she could recover, Libby took Max by the arm. "I have something to discuss, Maxey."

Maxey?

An unpleasant possessiveness gripped Angel as she watched her lead him to the sales counter, her arm intertwined in his—and Max allowed it!

Turning into the mystery stacks to compose her feelings, Angel bumped into a weathered brunette in jeans who stood at the end of the row. It was Greg's wife, Kim, the owner of The Pelican. With aimless reach, she took a book from the shelf and stared at the cover.

Angel felt she had interrupted a private moment and, wanting to dispel the awkwardness, offered a convivial comment. "My daughter loves mysteries."

"I've no time to read," Kim said, twisting the book back into place. "I wish I had more time. For everything."

"It goes fast, faster than I imagined."

"Greg says I put too much time into the restaurant. I suppose he's right but…" She looked towards the sales counter, where Libby was speaking to Max. His expression was intent—and much too interested for Angel's liking. For a moment, both women watched the unlikely pair.

As Kim turned, Angel read the harsh story her face told; the tired lines in her pale skin were like etchings in coral rock.

"I thought I'd see what's so great about this place. Personally, I don't get it. Sorry I can't stay for your talk, Angel." She made a brisk exit, avoiding the crowd.

Libby's voice cut through the chatter in the store. "Hey, folks, please be seated. You can purchase your books after the talk."

Angel made her way to the author's chair, stepping over children sprawled on the floor, smiling shyly at their mothers. With the earlier books, her readers were Faith's friends; the mothers, Angel's peers. She felt old among these lithe women and didn't know their kids, though they gave her an enthusiastic reception.

"Thank you for coming," she began. "How many of you already know Stella?"

Several small hands waved in the air. Angel scanned the eager faces, when she caught sight of Libby rushing to Max's side. He took her into his arms. Close. She nestled her head on his shoulder. They were entwined. *Max and Libby?*

He opened the storage room door in back of the counter, guiding her inside. Before they slipped from view, he caught Angel's eye. Her heart thundered high in her chest then plummeted, like an anchor thrown overboard, to the dark depths of her being, back where it belonged.

She reached for her marked copy and, with a jittery hand, knocked over the stand. A glass of water fell to the tile floor, shattering into pieces. Small girls shrieked. Helpful parents stepped forward. And still, despite the commotion, Max and Libby stayed out of sight, doing God knows what.

Angel tried to collect herself, snuffing out the ridiculous loving feelings she had nurtured for Max.

"You see," she told the audience, holding up the book cover. "The excitement Stella feels when she meets her new friend the Merman must be contagious."

She began to read the selected passage, her voice on automatic, her mind focused on the door that concealed Max and Libby and their secret tryst. Papi was right: *All men are bastards*. Even Max.

During her reading she noted their sly return, Libby's reddened eyes, Max's tender concern. When she finished, and the applause ended, Angel began signing books, a task she normally enjoyed. Now, from the corner of her eye, she watched her false lover show a collection of shells to a young family while her rival worked the cash register.

Once more Max turned to catch Angel's eye, though she pretended not to notice. Had she imagined a pleading look in his eyes? Did he regret the interest he once showed in her, or like a foolish lonely woman had she misinterpreted his desire in the first place?

As happy customers trotted off with their purchases, the front door repeatedly yawned, letting in the shrill sounds of children released into the world and motor engines carrying them away to their next adventure.

Angel moved a black Sharpie across the title page of her new book, inscribing it to a bespectacled, tow-headed girl who, in a shy voice, confessed her dream of becoming a writer.

"That's not your name," the would-be author said.

Angel turned to see her crestfallen expression; her slender finger pointed to the signature: *Angel Rose del Corazón.*

"Oh," Angel said, taking a fresh copy. "Silly mistake."

Clutching her prize, the proud book owner trotted off to meet her mother; they were the last to leave. Angel quickly gathered her things; she did not want to be alone with *them.* As she made her way towards the front of the store, Libby intercepted her.

"We're clean out of *The Merman* books," she said. "I've got six more orders."

"That's nice," Angel said.

"Guess it's in the air, huh?" At Angel's quizzical look, Libby added, "Stella got her man, love is in the air."

"Yes, well, thanks again for the reading."

"Come by next week, I'll have an accounting done."

Angel could feel Max watching her, but she couldn't bring herself to look at him. What did she know about love? She was treading without a life jacket in deep waters. *Forget it.*

HEAVEN HELP US

Shells evolved more than five hundred million years ago, using the basic building material of calcium, a major component of seawater. With an eat-or-be-eaten dynamic, shells grew beyond mere shelter for mollusks to offer a dazzling array of knobs, ribs, spines, teeth, corrugations, and thickened edges, which serve as obstructions to predators. This shell-building boom may have altered the earth's atmosphere, fostering the relatively mild conditions conducive to human evolution.

SANIBEL ISLAND, FLORIDA

SUMMER 1985

The X-ray technician stepped out of her protected cubicle into the cold room. Angel stood rigid next to a cone-shaped camera that aimed lethal radioactive rays at her left lung. A leaden apron hung below her waist. The heavy-set middle-aged woman swung the camera arm to the other side of Angel's chest as she repeated her earlier warning.

"Stay still till you hear the click," she said, as she lumbered back to her protected space. "It's the last one."

The partition door closed, leaving Angel vulnerable to the alien gray equipment that peered into the tissues of her body. The machine emitted a small whir as it recorded the state of her health. If only it were as easy to quantify her emotional life.

She ripped off the paper gown and dressed, anxious to feel the sun on her skin. Soon she was speeding across the bridge, San Carlos Bay glistening below. A stiff wind folded the choppy waves over like tatted lace handkerchiefs on the breast of the sea.

Now that Libby had her clutches into Max, Angel would not humiliate herself by attending class. Yet the thought of leaving another Valentine unfinished left her unsettled—would the cycle of love and loss never end?

On the sun-streaked horizon, she saw Tilly grinning at her. Once you possessed the Shell Queen, you were entitled to a wish. *It doesn't hurt to get a little magic for yourself.*

Motoring down the incline, Angel recalled the simple wish she had given Papi's beloved Sea Goddess. She sent her plea sailing across the bay and into the blue yonder where she hoped her old friend might conjure a little enchantment. *I want to be free and happy.*

The porch swing groaned under Angel as she reached for a glass of wine. A light breeze carried the vanishing trail of cigarette smoke into the air. In the distance, the ocean lolled at low tide, while the sun glittered like cheap jewelry on a tarted up hooker desperate to show her wares. In a corner of the fizzy, peachy-red sky, a crescent moon wobbled on coltish legs, a mere slip of a thing.

She sat at attention when she spied Max and Libby trekking across the beach. Of course it was Thursday, class day. They carried plastic buckets, probably full of shells for their Valentine projects. Barefoot and windswept, Libby looked relaxed; Max did, too, his khakis rolled ankle-high, the blue shirt loose. Angel couldn't deny how good they looked, like a handsome couple in an ad for resort living. A place she would never visit.

When they passed the nest that Max and Angel had claimed, he looked longingly in her direction. Or maybe he had sand in his eyes or saw a colony of seagulls flying inland. *Forget it.*

The sharp, unmistakable rattle of Faith's Beetle coming down the lane yanked Angel to her feet. Heart thumping, she flung open the front door just as the Red Bug swung into the front drive. Why the reckless speed? Was she on the run from that bastard Wayne?

Faith left the car door open, moving fast towards the house, her face a jumble of fear and excitement, and something else—a girlish vulnerability. She swept past Angel, heading towards her room.

"I'm not talking to you," she said.

Angel followed her. "What's wrong?"

"You mean, what's right. I found my father." She began throwing clothes into a suitcase. "Didn't I tell you I would? Santiago Valdes owns a construction company in Key West. *Construcción de fe*. It means Faith Construction—see? All these years, he was thinking of me."

The shock of it hit Angel like a slap in the face. *The shells say Santiago will see his daughter again one day. It won't be what you expect.* Tilly the Sea Sorceress had predicted it long ago, though Angel always hoped she was mistaken.

"Wait," she said, her decision made. "I'm coming with you."

"No way." Hot light flashed in Faith's eyes—just like her father. "You're never coming between my father and me again." She grasped a vinyl photo album with a psychedelic cover. "Dad wants me to fill him in on all the time we've lost."

"He said that?"

"He said, and I quote verbatim, '*Hija*, I never stopped loving you.'"

Faith had no idea who he was. How could she? Angel had not yet written the last pages.

"Can't you at least wait a few days until I finish the story?" she said.

Faith rolled her eyes. "Are you crazy?"

Hefting her suitcase, she cast a wistful look around the room. Like Daniel entering the lion's den, her daughter was heading into danger, her shield also made of faith, however misbegotten. Angel had run out of time.

"Your father has an explosive temper," she said. "You don't know what you're getting yourself into."

A look of disappointed certainty dampened Faith's expression. "I knew you'd try to stop me with more lies. Can't you just be happy that he wants me? He still loves me, Mom."

Faith left with a slam of the door that shook the house.

There was one slim hope: *Construcción de fe* might also imply building faith in God. How ironic if the Book of Life contained Santiago's name. People could change, couldn't they? In the crepuscular light, palm trees swayed at the edge of the beach like tall craggy wise men who shook their heads: *Could a predatory shark become a playful porpoise?*

* * * * *

Dear Faith,

Please forgive any errors; I hurried these pages, hoping they'll arrive before you leave town. Please be careful!

Love,

Mom

COMRADES IN LOVE

KEY WEST, FLORIDA

OCTOBER 1966

In the fall of my senior year at Key West High, the Captain's first mate passed away. The prize-winning duo never recaptured their glory days and I suspect Palo died of regret. The usual goings-on at church occupied Mother so she elected me to accompany my father to City Cemetery. By age seventeen, the realization that neither of my parents, or their respective gods and goddesses, would save me had left me sullen and moody.

Papi and I stood on a torrid Sunday afternoon with Palo's extended family among the stacks of graves that lay on top of the coral bedrock, which presented an impenetrable barrier to underground burial. For good reason, Key West's original name, *Cayo Hueso*, meant island of bones.

A young attendant held a black umbrella over the elderly priest to shade him from the red-hot sun as he gave the burial mass. The Captain's trembling hand clutched my elbow, radiating fear. I paid him little mind, distracted as I was by a dark, handsome stranger.

He dressed like no one I'd ever seen, in a rakish black beret, safari jacket, and high-laced combat boots. A beard covered his strong jaw, like the "*Barbudos*," or bearded revolutionaries, who had taken over Cuba. When our eyes met, his arrogant air inflamed my curiosity. Who did he think he was? I wanted to slap him.

After the funeral, I sat on a threadbare couch inside Palo's simple shotgun house on Tropical Avenue, crushed between grieving cousins, the air redolent of cinnamon, cloves, garlic, and cheap beer. The rhythmic sounds of Celia Cruz and *La Sonora Matancera* drifted in from a radio in the overgrown yard, where couples of all ages danced a salsa beat.

With furtive glances I watched Mr. Know-It-All accost the Captain, who stood dazed in a corner of the room. My father's refined Spanish accent gave him a cultural edge over the young man's rapid-fire guttural speech. However, his bowed shoulders and hangdog expression suggested he was the one begging for a favor.

After they shook hands, the guy stared hard at me. I straightened up and stared back, defying him, despite the wild beating of my heart. Like a stingray's wing in flight, a lazy smile curved across his proud face.

Bristling with indignation, I went to the porch, but soon heard him near. Rather, I sensed the signs that announced his presence: the earthy scent, a combustible thrum in my blood, the unwanted loosening of my limbs. I spun around, ready to put him in his place, but lost my way in the dark depths of his eyes.

"*Buenos días.*" Like shark's skin, his voice was both rough and smooth.

I ignored him, pretending keen interest in Palo's rooster, which stepped mightily towards the chicken coop. I took smug comfort in the knowledge that the Cocky Joe beside me was as pompous as the rooster and, therefore, beneath me.

Without warning, he reached for me. "A ladybug." He untangled it from my hair and offered it in the palm of his hand, as if it were a good luck charm.

Another dreamer, like Papi, I decided. "Am I supposed to make a wish?"

"Do I look like a man who believes in miracles? Wishes are for the rich who can afford to dream. I work for my bread and butter, like this little one." He paused to set the bug on the porch railing with a delicacy that belied his muscular build, and I found myself aching for his touch. "We're the workers of the world, *princessa.*"

"I work, I'm no princess."

He held me in his thrall, while his omniscient gaze traveled across my face, down my bodice, to my hips, and back to my bewildered stare. I felt naked and stupid. How I wished he'd go away or else take me in his arms.

His attention wandered to the rooster, which had flown on top of the coop, setting off the hens' mad clucking. He lit a smoke with deliberate motions—the sexy flick of the match, the strong mouth sucking on the cigarette.

His sudden indifference infuriated me, and once more I felt the urge to strike him. Instead, I marched away without a word. Despite the heat that shackled my legs, I began to run, stamping out disturbing thoughts of him. I never again wanted to set eyes on his handsome face.

The following weekend I biked as usual to the marina to assist the Captain. Reaching the end of our berth, I stopped short. There, on my ship, carrying fresh bait into my cockpit was Mr. Irritating. He nodded towards me, just barely; the brim of his straw hat obscured his eyes.

I shouted across the stern. "What are you doing here?

He shrugged. "I told you, I'm not a rich man."

My father appeared from the cabin and introduced us. "*Mi hija*, Angel." He jerked his head towards the interloper. "Santiago Valdes, Palo's nephew."

Papi paused to stare at me, as if seeing me for the first time. I've often wondered if, in that moment, Yemayá granted him a glimpse of what was to come. In any case, his comment surprised me. "Sometimes I think she knows the secrets of the sea better than me."

Santiago grunted at either the heavy ice chest or me, conveying how little I mattered. He began to hum a melancholy tune that further inflamed my hostility. Man, I hated him.

Cornering the Captain on the flybridge, I unleashed my fury upon him. "He's no fisherman, Papi!"

"*Shhhh, Hija.*" The Captain looked below at Santiago, who sat on the stern smoking a Marlboro cigarette, his bare muscular shoulders coiled with energy. With sad eyes my father pleaded for understanding. The local fishermen refused to crew for fear of catching the curse; he had no one. "*No tengo nadie.*"

"You have me, Papi."

He shook his head. It wasn't women's work. "*Eso no es para ti.*"

That day, we had a decent charter, and I aimed to prove him wrong. All through the long scorching day, I worked double time, anticipating the Captain's orders, nudging our new helper out of the way. I tossed him a smug look as I left that afternoon, hoping his wounded ego would keep him away.

But Santiago returned the next day, and, to my dismay during the following week, I had to suffer the Captain's increasing praise of his protégé during dinnertime. Each night I kneeled beside my bed and continued the family tradition of bargaining with God: *Please, Blessed Jesus, send Santiago Valdes back where he belongs and I promise I'll never again entertain sinful thoughts of him.*

I knew exactly who had put in my head visions of Santiago's hard mouth on mine, and the overwhelming desire to lie with him in the biblical sense, our loins pressed together. Therefore, I hurried past the living room hearth, determined to avoid Lucifer's evil influence. I suppose the danger of being a double agent is that you believe you can switch your false identity on and off at will.

Nevertheless, after another frustrating Saturday on board with Santiago, the devil caught me off guard at twilight, when the long shadows of trees and branches writhed like phantoms across the living room.

Hey, Angel Baby, long time no see. I've been keeping my eye on you. Santiago was a prize pick. Tailor made, wouldn't you say? He began to guffaw; his tail twitched in the air. I prayed that he'd choke from laughter. Instead, he snapped his fingers and, like a magician producing a bouquet of flowers out of thin air, regained his suave swagger.

Aw, don't pout, Angel. You know you can't fight it. What is it your old man says? Ven, ven, mi amor. Come to me, Baby.

Holy Crap! Was the devil in cahoots with Yemayá? I started to question Lucifer when he vanished with a wink, his parting words floating in the air. *Enjoy the ride!*

I doubled my resistance to Santiago. And yet, the more I attempted to banish the desperate longing for his touch, the stronger my attraction grew. Night after night, mind-boggling vulgar visions seeped into my dreams, until, to my amazement, I couldn't have cared less about my heavenly place in eternity.

The next weekend I stood on the bow of *La Libertad*, scouting for game, while an inescapable awareness of Santiago's presence at the stern wafted over me like the wind. As I rode the lift and roll of the waves, my attention followed him wherever he wandered, as if an enchanted string connected us.

When we entered deep blue water, not far from the bridge where the Captain proposed to my mother, Santiago spotted the long dorsal fins of dorados. Their dazzling colors—yellow, green, blue—flashed in the sunlit waters as they zigzagged alongside our vessel. The speedy fish with powerful tapered bodies promised a good fight.

The Captain cut the engines and slid down the ladder to the cockpit, spitting commands. Santiago cast an extra line from the gunwale and motioned for me to take it. In a split second, as if the future had hiccupped into the present, I saw our bodies pressed together. It's funny how fast one makes a decision, or maybe it's already made for you.

I watched myself move towards him, bend under his arms and seize the rod. The line ran out, throwing me forward—it was a big catch. I braced one foot against the railing, my arms waving the rod like a flag. *So much for superior seamanship.*

I expected my adversary to gloat. Instead, he encircled my waist with his rough hands, steadying me. I leaned against his bare chest, his heat as taut against my backside as the line in my hands.

He whispered in my ear, low and husky. "Easy, take it slow."

If it weren't for the fifty pound fight on my hands, I would have turned around and repeated those very words to him—*easy, take it slow.* Everything but the electric touch of our bodies fell away—the excited passengers' voices, the slap of waves against the hull, strident seagulls circling overhead. When my limbs began to shake from the pressure, he grabbed hold of the rod, sheltering me in the hollow of his arms, and the brave dorado fought for his life, while I gave mine away.

Santiago landed the catch, splattering sacrificial red blood onto the pristine white deck. What a pity Jesus had died to save me from my sins, when I had found the perfect savior here on earth.

The happy clients left with their catch packed in ice and fishing tales that grew taller by the minute. The dazed Captain stared after them, a fat wad of tips in his pocket. The turn of good luck may have perplexed him, but I knew that the powerful bond Santiago and I shared could create miracles.

The Captain mumbled something about an evil witch and told us to batten down the ship. I suspected he was heading to drink, and for once I didn't care. As Santiago and I moved round the boat in a quiet dance, I became overly conscious of the swing of my hips, the rise and fall of my breasts.

When we finished, I grabbed a can of Coca-Cola from the cooler, handing one to him. *Phsst!* The cool fizzy drink tickled my throat, but a lump remained. We moved, as if by silent agreement, to the end of the creaking dock, where we sat side by side with the Gulf spread before us, the heat from our tired bodies hanging in the day-old air. Water lapped against the seawall, rocking the boat in its slip. A school of minnows darted towards the channel; pelicans headed to roosts. The world, and us in it, fell into a natural order.

When the sun sank below the horizon, it emitted a brilliant emerald flash of light for a scant second. Santiago whistled in appreciation. I spoke in a rush.

"It's called the green flash. It's a lucky sign. I guess we were lucky today." A lazy smile curved across his sensuous lips. *Why doesn't he say something?* "The Captain is the best there is, you'll learn a lot from him."

Santiago chugged back the soda, then crumpled the can in his hands. "I'm not a fisherman, remember?"

"I'm sorry. I thought—"

"You were right. I like that about you. You've got *cojones.*"

"Um, thanks."

"You're welcome, *princessa.*" The title now felt like an endearment: the syllables dripped like thick guava juice from his mouth.

"Meet me after school Monday at State Beach."

I wasn't allowed to be alone with a boy—the Captain would kill us. Yet Santiago had the right to command me; that's what saviors do. In the end, I never had a choice, no matter what God says about free will.

I relied upon my early espionage experience to create the perfect cover: Angel the Artist. Specialty: nature sketches, particularly of the sea and shells.

As long as I continued to parrot Christian lingo, Mother paid little mind to my new hobby.

With sketchbook and pencil case in my bicycle basket, I hurried to State Beach for my first date. It was late in the day when I walked through the heavy pine grove, my flip-flops kicking up prickly sandspurs. I gasped when I saw his languid figure lying against a patch of white sand, his dark naked chest like ink on parchment; the ragged jean shorts stretched tight on his hips. Gray wisps of cigarette smoke curled into his hair, giving him a devilish air. He drew me to him with a single look—the omnipotent can do that.

I sat beside him on the blistering sand—which, as a testament to his power over me, didn't sting. He toyed with his cigarette, rolling it between his fingers, while he studied me. I feared he might see the blemishes on my soul. At some unseen signal, he nodded to himself and handed me a slim book.

"This is for you."

A gift from a boy to a girl signified a bond, and unlike a bouquet of flowers, a book could last a lifetime. However, I found the title far from romantic.

"*Guerilla Warfare* by Che Guevara."

"Don't you care about the revolution, *princessa*?"

I'd often heard the Captain curse Che and his cohort Raúl Castro for ruining his beautiful island. They were Santiago's gods, the Marxist book his Holy Word; and I decided to join his side, because the deities warring for my soul had never made me feel all warm and gooey. And that's how I found myself right back where I'd started—lying to appease my new savior.

"Are you kidding? Castro and Guevara are so cool. They help the poor, kind of like Jesus throwing the money lenders out of the temple."

"Exactly." His eyes crinkled with pleasure. "Read it."

"I promise." I would have agreed to anything as long as I could bask in his glow.

"What do you want, Angel?"

"What do you mean?"

"A person who doesn't know what he wants is like a man without legs. He dreams but he never goes anywhere."

"Like a sailor without a boat?"

"Exactly." His dazzling smile convinced me that he could change the world. He pressed his question. "What do you want?"

Recalling the coconut wish I'd made to Yemayá, I realized my dream had come true. "I want to be happy."

"How?"

There are moments you never forget, moments of quiet decision that propel you into uncharted waters. I didn't even notice the shift as I gave him the answer he wanted. "I'd be happy helping people." *Like you saving me.*

His eyebrows pressed together as he wavered on the verge of decision. I felt I had won a great prize when he nodded with satisfaction. "We'll be comrades. We'll go to Cuba. We'll be happy there, you and me, eh?"

I took it as a bona fide proposal. Someone would join us as man and wife, perhaps even Castro. "Yes, comrades."

At last Santiago drew me to him. We lay on the sand, our limbs entwined, hinged together like a bivalve shell—any common scallop or mussel, even a rare angel wing—each half integral to the other's survival. An intoxicating aroma of beer, cigarettes, and body heat enveloped me. He rubbed his hand up my thigh, creating a bloom of deep heat within. When our lips met, I responded tentatively at first, until irresistible desire loosened my inhibitions and our tongues began a primordial dance to which I was discovering the steps. Like Mary Magdalene, I was worshipping the Beloved. Not even the devil could touch me now.

Too soon, my comrade-in-love released me. “Be here tomorrow.”

I nodded, speechless. He had me hook, line, and sinker.

Soon my sins began to multiply faster than crabgrass in June. Mother circled around my excuses while I weaved and dodged with artful deceit, inventing new friends, imaginary outings. After each tryst with Santiago, I used breath freshener and changed my clothes to disguise our lusty smells. It was as unnatural for her not to track the scent of a lie as it was for a shark to avoid a pool of blood. She was often on the phone with Reverend Powell, oblivious to the guilt stamped on my forehead, where once I’d feared I would wear the mark of the Antichrist, 666. Now I only wanted to wear a wedding ring.

Nearly every afternoon, I met my fiancé at his shabby one-bedroom apartment in a bleak concrete two-story building in New Town. His musky scent permeated the dingy walls; dark hair strands littered the orange shag rug. In this divine oasis he reeled me in, inch by inch, leading me to salvation: he unhooked my bra and caressed my breasts; then days later, he slipped his hot hand under my skirt with a passing feel; another day, he rubbed my crotch until my panties were soaking wet.

The day of reckoning would come soon enough—even the best of spies get caught—and there would be hell to pay. There was, however, one surefire escape, though it was tricky. I had to be one hundred percent sure, because there was no turning back. Once I lost my virginity to Santiago, I would be his forever. Jesus said so in St. Matthew 19:5-6: “For this cause shall a man leave father and mother, and shall cleave to his wife.... What therefore God hath joined together, let no man put asunder.”

At home one night the unmistakable deep baritone of Reverend Powell roused me from sleep. I feared the Men in Black were coming to cut out my soul, just as they had done to the Captain. I crept down the hall and saw the Reverend and Mother at the kitchen table, their heads drawn close over tea and cookies, plotting in fervent whispers. I took it as a heavenly warning.

On a windy day in March 1967, a month before my eighteenth birthday, I decided to wed myself to Santiago. I sat on the edge of the bed, imagining his promises of undying love to mark the occasion. As he stripped naked, my eyes fell on his hard, bulging sex. It was angry and had a life of its own—it would free me. With expert hands, he undressed me and pulled me close. I shivered as our bodies melted together.

With the tip of a finger, he skimmed the wetness in my sex and brought it to his lips, murmuring. He threw me back on the bed and spread my legs. As he climbed on top of me, his eyes flared with the same look of devotion I'd seen in True Believers. Now I was the object of devotion and, at the same time, the adoring disciple ready to give my life over to the Beloved.

He put his fingers deep inside of me, and when I squirmed with pain, he admonished me. "Relax, Angel."

Time takes on the slow step of the surreal. I close my eyes and the next thing I know, he pushes his throbbing sex into mine. This, I understand, is my baptism and I rejoice, knowing Jesus also bled for love. Faster and faster, Santiago and I begin to rock when, man, oh, man, I'm flying. He's pulling me across flat water on a pair of slick new water skis. I skip over a wave and hover in the air—free—for just a moment, though it feels like eternity, until I land with a thundering crash. Deep moans shake my lover as he collapses on top of me. It's done; we're married in the eyes of God. No man can separate us now.

"I love you, Santi."

I spoon behind him, waiting for words of endearment. Instead, I hear a gentle snore. Though our afterglow fails to measure up to my dreams, I take satisfaction in my newfound power to affect him so profoundly. A warm stickiness on my inner thigh draws my hand there. The sacrament of blood! I breathe easy, knowing it has the power to wash away my sins.

Mother might have said I had fallen from grace. My interpretation was far more satisfying: I was born again through the miracle of sacred union with Santiago.

During the muggy spring of 1967, consumed by the heady discovery of sex and young love, I found a peace that passeth all understanding. Cuddled at Santiago's side, attentive as a front-row churchgoer, I would have followed him to the ends of the earth, even to Cuba.

Satiated with sex, he would lean against the pillows and punctuate the air with a cigarette as he envisioned our future. "In Cuba we won't have to worry about money."

"You won't have to work?"

"Everyone works; everyone eats. Fidel treats everyone the same."

"Sounds like heaven."

"Do you still need God, *princessa*?" He pinched my ass with a mixture of affection and pain, which I recognized as godly love.

"I have you now."

"Exactly. More important—you have the revolution. You'll work for the people. You can translate my newspaper into English."

"What newspaper?"

His chest swelled with pride. "*Las Noticias de Libertad.*"

"Freedom's News?"

"Not bad, eh? I know a guy who sails from Havana to Key West every month: Enrique, he has a small fishing boat. The stupid Coast Guard never sees his red sail—red like the communist sign. He's fast, invisible, like the wind." He drew a long satisfied inhale of smoke. "Enrique will smuggle our paper to the cigar workers and comrades here. Screw the FBI."

I sensed danger, the kind I'd felt when a six-foot barracuda slid beneath me. What did I really know about this man to whom I had pledged my life? Was he a criminal on the run? And yet, I denied my fears because I had everlasting faith.

As the weeks went by, I let my cover slip: disheveled hair and dazed eyes, unaligned shirt buttons, the pungent trace of carnal knowledge. Let me tell you, a spy in love is a sloppy spy.

Late one afternoon, as the light paled through Santiago's bedroom window, I tugged on my bra. Though we'd made love an hour ago, Santiago grabbed my hand and thrust it against his hard cock. With feverish eyes, he pulled me to the bed.

I closed my legs. "I'll be late for supper."

"You're mine, Angel, don't forget it." And he took what was rightfully his.

Darkness crowded out the day by the time I pedaled home. I was tired of inventing stories and longed to drop my cover. Hadn't Jesus commanded his children to love one another? At least, the Captain knew about love and might sympathize.

The minute I stepped onto the front porch, I understood my tragic miscalculation. My father yanked me inside; a hard slap across the cheek sent me reeling onto the living room floor. He loomed over me, the last strands of sunset reddening his angry face, as he heaped upon me curses of shame and whoring.

"*¡Puta, qué verquenza!*"

Another slap; salty blood webbed my mouth. I watched a red stain spread on mother's precious needlepoint rug. I became aware of her standing at the hearth—no doubt blocking Lucifer's passage—with grim Reverend Powell by her side.

The Captain threatened to kill the bastard. "*Voy a matar ese cabrón.*"

He moved to hit me again, when the Reverend interceded, strong-arming him to an upholstered armchair. "Let us turn to the Lord."

I caught the preacher's smug look at Mother: *Jesus and I will take care of this.*

Her stern countenance softened with something close to coquettishness.

The Captain smashed his fist on the chair and uttered the words that would brand my heart: All men are bastards. "*Todos los hombres son cabrones.*"

If only he could have channeled his fury to recapture his buccaneer spirit. At Mother's disapproving look, he disappeared back into his shell, a spiritual vegetable.

Reverend Powell sat by Mother on the couch, commanding me to join the cozy circle. I stumbled to my feet, avoiding the Captain's hard stare, as I perched on the chair across from him.

The Reverend began. "Let us pray."

As they bowed their heads, the childhood fear of being left behind on Judgment Day haunted me. I prayed to my new savior, Santiago, for salvation, while the holy man invoked the Almighty's presence.

"Dear Lord, let your eternal light shine upon Angel for whom you sent your Only Begotten Son to die on the cross to pay for her sins so that she might know everlasting life. Amen."

"Amen." Like obedient children, my parents waited for him to continue.

"Angel, as your brother in Christ, I beg you to unburden your heart and confess your sins."

A captured spy reveals nothing but basic facts. “Santiago and I are married in God’s eyes. There’s nothing to discuss.”

The Captain, nearly apoplectic, jumped to his feet. “He’s using you.”

“He loves me.”

Reverend Powell restrained him once more. “Rafael, I beseech you. Give the Lord the opportunity to work his grace upon your daughter.”

As he slumped back into his chair, he yelled at Mother. “Give her the paper!”

“Not yet.” She fingered a sheet of paper that lay on her lap. What dreadful plan had they concocted?

The preacher continued, his solemn demeanor forcing quiet upon the small congregation. “The Bible tells us, in John, chapter three, verse three: ‘Verily, verily, I say unto thee, except a man be born again, he cannot see the kingdom of God.’ Now, the Scriptures don’t say unless a man be an American born in Key West he cannot be saved, does it?” He chuckled at his cleverness. “Tell us, Angel, is Santiago saved?”

“Technically, no, but it doesn’t matter.” From the corner of my eye, I saw Mother wince.

“Would Jesus want you to bind your heart to a man who knows him not?” Meaning: would I risk a spot in eternal heaven for a paltry life of human love?

Mother urged me in the steely, metallic voice with which she had commanded the Captain to quit Miss Virginia. “Answer him, Angelica.”

Unable to contain himself any longer, my father flung the ominous paper at me. It was written in Mother’s precise script.

“Read it!”

I, Angelica Rose del Corazón, do solemnly swear upon my eternal soul to abide by the following God-given rules in order that evil might not find purchase in my soul and I might find salvation in the Lord Jesus Christ, our savior.

1. I, Angelica Rose del Corazón, promise never to see Santiago Valdes again. "It is said, Thou shalt not tempt the Lord thy God." Luke 4:12

2. I, Angelica Rose del Corazón, promise never to speak to Santiago Valdes ever again, in person, on the phone or through an intermediary. "I am the way, the truth, and the life: no man cometh unto the Father, but by me." John 15:6

3. I, Angelica Rose del Corazón, promise never to imagine sinful fantasies about Santiago Valdes. "God is a spirit: and they that worship Him must worship Him in spirit and in truth." John 4:14

4. I, Angelica Rose del Corazón, promise never to dream about Santiago Valdes ever again. "He that believeth and is baptized shall be saved; but he that believeth not shall be damned." Mark 16:16

*Signed:*_________________________ *Date:*________________

Good God, it was a contract for possession of my body and soul—*cuerpo y alma.* If I signed it, I would become like the Captain, a spineless urchin scraping the bottom of the sea.

"You can't do this!" I ripped the document to pieces.

The Captain demanded I leave home. "*¡Vayáte!* No whore lives under my roof."

"Santiago loves me! You'll see."

I fled to my room and with surprising calm gathered my clothes and a few books into a large canvas bag. At least the war was over. From the living room I heard the Captain's repeated threats to "kill that bastard," followed by the slamming of the front door. He would soon be too drunk to lay a hand on my husband—at least now I could claim that title. I heard the front door close again and figured Reverend Powell had left, his mission a failure.

I stepped onto the front porch to find Mother standing there, her features hard as stone. She held out my mod-covered King James Bible.

"You always were hell bent for leather, Angelica Rose. I guess the devil's not done with you."

Poor Mother didn't understand that I was already headed to the Promised Land. As I swept past her, I heard her terrified whisper. "Whenever a star falls, a mermaid is born."

* * * * *

SANIBEL ISLAND, FLORIDA

SUMMER 1985

Soft rays of sunlight warmed the coffee pot, as Angel held it under the tap, turning the water into a golden elixir. She watched a hummingbird hover at the stem of a bright pink hibiscus, like a rare iridescent green jewel. Where was Faith right now? In the Red Bug, puttering up Duval Street, eager to meet the father she never knew.

Perhaps Angel should have taken her for a visit years ago and set things right. And yet, the idea of putting either of them in harm's way reminded her why she had closed that door long ago.

The insistent buzz of the doorbell startled her. *For heaven's sake, this early?* Peeking through the front curtains, she was surprised to find Max on the porch, looking oddly intent.

"Just a minute please," she called, and hurried to her bedroom.

Why bother to look her best when he belonged to Libby? To show him what he had missed? Not likely. She scanned her closet for the perfect thing to wear on the occasion of receiving a man who had kissed her—the first man in decades—and then chosen another woman. *Let him wait.*

She decided upon her coral-colored sundress, the one she'd worn when they met. He wouldn't remember, anyway. As the smooth crepe material fell over her hips, she recalled his hands on the hem, his face close to her thighs, his expression like the welcome embrace of morning light across her bed. *Oh, forget it.*

When Angel opened the door, she saw the cloudy tiredness in Max's eyes. His unkempt appearance took her aback: the uncombed hair, stained rumbled clothes.

"*Sehr shön,*" he said, his voice rough with pain. "I remember you so pretty at the party for Maeapple. I apologize for the early hour, but I wished to talk." He combed a hand through his tousled hair. "You are missed…at class."

"I simply don't have the time, Max."

"Ach! How can I explain?"

As he turned his head, Angel noticed an octagonal frame of a Sailors' Valentine propped against the porch railing, its back facing out. He was stubborn, wasn't he?

"I don't need it," she said. "Maybe Libby can use it."

Max shook his head. "It isn't the same."

She searched his troubled face, wondering if he meant class wasn't the same without her. Or possibly, could it be, life in general was pointless without her? Oh, but he was referring to the Valentine.

Despite her resistance, she felt drawn to it. As she took hold of the frame, the past rushed up to meet her. The simple design depicted a schooner under a blue sky dotted with seagulls. She knew it well, and as she pondered the mysterious steps that had brought it to her doorstep, she heard her mother's voice. *Whenever a star falls, a mermaid is born.*

She had adopted the phrase from her mother Willow and used it sparingly to convey an irrevocable change in life. She said its true meaning only could be grasped in the world of mermaids and sea goddesses.

"Where did you get this?" Angel said.

"As I told you," Max replied. "In my Shell-Mobile, I have traveled many miles. This is an antique. I want you to have it. Perhaps you will remember me by it."

"But how did you come across it?"

He hesitated, and uncharacteristically avoided looking at her, or so it seemed. "It was long ago," he said. "The details are unimportant. I wish to convey the sentiment of the Valentine. Please forgive me." With one last searching look, he turned away.

"Max?" She called to him, but he continued on, and soon she heard the putter of his car engine.

Angel smoothed her hand across the empty back of the frame, where once Papi had taped a handwritten note. In the soft tropical air, she heard him whisper. *Forget Me Not.*

A TEST OF FAITH

Nineteenth century collectors perceived shells as a gift from God that "declare the skillful hand from which they come," revealing "the excellent artisan of the Universe." A shell's spiral chamber suggested climbing a staircase to attain a closer connection to God. The departure of the mollusk from its shell represented the passage of the human soul into eternal life. Oliver Wendell Holmes conveyed the spiritual ideal in "The Chambered Nautilus," one of the most popular poems of the era: "Build thee more stately mansions, O my soul, / As the swift seasons roll! / Leave thy low-vaulted past! / Let each new temple, nobler than the last, / Shut thee from heaven with a dome more vast, / Till thou at length art free, / Leaving thine outgrown shell by life's unresting sea!"

SANIBEL ISLAND, FLORIDA

SUMMER 1985

The dark, screaming storm descended in the thick of night like a coven of witches in heat. It barreled across the gulf, raking long fingers of wind over the water and into Angel's home, shaking the rafters and her soul. Huddled under the covers, she heard a crash overhead and hoped her roof was intact.

She prodded herself to investigate, but old fears of the Second Coming chained her to the bed. After all these years, the details still worried her: would she hear the jetliner takeoff of the Chosen, and when would she realize she had been left behind? She burrowed into her pillow. If the reign of the Antichrist was upon her, she would need her sleep.

When day broke with a startling wash of stark light, Angel threw open the curtains, relieved to find the world intact. A look in the mirror revealed a clean forehead, free of the mark of the damned. Eager to stand in the sun, she hurried to her morning coffee. While the pot brewed, she lit a cigarette and studied the Sailors' Valentine that sat serenely on the dining room table.

What were the odds that this particular Valentine, which had once belonged to her grandmother and her mother, and had been given to Angel by her father, had ended up in the hands of a man with whom, if Angel were honest, she was in love? She wanted to believe she was independent, that she had carved her path as a writer and mother without the help of anyone, least of all her family. This potent symbol of the past threatened that illusion, raising the possibility that they had never forgotten her, no matter how long or how absolutely she had banished them from her life.

The urge to run to Max's house and demand answers tempted her. She recalled the evasive look in his eye when she asked how he found the Valentine. *I wish to convey the sentiment of the Valentine. Please forgive me.*

Forgive him for what? And how could she demand the truth when she was not also willing to reveal it? She looked up at the vast cerulean sky, picturing Max on her doorstep. *Forget me not.* Did he really want her? There was only one way to know.

Angel set out on a mission, rehearsing an inner monologue to Libby Belle: *You don't need Max, you have your pick of men. Max isn't your type, he's mine. Of course, he's in your thrall, but he'd be happier with me.*

A large angry hand had shaken the town upside down and then, perhaps interested in a more orderly locale, left mid-chaos. Angel pumped her brakes through deep puddles that clotted the streets, skirting a litter of denuded palm fronds, their curved stems like the bones of ancient vessels, and a random trail of objects that included a tire truck, a baby carriage, and a large stuffed sailfish that must have fallen off the Bait Box.

The blue-and-white awning over Seaside Books tilted like a windmill; from a large rent in the middle, the fabric hung at opposite angles. The parking lot in front of the store was empty. On the verge of leaving, she noticed Libby's car parked in the lane near the storage entrance.

As she passed under the broken awning, a thoughtless seagull landed on top, tipping a stream of water onto her head. The front door locked; the store wouldn't open for another twenty minutes. She scanned the street, wondering if Libby had gone for coffee, when a jeep pulled up and parked with a view down the alley.

It was Kim Goodwin. She wore a pair of dark sunglasses and stared straight ahead, ignoring Angel. Why was she here during the Pelican's busiest hour? She wasn't exactly a book lover.

Walking down the lane, Angel spotted a truck's fender jutting from behind the store. She knocked on the side door. Waiting in the cauldron of heat, time ticked as it had in her youth when life had not been hers to control and the dog days had dulled her senses.

She cried out as the door hit her in the shoulder. A car door slammed, and before Angel knew it, she was standing in the crossfire as Kim barreled down on her husband Greg. She had shed the sunglasses and her bloodshot eyes spoke of deep pain.

Angel heard a gasp and turned to see Libby standing behind Greg, her skirt askew, the helmet of blond hair mussed.

Kim called out from several feet away. “You lying cheating no good bastard.”

“Kim.” That was all Greg said.

She unleashed her fury upon him. He took the blows and kicks without protest, sinking lower by the inch until he lay beneath her in a fetal position.

Kim spit out the words that perhaps every betrayed woman has ever uttered. “I trusted you.”

Angel recalled Papi’s disheartening warning: *All men are bastards.*

Libby shrank back beside the door, watching the seamy spectacle, her blank expression unreadable.

“And you,” Kim said, turning on her. “I have no words for your kind.” She spat at Libby as if she were dirt, then walked away.

Libby offered Greg a hand, but he waved her away as he hobbled towards his truck. He peeled out with a squeal of rubber. Once more, quiet descended on the wind-swept morning.

Libby stared at the wall as she spoke. “It’s not easy. All the good men are taken.”

“He’s married,” Angel said, wondering how she had ever rooted for Miss Virginia to steal away the Captain.

“What do you know about love?”

“I came for the accounting receipt.”

“Just a minute.” The door slammed behind her as she disappeared inside.

A small bubble of glee popped in Angel. Perhaps Max had never been anything more than a confidant to Libby. Perhaps he didn’t want Angel to forget him, after all.

* * * * *

Dear Faith,

I’m happy, at last, to introduce you to Tilly in these pages. If only you could have known her, how different things might have been. I’m hoping there’s still a chance her strong spirit might inspire courage as it did for me.

Are you in Key West? Will Wayne forward your mail? Please contact me.

Love,

Mom

A GOOD WITCH

KEY WEST, FLORIDA

MAY 1967

Exiled from the marina, Santiago got a job working construction, while I finished the last few weeks of high school. As soon as I graduated, we planned to have a civil marriage ceremony, but life got in the way. To tell you the truth, I couldn't face such a dismal affair. One day, I imagined we would prove my parents wrong and enjoy a belated ceremony with family and friends.

I began plodding up and down Duval Street, filling in job applications for shop girl, bar maid, waitress, and tour guide. The locals joked that Duval, which ran under a mile long but started at the Atlantic Ocean and ended at the Gulf of Mexico, was the longest street in the world. After one week, I felt as if I'd circled the globe and had nothing to show for it but tired feet and a broken spirit. Due to my lack of experience other than fishing—or, more likely, Parrot Line gossip about the Old Town girl who ran off with a revolutionary—no one would hire me.

I had no choice but to seek employment in New Town, the northwest area of Key West, which Conchs like me shunned. As I chugged up North Roosevelt, I spied Howard Johnson's trademark orange roof with a weathervane of Simple Simon and the Pieman spinning in a stiff breeze—the perfect hiding place for a pariah.

I stood my bike beside a pastel-pink Cadillac with white fur seat covers that screamed "tourist" and entered the air-conditioned restaurant. Sunlight streamed in through a row of long windows, highlighting shiny vinyl booths. A handful of customers, most with red-lobster sunburns and loud cheap clothing, lazed over their heaping plates. As I approached the counter, I caught my reflection in the gleaming cash register; for a young bride, I looked weary.

"Can I help you?"

A blowsy middle-aged woman barreled towards me, her bright blue-and-white-checkered uniform a garish contrast to her red dyed hair. A plastic badge on her uniform read: *Matilda*. I knew at once that she must be the owner of the tacky pink car outside. Her scruffy sneakers gave the carefree impression of a Conch, but the staccato rhythm and short vowels of her speech revealed a transplant—a Fresh Water Conch, one of the many shipwrecked souls who washed up on our shores, seeking refuge.

I might have been down, but I was the real deal, a Salt Water Conch. Under her withering inspection, however, my confidence sank. I'd rather have gone hungry than work for her.

"May I please have a glass of water, Ma'am?"

She filled a plastic glass and set it on the bar, scowling at me with owlish eyes, steam from the pass-through kitchen window tufting behind her.

"Thanks."

I gulped it down and started to leave when her sharp voice accosted me.

"Didn't you forget something?"

"Isn't water free?"

From underneath the counter, she pulled out a job application and slapped it down in front of me. "Isn't this what you came for?"

I was speechless. Maybe she was a witch, escaped from a Northern coven.

"Go on." She pushed a pen into my hand. "Fried clams?"

Again, she'd read my mind. The greasy kitchen smells had my empty stomach churning, but my pockets were empty.

Before I could respond, she barked an order to the Cuban cook. "Give me a number one, handsome!"

"I can't pay for it."

She winked at me. "Applicants get a free meal."

My Mother might have said no unclean person hath any inheritance in the Kingdom of Heaven. But to me, this witch was an angel of mercy. By the time I'd finished filling in the blanks, she'd placed a hot plate in front of me. As I devoured the meal, her focus alternated between the application and me.

She squinted over a pair of dime-store bifocals. "That right, you live in New Town? I took you for Old Town."

"I just moved; my folks are on United."

"Uh-huh. You're a newlywed, Mrs. Valdes." It wasn't a question.

"Yes, ma'am."

Her eyes cut over to my naked ring finger. "So your parents disowned you. What's wrong with the guy?"

"Nothing! He loves me."

"That's what they all say."

She cackled with abandon, when a melancholy mood flitted over her. She muttered something like, "Too late now." Just as quickly, she recovered her intimidating mien. "Be here tomorrow, seven o'clock. Don't be late, and wear a dress."

Freed from the daily battle for my soul, I had decided to abandon espionage work. This seemed like a good moment to start telling the truth. "I won't be permanent, ma'am. Soon as we save enough money, we're going to Cuba. I understand if you want to reconsider. Otherwise, I'll work harder than you imagine."

"Is that right?" She peered over the top of her glasses, scrutinizing me with such intensity that my cheeks burned. "You don't look like a revolutionary. That man of yours must be a hunk." Again, that witchy cackle—part hyena, part Mae West. I wondered whether to join the laughter or run away.

She tightened an apron over her abundant hips. "Honesty goes a long way with me, Kiddo. See you in the morning." She held out her hand and I shook it. Like her face, her grip was strong, with a surprising vein of compassion.

"Thank you, ma'am."

"If you say that again, you're fired. Call me Tilly."

"O.K."

As I left, she thrust a rock-solid frozen tub of HoJo's butter pecan ice cream into my hands. "Freezer's on the fritz. Don't know when that lazy sonafabitch repairman's gonna get his butt here."

We shared a giddy secret smile. Maybe all lies were not equal and some were downright merciful. Grateful for the lifeline, I decided to be the best damn waitress ever.

As I biked home, I wondered if witches could enter heaven. It seemed unfair to doom someone as kind and generous as my new boss, no matter how close a relation to Lucifer she might be.

I arrived early the next morning in my Easter dress, a simple white linen shift with yellow rickrack trim. Tilly was a fast talker and waitressing was harder than I thought. I created a mental flow chart, cross-referencing my tasks with the stations and duties onboard *La Libertad*: Tilly was the Captain; I was her first mate; the customer was our client; the meal was the catch. My job was to send our well-fed customers sailing out the door with a smile.

Whenever traffic slowed, I married saltshakers, topped ketchup bottles, memorized the menu, and learned to operate the cash register. Soon the corkboard tray felt like an extension of my arm; my movements became balletic. My cheap HoJo uniform paled in comparison to the finery of a Pan

Am stewardess, and I hadn't traveled past the end of the Rock, but I felt proud and soon earned Tilly's respect.

"Keep it up, Kiddo. You're almost ready for the next level."

I assumed she meant a job promotion, when all the while she was clocking my readiness for entry into a mystical world, my hidden birthright.

As soon as I received my second paycheck—which, of course, I signed over to my husband—he quit his job. Naturally, he couldn't continue to work for the very system he aimed to destroy. Besides, his vision of a Communist newspaper required many hours of undisturbed reflection. Who was I to question the wisdom of his decision? I'd bet my future on him, and no less than eternity.

Late one sweaty midsummer night, Santiago stumbled into the apartment, stinking drunk, and climbed on top of me. While we made love, a startlingly clear vision came to me: Yemayá rode over moonlit waves on the back of a dolphin, iridescent pearls dripping across her naked breast, a crown of shells atop her long green hair, while above her flew a purple banner that read: *You're pregnant*.

I drifted back to sleep and, by morning, forgot about it in the scurry of life. Three weeks later, when the smell of fried grease made me sick to my stomach, I remembered the prophetic vision.

"Angel, are you okay?" Pushing open the bathroom door, Tilly caught me vomiting into the toilet. "Good grief! You got knocked up."

I slumped against the tiled wall. "Don't worry, I can work."

"That's not the problem." A sigh heaved her huge bosom as she placed a cool wet cloth on the back of my neck. "What are you going to do? You're too young to be a mother. Why, you're just a baby yourself."

"I'm married."

"You have plenty of time, Kiddo."

The implication shocked me. "I would never do that. Marriage is sacred in the eyes of God."

"Oh, boy." She gave me a pitiful stare. "It was worth a try."

Poor thing, she didn't understand Jesus's example: love required sacrifice. Besides, I already loved you, Faith, and I hoped your arrival would bring your father and me closer, even restore our social standing.

Woozy, I struggled to my feet. "Aren't you happy for me, Tilly?"

Snuffling back tears, she wrapped me in her huge flabby arms. "A child…long ago. Oh, heck." She blew her nose as she hurried out.

That night, I splurged on steak dinner at Winn-Dixie and dressed in my Sunday best. I waited until Santiago had finished supper before I sprung the good news.

"Guess what?"

A scowl made plain his disdain. Nevertheless, I had won the prize and, for once, I deserved to call the shots. I sat back with a crocodile grin.

"Please guess."

"Stubborn." He swilled back a beer. "You got a raise?"

"I'm pregnant. We're going to have a baby!"

His eyes widened in shock, as he rolled an empty beer bottle on the rickety table. He spit out a single word. "*Gonjo.*"

Shit? Hardly the joyful response I expected.

(Faith, I wish I had a prettier tale to tell. Considering my sorry lies, I see no reason now to sugarcoat the past.)

Santiago pushed away from the table, while I sat frozen. Behind me, I heard the scrape and slide of spare change on the kitchen counter. He was gathering my tips for his nightly bar stop.

The leftover gristle on the plate mocked my efforts. Why hadn't he delivered the adoring words I'd written in my head? For one horrible moment, I fell between the yawning gap of my imagined life and the depressing reality.

As he sauntered towards the front door, I blocked his path. "Where are you going, Santi?"

"None of your business."

"When will you be back?"

His eyes iced; his body tensed. "Are you *loca*?"

"It's just that I thought—"

"The man thinks. You obey. *Comprendes*?"

"I understand, but—"

"Always 'but.'"

"I'm sorry, but the baby will be here by spring and—"

Here came the very first slap, white-hot across my cheek. "Stubborn *princessa*."

My husband slammed the front door behind him as he left. Blind with tears, I fell onto the bed, wondering why my heart was full of sin. I recalled the Epistle to the Ephesians: "Wives, submit yourselves unto your own husbands, as unto the Lord." I simply had to try harder.

* * * * *

SANIBEL ISLAND, FLORIDA

SUMMER 1985

A snippet of energetic punk rock drifted in the office window from the beach. Angel looked up from her typewriter, blinking into the bright glare of sun, as the door closed on the nebulous world where memory and imagination mingled. She drew on a cigarette and, stifling a hacking cough, contemplated the stack of carbon copies. One woman's life fell onto the next, her experience forever printed on successive generations. She thought of Willow's Valentine and its deceptively simple message, *Forget Me Not*.

The women in her line were as interconnected as the shells in a Sailors' Valentine—the placement of one shell affected the next. If only Faith could recognize the tapestry of their lives, perhaps she could write an independent chapter. Or would the familiar pattern of loss and longing she had unknowingly inherited leave her broken and alone, perhaps saddled at a young age with a child?

And what about Angel? Couldn't she also make a new start? Papi had it wrong—all men were not bastards, least of all Max. If she never risked her heart, she might break both of theirs.

She studied the shoreline, where a hedge of clouds layered the beach in swaths of gray haze, wasting into dim crepuscular light. Like the female loggerheads that swam for endless miles past predators and manmade obstacles, such as garbage and heavy anchor lines, to nest on this shore, she must summon courage from the sea. *You got seawater in your veins, Kiddo.*

Quickly now, before she could change her mind, Angel put a copy of her story in a manila envelope and wrote a note:

Dear Max,

Forgive me if I have misjudged you. I now understand that the secret you hid was not yours to tell.

If you have the time and interest, I hope you will read the enclosed story of my early years. I did the best I could and must face the consequences of Faith's anger, and maybe your disappointment, as well. At the very least, perhaps you will find it in your heart to consider me a friend.

Yours truly,

Angel Rose del Corazón

On cat's feet she crept to his porch, where a night heron trained one suspicious eye on her from its perch on the railing. As she laid the package against the front door, she offered a heartfelt plea. *Forget me not.*

* * * * *

Dear Faith,

Would you please call me? Just let me know you're okay.

Love,

Mom

SHELL TALK

KEY WEST, FLORIDA

NOVEMBER 1967

By winter, my belly had swelled, just like our local population, which saw the annual arrival of northern Snowbirds. The slight drop in temperature did little to alleviate my discomfort, while the days pressed upon me with suffocating sameness: I waddled to work in the morning, returning to a lonely apartment at night.

If I happened to lay eyes on my husband, he was either passed out with drink or we barely spoke. Frankly, I was sick and tired of hearing about Evil Capitalists and his grandiose plans.

I deserved God's punishment for my lack of faith; even Yemayá had abandoned me for deserting the Captain. In the solitude of my daily walks, I sent a vague prayer for help to anyone who would listen, even my old ally Satan, like casting a line into the ocean hoping it would catch onto something, even a rock.

One drizzly afternoon, I sat at the counter, counting tips, wishing I didn't have to go home. Tilly shrugged on a jacket and, with a peculiar look in her eye, studied me.

"Come with me, Angel. I want to show you something."

"What?"

"My sanctuary."

"Oh, what religion are you?"

"*Ha!* Maybe you'll tell me."

Intrigued, I rode with her in the fur-lined Caddy several blocks away to the Tropical Arms Apartment House, a collection of one-story bungalows that sat in the shade of a huge magnolia tree. A small patio, artfully decorated with driftwood and conch shells that sprouted air plants, fronted Tilly's unit on the west end. A pair of dainty jingle shell chimes hung from the eaves, on either side of the front door, tinkling in the breeze.

I don't recall what we said; I can only tell you that once I entered her front door, my life changed. I first noted the typical Key West décor: muted pastels, rattan furniture with tropical print cushions. Soon, a subtle, pervasive calmness—not what I expected from my boisterous friend—took me by surprise.

"Do you live alone?"

Tilly chuckled. "I guess you could say that."

She looked at the living room wall, where several octagonal shadow boxes hung higgledy-piggledy. Upon closer inspection, I saw they contained intricate mosaics of flowers, objects, even figures, made entirely of shells. Most included a catchphrase, written with tiny seed shells, such as: *Remember Me*, *Love Always*, *Today Is A Gift*. Picture and verse often complemented each other: *Love Points The Way* encircled a nautical compass. The artistry reminded me of a tapestry I'd once seen in a schoolbook.

"Wow. What are they?"

She continued down a hallway, indicating that I should follow. "Come on."

We entered a room lined with more mosaics, where my awareness of a benevolent presence increased. The last light of day slanted through the window onto a long folding table that took over the room. A few shadow boxes in various stages of completion, along with colorful piles of shells, cluttered the surface. Dozens of boxes, labeled with names of shells, were crammed into a pair of bookcases: tellins, augers, ladder horns, slippers, limpets, lucines, murex, moons, many olives, and all kinds of scallops from Calico to Lion's Paw, Rough and Zigzag.

I didn't recognize the meekness in Tilly's voice. "This is where I find God."

"Are you saying you made these?" *With her gruff manners and bloated hands? Tilly, who didn't believe in love?*

She pointed to a shell mosaic designed around a small watercolor of two heavy-set women, one black, the other a red-head. They were gathering shells on a sun-drenched beach made of rows of different cockles—Velvet Egg, Yellow Prickly, and Painted Egg. Underneath, the message read, *From A Friend.* It was beautiful, and I told her so.

"Gladys taught me Shell Work. She was a wonderful woman from Barbados. Unfortunately, she died before I could finish it."

"I'm sorry."

"Yeah. Me, too." She paused to brush her hand over her face. "You know the true power of a Sailors' Valentine is revealed when you give it to someone you love."

I traced a finger across the laborious detail in Gladys' Valentine, trying to imagine Tilly at work in her "sanctuary."

"I don't know what I expected. I'm impressed."

"Ah, don't be." She fanned the air with annoyance, though I could tell she was pleased. "Mine are lousy compared to some. They're called Sailors' Valentines." She poked me in the arm and winked. "I once saw a kinky one, you know, a couple of horny sailors with a beautiful island girl, all in the buff." Her hearty laugh boomed in the small room.

As I took in the beauty and the serene energy of her work, I thought of Papi's obsession with Yemayá. Maybe he'd been on to something, after all.

"I never imagined you could do so much with shells."

She swept away a stray lock of grayish-blond hair that had escaped her dye job. "I'm surprised you've never seen one, you being a Conch and all. I bet your ancestors had one or two."

I hope you don't mind me saying this, Tilly. But I didn't take you for the sentimental type."

"It's no lie; Shell Work saved my life. Key West was the end of a long road. I finally found peace making these. To tell you the truth, the Valentines make themselves; my fingers just do the shells' bidding." She spoke in a high-pitched, cartoonish voice. "'Here, put me here, no not there, you dumb broad, over here.' They're bossy little suckers."

She picked up an empty frame and stared at it with such intense recognition that I had a funny feeling she could see the arrangement it was destined to contain. "Now you need it more than I do, Mrs. Valdes. Take a seat."

Why deny it? Hadn't I been begging for help? My heart whispered, *this is the way*. I did as Tilly said, and she set the frame in front of me.

"First off, Kiddo, you gotta find your Shell Queen. That's the key. Trust me, everything else follows. The Queen holds the message in her chambers. Once you've got the right shell, you've got the whole shebang. Go ahead."

"But how? There's so many." The overwhelming number of boxes of shells offered an array of possibilities and, also, of failure.

She had a mischievous glint in her eyes. "I'll share a trick of the trade. Let the Queen call to you. Why work hard when she'll speak to you, plain as day? All you gotta do is listen."

"That's it?"

She plunked down across from me in a padded chair. "Are you kidding? That's everything! It took me years to learn that."

I folded my arms across my chest, my jaw set. "It makes no sense."

"Go on, Miss Key West Conch, pick the shell you think oughta be the Queen. See how far it gets you. Trust me, you'll feel like you been scrubbing floors all day long. You'll never finish the damn thing, either." She challenged me with a pointed stare. "Give it a whirl."

A zoo of questions ran amok in my head. I began to question my instructor, but as soon as she started her handiwork, an invisible shield seemed to surround her.

Most of the shells were old childhood friends: Atlantic bubbles, Deer cowries, Volute turrets, Razor clams, and Angel Wings. However, no Shell Queen "called to me," whatever that meant. I ran my finger along the smooth, brownish cup of a Glory-of-the-sea cone, surely a name worthy of a queen, and showed it to my mentor.

"How about this one?"

She peered over her glasses and shrugged. "Let the shells talk to you, Angel."

"Talk how?"

"Just like we're doing—Shell Talk." She jutted her chin at the pretender. "Well, is that the queen?"

"Guess not." I dropped it back in the box. "What do I do?"

Tilly screwed up her face. "Just listen!"

I marveled at the nimbleness with which she glued a False Red Strigilla into a small floral-like bouquet. As she continued working, her face softened and, once more, her attention slipped away, as if in a trance.

I moved behind her to read the unfinished legend. "What's that going to say?"

Her voice sounded faraway. "*Peace and Happiness.*"

"Is that what the Queen Shell told you? What if you want to say something else? Maybe I'll make one for Santiago that says, *I Am Yours.*"

"It's not hard to listen, Kiddo. We just forget how. I tell you, over time I've come to believe the Valentine already exists—I can't say where, I'm not that smart—it's like I'm just brushing sand away to uncover it."

Twilight flickered outside, and I grew weary. "I should go."

Tilly wagged her finger at me. "I couldn't sit still in the beginning, either. Boy, did I have a bee up my butt! I fought salvation tooth and nail. Gladys would just smile and say, 'You got somewhere to go?' Course I didn't. I finally finished that one, my first." She pointed to a simple Valentine that hung in front of her chair. Though cruder than the rest, its message carried quiet power: *Love Yourself*. "By then I was hooked. And maybe I'd learned to love myself a little, too."

"Is that what mine should say?"

She chortled to herself. "If I could tell you that, I'd be a rich woman. Only you know what's in your heart. Like I told you, listen, and the Queen will come."

"But I don't hear anything."

Tilly shifted her big hips in the chair, as if batting my resistance out the door.

Eyeing a box of Brown augers, I decided it was as good a choice as any. For dramatic effect, I spun one inside my empty shadow box, hoping for inspiration, but none came. I tried again, this time with a Lightning Whelk that, unlike most shells, coils to the left. Still nothing.

"Ugh!" I sank back in the chair, while my crazy friend ignored me.

How was this any different than the Captain sending a dolled-up coconut shell to sea? Or Mother taking the sacraments? Where had any of their rituals ever gotten me? Shell Talk was another silly superstition.

I pushed my big belly from the table. "I can't do it. I'm sorry."

She squinted over the top of her glasses. "You'll be back. You got seawater in your veins, Kiddo."

Tilly ignored me the next day at work, which was fine by me. I had no interest in her shell games. And yet, all through the day, at the oddest moments, a parade of sea-born images floated through my mind: a lovely Sunrise Tellin half-buried in the sand, its pink-banded shell aching to be plucked; the afternoon tide rolling in with a popping mix of shells; the call of the sea echoing inside a conch; a coral reef teeming with life, another world unto itself. Not exactly memories, more like impressions unwittingly gathered in my youth, the images softened my heart and filled me with longing, not unlike the wonder of falling in love.

When quitting time came, Tilly and I sat side by side at the counter with the supper special and not a mention of shells. Afterwards, without a word of discussion, we drove to her apartment and picked up where we had left off.

Eager now to find my Shell Queen, I surveyed the many possibilities. On a whim, I jockeyed several turrets in my hand. The sound of shells grinding against each other recalled waves raking shells along the ocean floor. In time, they would be worn down to sand, only to be reformed into wondrous shapes all over again. Perhaps, someone or something larger than myself—who or what I couldn't say—also was wearing me down.

I tested the Rough scallops and hesitated. No, maybe not. Next, bubble shells. At once I sensed a wrong turn. In fact, wherever I looked, I hit a dead end; I was trapped in a maze. How had I gotten so lost?

And then it struck me: For so long, I had buried my natural instincts under survival camouflage that I was a stranger to myself. The Captain's admonition came back to haunt me: *Nunca olvides quien eres.* Well, the joke was on me because I had no idea who I was. He said I was the daughter of the Sea Goddess and Mary believed I belonged to Christ, while I'd given myself to Santiago, body and soul.

A dam inside me burst with a gush of tears that I thought would never stop. Tilly wrapped me in a bear hug, her body warm and comforting.

"Don't you worry, Kiddo. Ain't nothing that can't be undone, except that baby, and she'll be just fine. All you need is a little peace and quiet, and it's right here for the taking."

At the time, Faith, her reference to you as a "she" slipped by me. I only thought of it after your birth, though by then I had grown accustomed to her sorcery.

I dried my eyes on the sleeve of my uniform and sat empty as an indifferent shore. Through the haze of inertia, I watched my kind teacher return to work, marveling at her capacity to love. Maybe I didn't know a damn thing about it.

If she could make such beautiful things, why couldn't I? And if I could make a Sailors' Valentine, maybe I also could accomplish other things, goals I'd yet to imagine.

Without a conscious thought, I found my hand lingering upon a heap of Sunrise Tellins. My heart skipped a beat. Tilly's head jerked up. She spoke in a low whisper, so not to break the spell.

"Follow that."

My attention swept over the shells, as purposefully as the tide, toward one in particular. Not as pretty as the rest, I found it compelling, nonetheless. When I grasped it in my hand, hope filled my heart and, for the first time in months, I smiled.

The mysterious was revealed. "My Shell Queen."

A wide grin creased Tilly's face. "Now make a wish. It doesn't hurt to get a little magic for yourself; I always do."

Magic for which of my lives? The actual depressing reality or my fantasy escape? If only I could knit them together with a single stitch.

"Just one wish?"

"Don't be greedy! You got plenty of time. I'll tell you, when I want to find a particular shell on the beach, I see it in my mind first, and sooner or later it appears. Just ask yourself what you want—it'll come."

I didn't know what I wanted other than the same plea I'd once sent skittering out to sea in a little coconut boat: to be free and happy. I still had no idea how to get there or what it would look like. Show me the way, I prayed.

And the answer came: *Have Faith.*

I blurted it out loud. "Have Faith? Is that it? That's the message?"

Tilly laughed. "What'd you expect?"

"I don't know, something romantic. Faith in what?" Jesus, Yemayá, Castro, or my husband? Were the shells accusing me, rightly so, of having lost faith in all of them?

"This isn't a debate, Miss Hardheaded Conch! One day you'll understand the message."

If I'd known how long it would take to grasp those two little words, I might have quit right then.

That night, as I walked home through the dark balmy night, the world looked fresh and new. In the dim moonlight, an old woman in a rocking chair waved to me from her porch. Smells of grilled fish and fried clams wafted from an open window. A woman cooed to a crying child. And, to my surprise, I found it a friendlier place.

A PEACE THAT PASSETH ALL UNDERSTANDING

The fragile white Sand Dollar is sometimes called the Holy Ghost Shell: the five-pointed star etched on top is believed to represent the star of Bethlehem, while the five oval holes show the wounds Christ suffered on the cross. The shell's five interior teeth form another star until broken apart, at which point they resemble white doves in flight or the five angels that sang to the shepherds at Christ's birth.

SANIBEL ISLAND, FLORIDA

SUMMER 1985

Angel stood naked and afraid on a rocky cliff, where huge waves crashed, hard and urgent, and the full moon laughed at her plight. Terror anchored her to the spot until a glint of sunshine through the lace curtains roused her from the nightmare.

Or had it? An urgent pounding continued to disturb the night air. A trumpet, she realized, as the terrible childhood fears surfaced. What if the archangel Gabriel was blowing his horn? Was this the Lord's Second Coming?

Tying on her robe, she rushed to the back porch, shocked by what she saw in the stark stream of moonlight. No great celestial power but a flesh-and-blood man stood behind her cottage with a large Queen Conch in his hands. Maximillian Sussmann was calling to her with deep desire. He had read her story; Angel could see it in his eyes, soft acceptance tinged with something she couldn't name—pity? *Una Hija del Mar* would never stand for that, and so she held her ground.

In her mental Laboratory of Love, however, vials spilled, scales crashed, notes were ruined. She struggled to examine, to weigh, to postulate. For heaven's sake, she wanted to throw herself into his arms.

Again, he lifted the shiny conch in the air. The haunting bellow tugged at her heart and she found herself running towards him. He dropped the conch onto the sandy verge, sweeping her into his arms.

"*Liebshen*," he said. "Again, I heard you. In my head, like the day you fell into the sea. I was resting, even thinking of you, when you called to me. I went to the door, certain to find you there. Instead, how puzzled I was to see the package. I read through the night. And when I finished now, I thought, I must see you right away."

"Max." She knew she must tell him the story wasn't finished. "I ran away with Faith when she was a baby. I had no choice but to abandon her father, at least I thought so at the time. Do you think less of me?"

"My dear, in this life we must survive. If you regret the past, only you must forgive yourself. For me, it does not matter. I want you, always."

Buoyantly, they kissed, without restraint, and she gave in to the warm slide of his tongue. She wrapped her arms around his neck, clinging to him, as he trailed his lips along her throat. The heat of their bodies, like gravity, pulled them deeper into each other.

"Shall we go inside?" Max said in a throaty voice.

Angel led him inside without a smidgen of hesitation, until she froze at the bedroom door.

He pulled her close and whispered, "I love you."

Did she love him, too? She thought she might, but was she required to say those three little words, so potent and overwhelming, simply because he had? And yet, she did not want him to lose faith. Ill-equipped to navigate the minefield of romance, she laid her head on his chest, reassured by his steady heartbeat.

"I see," she said.

"Do you?" He stroked her hair. "Angel, I'm here for you. Whatever you want from me, I will give."

Her frustration increased—what kind of wordsmith was she? Like the Captain might have done, she weighed the subtleties between expressions of love. In Spanish, the options were more apparent: *te quiero* could mean I love you—though, literally, it meant I want you—while *te amo* could only signify I love you with deep sentiment.

"I want you," Angel said, at last, which was also true in the carnal sense. "Please be patient with me."

"You know we don't have to go further," he said.

She answered with a luscious kiss that lasted until she could no longer tell where he began and she ended; they were merging into something she did not recognize but longed to fling herself into. She pressed her body against his, communicating her growing desire, and he gently guided her to the bed.

The exquisite feel of their bodies intertwined caught her off balance, as did his hand that ran up her nightgown, covering her curves—her hips and breasts—with the same devotion she had seen him give a rare shell. His hot touch sent a shiver up her spine and into her brain, exploding with pleasure.

This was not the urgent lust of her youth, but a heady sensuous world that awakened a willingness to explore, where pleasure was received and given, and delicacy rode an increasing trail of passion. She unbuttoned his shirt while he watched with a captive look. She marveled at how much he enjoyed this small act of love. He undressed her, kissing her smooth thighs, her womanly breasts, her perfumed neck, in a mutual exploration that might have lasted minutes or hours; she couldn't say.

Fumbling and laughing, like two kids who have happened upon a secret room, they yielded to each other. She guided him to her wet wanting sex, so long without a man's touch, and, moaning with hunger, felt him enter her. Together their hips rocked, gentle at first, then hard and long. To her astonishment, she felt her body quiver with pleasure.

"Max." She repeated his name, softly, distractedly, while she climaxed. "Max."

He groaned and together they peaked, easing into the afterglow.

"Thank you, *Liebshen.*" He kissed the top of her head.

"*Hmmm.*" Was anything in the world more wonderful than love?

"I love you, Max."

Angel snuggled beside Max as he slept, warm in the wing of his arm, while a gentle breeze batted at the curtains, carrying in the sounds of early beachgoers. In her mind's eye, she replayed the exquisite moments of their lovemaking. It had been easier than she expected, despite their initial awkwardness. Max's strength and, even more, her relaxed willingness surprised her.

All these years she hadn't had time for love and now, as the minutes ticked by, without a single page written or line edited, she couldn't imagine being anywhere but at his side. Soon, she decided, she would confess details of her past. She had many questions for him, too. Chiefly, how had he obtained Willow's Valentine?

But as he rustled beside her, they giggled at the sight of each other and all her pressing points fell away.

Max squeezed her tight. "Good morning."

"Would you like breakfast?" she said, overcome with shyness.

He glanced at the clock on the bedside table. "Ten o'clock? Such gypsies we are."

"It's okay if you have to go."

"I must only be with you."

"Okay, breakfast then. Use Faith's bathroom. I'll just be a minute." Before she closed the bathroom door, Angel turned to smile, happy to find him watching her.

She stared at herself in the mirror, examining the glowing effects of lovemaking or perhaps, happiness settling into her rusty heart. A few minutes later, she heard the pleasing sound of his footsteps on the pine floor, the pulse of the shower in the other room. How had she lived so long without a man, without this man?

When she walked down the hall, she felt as if the photo of her and Santiago belonged to a different woman. The smell of eggs and bacon wafted towards her, and she saw Max at the stove, grinning.

"We will need nourishment," he said. "That is, since we are together."

"Pretty sure of yourself, aren't you?" she said.

He looped an arm around her waist and kissed her. "I only know I love you."

"You're such a romantic."

His eyebrows arched. "This is a crime?"

"Not anymore."

They took their plates to the sun-soaked porch and ate hungrily in the warm air, which carried the smell of suntan lotion and the sounds of soft rock tunes and speedboats buzzing offshore—the fertile abandonment of summer. Grasshoppers hummed, the surf rolled, and the old swing creaked.

When Angel had her fill, she sat back to light a cigarette. Max regarded the smoke suspiciously, and before he could protest, she waved away his concern.

"I want to make an experiment with you," she said, with a raspy cough. "Since we are together."

"An experiment? Shall I be Dr. Frankenstein and you my wonderful exotic creature?"

"There's no *Dr. Fhran-ken-shtein.* We have to be equals."

The way she rolled the German accent as flat as a piecrust delighted him. "*Ach!*" he muttered, shaking his head.

"What is it?"

He looked to the heavens. "God should not know how happy I am or He might snatch it away."

"You're superstitious, Max." *Like Papi, and Mother, too.*

"For life's unexpected changes I have great respect. I want to protect you, *Liebshen.*"

"But you can't." She held one hand on top of the other, as if holding an imaginary ball. "I don't want to look up at you—from the bottom—with you always on top." Then she held her hands parallel. "It has to be like this, an equal partnership. Not draining or holding up the other, but side by side. What do you think?"

"Extraordinary," he said. "This word 'experiment'...a bit crude, no? Perhaps, a grand adventure. I would gladly go on any adventure with you, but no experiments, please."

"It doesn't matter what we call it. Are you in?"

"Ah, my Angel. I believe each name reveals an essential quality. For example, a Lightning Welk, *Busycon contrarium*, appears to twist from a powerful spark and cannot ever be a sunrise tellin with pink rays that stretch like dawn. Experiments can fail, especially when fear, its panicked head raises. On the other hand, once you set out on an adventure, there is no turning back."

"Do you want to turn back?"

"Never. I am committed till the end of time."

"Yes," she said, as she accepted the fullness of love. "Me, too, Max."

* * * * *

Dear Faith,

I hope you are forming a better relationship with your father than this story might suggest. Perhaps people can change, after all, even me.

Love,

Mom

THE GOOD WIFE

KEY WEST, FLORIDA

MAY 1968

As my confidence in my handiwork grew, so did my boldness in life. Mind you, nothing else had changed. Santiago was still jobless and drinking away my hard-earned money. I never mentioned my shell hobby and he never complained about my prolonged absences or distraction. I suppose he lumped it all together with the changes I underwent during pregnancy, or maybe he just didn't care.

Once again, I became a double agent in my own home. I wore the mask of a Good Wife, while, inside, *dentro*, I questioned everything. I went through his pockets, discovering women's telephone numbers scrawled on matchbooks and the scent of their sex on his clothes. The Sinful Spy, who deserved punishment, suffered these betrayals, while the Devoted Wife believed that, once the baby arrived, we would be a happy family and all would be forgiven.

Only at Tilly's did I feel whole. If you could have seen the excitement in my eyes as I hurried to her apartment each afternoon, you might have suspected I'd taken a lover. In a way it was true. I was falling in love with Shell Work as well as my newfound inner freedom.

My Valentine had begun to blossom, too. Working from the center, I cut a heart shape and filled it with different shell flowers, which I fashioned together with hot glue, a fine-tipped brush, and tweezers. I especially liked the three I created with translucent jingle shells, sometimes called mermaid's toenails, one each for mother, father, and baby.

When it came to creating words out of tiny rice shells, however, I balked after a few failed attempts. Here, I called upon a biblical verse: "It's easier for a camel to pass through the eye of a needle than a rich man to enter heaven."

"I'm warning you, Kiddo. Anything is possible with Shell Work."

One look at the miracle of our friendship and I had to believe in magic. Wary but willing, I created a grid on a piece of thin board, measuring five-eighths of an inch. I wrote the letters in neat capitals, two squares for a letter, and one between each word, *Have Faith.*

The next step required infinite patience, which I was sorely lacking. Using tweezers, I attempted to glue rice shells into the shape of a letter. Often, shells slipped from my grip or I'd be overjoyed to finish a letter only to discover a glaring disparity. One vexing evening I began to wonder if I'd ever finish the damn thing.

"How long does this take, anyhow?"

"Three hundred hours, minimum. For a simple one."

"No way."

"Heck, I never said it was easy, but it's the best game in town."

Three weeks later, when the message looked fairly neat and proportioned, Tilly pretended to take my success for granted.

"Like I said, you got seawater in your veins."

Maybe she was right.

By the time the magnolias were in bloom, my feet jutted out the sides of my frayed white sneakers and I felt like a fat cow. The shells often slid through my swollen fingers and I hadn't shared a civil word, let alone a kiss, with Santiago in months. Still, the fantasy festered like a cold sore: Once he saw our beautiful baby, we would live happily ever after. I simply had to have faith.

On Saturday, May 4th, 1968, a tropical storm tracked a steady beam from Havana towards our shores. HoJo's air conditioner was no match for the soppy humidity; perspiration slid between my milky breasts; the low-pressure system left me breathless.

Our new Cuban cook, Carlos, set a plate of mac 'n' cheese in the pass-through. Leaning his boxer's frame out the window, he commented on the storm brewing outside.

"*Viene una tormenta.*"

Tilly sent him a sexy wink. Half a foot shorter, with a shaky command of English and no visible means, he seemed an unlikely catch. However, ever since he'd started several weeks ago, she'd displayed a brazen lust for him. He pushed back his bandana and rubbed his head with befuddlement. My bet was on her.

Faith, dear, as I picked up a hot plate, I felt you roll hard against my belly, like a diver's bounce off the high board, followed by a plunge into deep water. Your due date wasn't for another two weeks, so I wasn't concerned. Halfway to my table, I doubled over in pain and dropped the order on the floor. My time had come.

Tilly hurried over. "You rest now. You're in for a fight, Kiddo."

Too frightened to resist, I let her help me out the back door. She shouted into the wind. "Call me the minute the pain comes regular. I'll be there in a jiffy."

As I wobbled home, white magnolias floated like tiny white boats in beaded rivulets of rain that streamed past me on the sidewalk. Given a few hours, I thought I'd finish my Sailors' Valentine. How perfect it would be to deliver it to my husband along with our child. I did an about-face, heading to Tilly's.

Thunder drummed the air, rending the dark sky, which unleashed a heavy load of rain. Struggling forward, head down in the cutting wind, my wet uniform plastered round the oval basket of my womb, I came upon Mother's church and decided to take refuge there.

Now, the nasty weather could have cornered me at the library or coin laundry, but I soon understood my arrival here was no accident. While shell work and pregnancy had occupied me, the Good Lord had been biding His time.

A viselike contraction left me panting against a pew in the empty sanctuary. Lightning flickered through the stained glass windows, illuminating the huge wooden cross on the far wall. Underneath it, lounging about in the choir stall, I saw the celestial duo. They nodded, and of course I realized they'd been expecting me.

I stared down the nave at them, as time moved in surreal opposition to the fast-moving events, etching the moments forever into memory.

Of the two, Jesus seems more in command—he's on home turf, after all. Satan, fidgety as a fish out of water, leaps onto the rafters and taps his cloven hooves on the wood beams as he whistles a tune.

Jesus addresses me. *Angel, what right do you have to deny your child salvation?*

I hang my head in shame as, unbidden, images of my innocent baby thrown into the lake of fire and brimstone flash through my mind. *I have no right, my Lord.*

I died so that you and your child might find eternal life.

I know, for John 3:16 tells us so.

If you will accept me as your savior, Angel, you will know my love.

Psst! Cupping one side of his mouth, Lucifer speaks with the oily confidentiality of a slick car salesman. *Don't believe a word He says, Angel Baby. It's all a con game. Don't take my word for it; ask your mother.*

His fiery eyes cut to a door that leads to the church offices. At the end of a clap of thunder, I hear a woman's high-pitched scream coming from there, perhaps magnified for my benefit.

Satan grins, his beastly eyes twinkle. *Told ya so.*

Cradling my belly, as if to ward off competing claims, I exit through the door into a dimly lit hallway. The lights flicker at another burst of thunder, which drowns out the squeak of my wet sneakers on the parquet floor. Again, I hear a wail…of pain or pleasure?

A thread of light edges Reverend Powell's door. The rumbling of the heavens shakes the walls, as a contraction steamrolls through me. This time, when I hear the rapturous cry, I rush into his office.

Wrapped in a lovers' embrace, half-naked upon the massive oak desk, they don't notice me. For a moment, I wonder if birth has induced hallucinations, but there's no mistaking the preacher and Mother, even in the throes of passion.

Anxious to leave unseen, I turn my back on them as another powerful contraction roots me to the spot. Catching the doorknob for support, I moan in pain, when a gush of water spurts between my legs. I watch it pool beneath me with the unhappy realization that I am caught here.

Behind me, I hear Mother's startled cry. "Angel!"

Gently, I slide to the floor. "Help."

Pale as the saints in her nakedness, she kneels beside me. Her warm hands tear away my underpants and spread my thighs. "The baby's crowned."

The Reverend shouts for help, while he drapes Mother in a black robe. The church secretary appears at the door, bewildered by the scene.

Always capable, Mother takes charge. "Get towels, hot water. Hurry!"

My fallen mother consoles me. "Just breathe, Angelica. You'll be fine."

I close my eyes against a tidal wave of pain. Suddenly, I find Tilly beside me.

"That's right, breathe, Kiddo."

The Parrot Line has alerted the town; the virile Captain, now a cuckold. What a pity—*qué lastima*—poor Papi has traded in his soul for a ringside seat in heaven, but it's all for nothing.

Fué todo para nada.

I utter a sharp cry as you move down the chute, Faith, splitting my bones. (Some day, I hope your turn will come and you'll understand the fleeting pain of birth.)

Mother urges me. "Push!"

Tilly repeats. "Push!"

Each of these women has birthed me—one in body, the other in spirit. Now their combined calls guide us.

"Again!" Their joint command competes with the rolling thunder.

Just this once, Jesus and Yemayá appear in harmony. In the electric light, I see Him place a collegial arm around her bare shoulders. I suppose the arrival of a new soul, one that might pledge to either camp, is reason for détente. Even Satan hides in the shadows.

The Sea Goddess wears a helmet of angel wing shells atop her flowing locks; a necklace of tiny pearls hangs from her hand. Jesus, who has never looked sweeter, dips a finger into the blood of His Calvary wounds and draws a cross on my exposed belly. Ever eager, the Evil One pokes his horned head into view, when the goddess blocks him with a swish of her tail.

Like the frightening yawn of a ship crashing upon a reef, the pain splinters open a pathway for your deliverance. The fever-pitch blows nullify fear, tissue, even my willpower: I am nothing but a vessel.

Together, the ethereal company summons you, and at last you reach your grandmother's arms. Your cries, robust and high-pitched, thrill the room. The Lord touches the crown of your head. *Blessed be the child.* You coo as Yemayá lays the pearl necklace over you.

And the Good Company disappears into the shadows, trailed by Satan, whose parting words earn him another jab. *Good luck, Angel Baby, you're gonna need it.*

Mother wraps you in a red cloth, a sacrament of Christ's blood, as she cups your small downy head. She places you at my breast without a word, her shame a barrier between us. As Reverend Powell coaxes her away, she tucks herself beneath his arm. What will she do now that she's forfeited her place in heaven? Those two pillars of righteousness may be undone, yet their love is plain to see.

And love, glorious perfect love, shines in the gilded light, in the beating of your precious heart, in the tears that run down Tilly's face.

She holds your tiny fingers. "She's so damn beautiful. You did good, Kiddo."

For once, I have to agree.

I awoke in Tilly's bed to sweet gurgling sounds, your perfect smallness snug beside me in the soft dawn. The dachshund yapped in the apartment next door; a sanitation truck rumbled to a stop in the street, with a clang of metal garbage cans. To my amazement, life had gone on while I had stopped to bring you into the world.

I studied your every movement, the small rise of breath, the way you pursed your lips, the feathering of long dark lashes on your round cheeks—your father's lashes. The night before, I'd telephoned him about a dozen times before Tilly took the phone away. For heaven's sake, what kind of husband was he? Why hadn't he arrived to greet his newborn child? Such dangerous questions were new. I had not yet realized the great strength motherhood would bring.

I laid you in a swinging cradle Tilly had procured and wrapped her huge robe around my lumpy belly. As I shuffled down the hall, I heard her humming in the kitchen. She wheeled round, a hand on her hip, scowling over a hot coffee cup.

"What are you doing up?"

"Did Santiago call?"

"No, he did not."

At last, however, he answered the phone. "*Digáme.*"

"It's me, Santi. I had the baby last night. Oh, she's beautiful. She has your lips and my eyes." His deafening silence gave me pause. "What's wrong?"

"A girl?" To most Cubans, a boy child, *el baron*, especially the firstborn, proved the father's manhood.

"She's perfect, you'll see." How I hated to plead. "Come quick, I'm at Tilly's."

"You don't tell me what to do, *princessa*."

"Sorry, but—" He hung up. "I miss you." Or did I simply miss being saved?

Tilly washed out her empty cup. "Well?"

"He's coming to get me. I need a shower."

"*Ha!* You need more than that, Kiddo."

As I hurried back to the bedroom, I fell back into the dream of happily ever after. I kissed your forehead and whispered in your ear. "Papi's coming."

My hostess rapped on the door. "I'm off. You rest up or I'll report you to child welfare."

"I won't be here when you get back."

"Uh-huh. I'll bring dinner. You be careful."

I showered and prettied myself for our imagined reunion: *Santiago will take me in his arms...Forgive me, Angel, I've been weak, but I never stopped loving you. I'll caress his cheek. There's nothing to forgive. And here, I'll produce the Sailors' Valentine and say, We must have faith in each other. He'll promise to take good care of us and finally, kiss me like he used to.*

By that evening, my clothes were rumpled, my makeup unfresh. The day ended as it had begun—with failed expectations.

At dusk, Tilly banged the front door open. "Anybody hungry?"

I considered possible excuses to explain Santiago's absence: he was working overtime to provide for his new family; he was busy getting the apartment ready for our arrival. But she never asked, and her unspoken assumptions only increased my depression.

Despite my hunger, I glumly picked over a plate of fried scallops with mac and cheese.

"You got to make hay while the baby sleeps," Tilly said. "I'm talking about the Valentine. You got to finish it tonight."

I scraped my teeth against the cheesy fork tines. "I'm tired."

"Trust me, you'll turn a corner when it's done. Life will still be hard, but sweeter." The faraway look that transcended time clouded her expression. "Otherwise, you'll lose your way. I sure hate to see that happen."

"I'm fine, Tilly."

She manhandled me into the hobby room, anyway, and I began work on the border. I cut a manila folder into thin short strips and, using pushpins to keep them in place, glued them at intervals around the edge of the frame.

In the quiet, meditative space, I tried to nurse my Dream Life. Yet, as all handiworkers know, truth slips in between each glued shell, each square stitched, each purl knitted. For months now, my fingers had penetrated the veil of illusion, bit by bit, and, with your birth, any remaining resistance was crumbling.

Several hours later, I quit with a heavy sigh. "I'll finish it later, I swear I will."

Tilly never looked up, as she repeated her advice, "Just remember, the true power of a Sailors' Valentine is revealed when you give it to someone you love."

Teetering between hope and despair, I waited the following day for Santiago's visit. His demanding knock came in the late afternoon. He stood in the courtyard in the lacy light that filtered through the palm fronds, without flowers or chocolates or even a baby present, scruffy and unshaven, with the off-kilter manner of the inebriated; hardly the romantic picture I had conjured.

But never mind. He rewarded me with a dazzling smile and a peck on the cheek as he swept into the apartment.

I hurried after him. "Wait till you see the baby. Come, she's in here."

As usual, he failed to follow my imagined scenario, drifting instead to the workroom. He flicked a shell across the table. It bounced off the wall and skittered across the tiled floor. "What's all this stuff?"

I edged away, coaxing him. "The baby's asleep in the back room."

He fell into my chair, examining my nearly finished Valentine with keen interest. I cringed at the sight of my hard work in his drunken hands. When he tumbled a series of Transverse arks, which I'd spent hours arranging as flying doves, I cried out.

"For God's sake, be careful!"

Like a bully who has found a weak spot, a satisfied look sparked his eyes. "You did this?"

"It's something Tilly taught me. I'll explain later."

He sat back and lit a Marlboro, blowing smoke with lazy abandon onto my precious creation. Would our daughter equate the smell of alcohol and cigarettes with love?

He rolled a snail shell back and forth between his fingers. "Do you remember what I asked you on our first date?"

I sensed the menace curled beneath his casual words. But, as I said, motherhood had emboldened me.

"We talked about a lot of things, Santi."

Again, he sullied my handiwork with the stink of smoke. "Comrades. Isn't that what you wanted?"

"Yeah, sure."

"*Yeah, sure*?" The sneering words brought the danger closer. "You're like a lazy Capitalist. You don't work for us. You work for these stupid shells—for yourself."

With a nimble trick of the spy trade, the Good Wife slipped on a compliant mask. "It's relaxing, that's all. Please, don't be upset."

He held up a warning finger. "*Nada mas.* This stops."

First thought: It'll be a small sacrifice for his love. Second thought: Shell Work was my way out.

"Yes, but—"

"*But*?"

I'd forgotten how that one little word enraged him. He shot up, cornering me against the table. "You the boss now, eh? It that what you learn from that *puta*?"

"Tilly's no whore. At least she keeps me company while you're out with God knows who."

Crack! His fist caught my jaw. As I fell backwards onto the table, it collapsed under me with a loud crash. Shells flew into the air, and in the raining patter, I heard the ridiculous message: *Have Faith!* Where had it ever gotten me?

As I wiped the bloody spittle from my mouth, I lost all remaining hope that Santiago would ever save me.

"Get out. I never want to see you again."

His eyes widened in disbelief. "You don't leave me."

He leaned over me, ready to strike again, when the front door slammed with a bang. Tilly rushed in, taking in the scene with an angry scowl.

She turned on him. "Why, you damn coward!"

They tussled and called each other every name in the book. With his drunkenness and her wrestler's arms, she managed to shove him outside. To my surprise, he howled from the courtyard the very words I'd longed to hear.

"Please, Angel, I love you, I'm sorry."

I pictured myself rushing to his side, begging forgiveness, reunited at last. My body pitched forward, ready to leap, when your hungry cries stopped me. Torn between the two of you, I was grateful when Tilly strode past, "I'll get her."

I righted my chair and sat staring at the terrible mess. Soon she reappeared, rocking you in her arms.

"He's not worth it, Angel."

I started to protest but my fantasies had run out of steam. I heard Santiago shout a final parting curse. Then he was gone, and so was my Sailors' Valentine.

"It's ruined."

"You can start again." She burped you on her shoulder. "That'a girl. Now, what's your name, honeybunch?" She looked at me. "Have you decided?"

How could I choose all by myself? Names were holy and, for those chosen souls, written into The Book of Life.

"Well?" Tilly prodded. "It's probably right in front of you."

I peeled off a scallop that was stuck to my thigh. Some day, I decided, I would teach you Shell Talk so you would never blindly give away your power to anyone. And I would rebuild the Valentine and hang it over your crib, as a reminder. *Have Faith.*

A startled laugh escaped my lips as I took you in my arms. "Hello, Faith."

My friend beamed. "I told you, anything is possible with shell work, Kiddo."

* * * * *

SANIBEL ISLAND, FLORIDA

SUMMER 1985

In a matter of days, the quotidian rhythm of Angel's life happily changed. She found Max snuggled in bed beside her when she awoke. At dusk they shared a meal, discussing the day with pleasant detachment, as if its events presented nothing more than inconvenient but necessary obstacles to this sweet reunion in which they had no need of anyone else. In their lovemaking she discovered a refuge and grew unafraid to relinquish the last light of day.

She clung to him as they said goodbye early on a sun-swept summer morning, her body rumpled from a surfeit of caresses. She had nothing to fear, as if the alchemy of Max's love had turned all the mistakes she'd ever made into well-planned decisions that had led her to this perfect moment. Since Faith had not called with bad news, Angel even began to believe that Santiago had changed for the better. At last she was free and happy.

With an easy heart she entered the stuffy old Cracker house where Dr. Nash kept his family practice. A stuffed sailfish and a bluefin tuna hung in the wood-paneled reception area, better preserved than the threadbare living room set.

Helen slid open the reception window and, without missing a beat, said, "How's Faith?"

A thin chain of green plastic ovals hung round her neck, attached to bifocals. Thick gray hair framed her fine-boned face, which was remarkably unwrinkled. All her worries resided in the pained cornflower blue eyes.

"A high school graduate," Angel replied. "Can you believe it?"

"Time sure does fly."

Angel handed her a copy of the latest *Stella*. "I signed it to your granddaughter."

"Well, aren't you the sweetest."

She led Angel to a room with an old-fashioned glass and steel cabinet. Pointing to a folded paper gown on the examination table, she said, "Front first. Keep your slacks on." Without another word, she closed the door.

Angel sat on the edge of the table in the pauper's robe. Perhaps she'd surprise Max with his strudel tonight.

Dr. Nash gave a cursory knock and entered, studying her chart. "Angel."

She coughed on cue. "Hello, Edgar."

All business—why waste precious time when he could be fishing?—he held a stethoscope to her chest. "Breathe normally. Any blood?"

"A few times. Nothing significant."

He rubbed his glasses clean, avoiding her scrutiny. "Meet me in my office."

"Is something wrong?" But he was already out the door.

Angel stuffed the gown into the waste can. For a moment she stood half-naked, staring into a faraway world of mermaids and cursed fisherman. *Ven, ven, mi amor. Tu eres mío, todo para mi. No luches mas. Ven aquí.*

She dismissed the vision for she had no need of the Sea Goddess or any other supernatural presence these days. As she passed down the hall, however, her early seaborne days came alive: the swell of the sea crashing against the hull of *La Libertad*; the exciting tug of a fish on the line; seagulls flocked at the stern, eager for scraps. It was nothing more than the plague of family superstition. Love was stronger than fear, and she had claimed it.

Nash sat at a massive oak desk, her black and white film X-rays spread out before him. He pointed to a dark mass blotted on the delicate ebb and flow of her life.

"Do you see that?" he said.

Angel could see that the black bloom threatened to snuff out the tenuous gray buffer. "What is it?"

"A tumor on your left lung. We'll have to do a biopsy to determine whether or not it's malignant."

We? Ah, the old saving game.

She sank into a chair across from him. Outside the window, a hibiscus bloomed with bright yellow flowers, the same as the one beside her house. She remembered the Queen Conch she'd found here a few months ago. Had Yemayá sent her a courtesy warning? Hadn't Angel known for some time what was coming?

"Let's kept it simple," she said. "Some awful beast is eating my lungs, right?"

"That's one way of putting it," he said.

"Have you ever seen X-rays like mine that aren't malignant?"

He heaved a long sigh. "There's always a chance."

It must be exhausting, standing between life and death. At least, earthly custody of the body was short-lived, while the interminable care of the soul never ended.

Angel shook her head. "I'm not going down the road of tubes and tests and waiting and hoping if the end is clear. I'm going to live every day I have. Just tell me, how much time do I have left?"

A thin smile creased his face. "If I could tell you that, I'd be a rich man."

"You must have some idea."

"Chemotherapy can extend—"

"Forget it." That was no way for a buccaneer.

"Are you sure?"

"Never more sure of anything."

Again, he sighed. "A year, if you're lucky."

"A year," Angel repeated.

A year of loving Max. A year of true happiness. More than she'd ever had.

The world sparkled with light as she left the office. She spun the dial on the car radio to a Spanish station and heard the familiar lusty sound of the queen of salsa, Celia Cruz. Angel gyrated her hips to the beat, wondering why she hadn't she spent more time dancing.

A strong breeze billowed the trees along Periwinkle Way. She longed to sail over the graceful palm trees into the ever-young blue horizon. An intoxicating radiance permeated the air—it emanated from her diseased flesh. Checking herself in the rear view mirror, she smiled.

For so long she had looked into the abyss of eternity and been afraid. Now that she was certain to fall, a great burden had been lifted. Here, on the precipice of death, she was drunk on life. A mysterious stranger was taking up residence in her heart, showering her with incredible sweetness.

It seemed incredible that people driving past didn't marvel at her electric presence. Their short-term vision blinded them while her blinders had fallen away. She wanted to flag them down and shout: *There's nothing to fear!* But she lacked the energy to save the world; only her daughter and Max mattered now.

As Saint Michael's and All Saints church came into view, Angel decided to have a chat with her Old Friends. She no longer came as a spiritual beggar, as she had in her youth. Having gained a foothold beyond this life, she simply wanted to talk shop. The cool cosseted interior and stained glass quiet greeted her like a long lost friend. She took a seat in the front pew, its hardness a tangible reminder that the here and now was nothing more than a testing ground for eternal life.

Let the show begin.

It didn't take long for the Prince of Darkness and the Prince of Peace to appear. Time hadn't changed them a bit, while it had ravaged her inside. She regarded them with cool appraisal.

Welcome back, Jesus said.

A nasty smile slid across the devil's face. *Nice to see you, Angel Baby.*

She got right to the point. *I finally get it.*

Funny how life distracted you, until you cozied up to death and realized that heaven was in front of you all along. Of course, if everyone understood the game, they'd be out of a job. The joke was on her. She'd wasted a lot of time playing the part of Sad Lonely Girl, when she could have enjoyed the beautiful bounty life offered.

After all, the Bible was chock-a-block with clues, such as this one: "Except a man be born again, he cannot see the Kingdom of God." Like a mollusk discarding its shell, Angel would release her body, while her inner being wouldn't die, just dip back into the ocean of life.

Jesus wrapped her in a benevolent smile, while Lucifer bowed with exaggerated grace. Their simple acknowledgements felt as profound as finding true coordinates after years lost at sea.

Just one more thing. They'd gotten their kicks and, well, she wanted a little tit for tat. If they would free Faith from the greedy claims of the past, Angel would go without a fight to whichever party wanted her. *Not a peep.*

She left them huddled together, plotting her future in soft whispers. As she stepped into the startling light, Tilly's words echoed on the warm breeze. *I'm warning you right now, Kiddo. Anything is possible with shell work.*

The scene was set: Yemayá's full moon lit a splendid path across the beach. Pinpoints of stars freckled the sky. Limp waves drifted aimlessly to shore. Calmed waters, midwife to nature's birth, waited to receive the loggerhead hatchlings. Angel, restless as a mother-to-be, kept vigil beside her birthing partner, Max.

As she dug her toes into the warm powdery sand, a knowing feeling, no heavier than a sea urchin shell, more powerful than a hurricane, passed through her.

She whispered. "It's tonight. I know it."

Max squeezed her hand. "My beautiful sorceress."

"You'll see."

Wrapping a blanket around her legs, Angel shivered despite the summer heat. Even before the prognosis, she had noticed an increasingly unpleasant sensitivity to the oddest things, with no rhyme or reason other than her body's incremental retreat from life—spicy foods, cold drinks, a hard wind. This she kept to herself.

As Max handed her a steaming mug, his devoted look gave her a pang of conscience. Was it wrong to let him love her? And yet, already, they were inseparable. If the tables were turned, wouldn't she want to share every last minute?

The heartsick lament reached Angel on a sudden sea-swept breeze. *Ven, ven, mi amor. Tu eres mío, todo para mi. No luches mas. Ven aquí.* She knelt beside the sandy nest, her ear to the earth. A low rumble could be heard within. The mound shook as the walls began to crumble.

"Take off your shoes, roll up your pants," she said, lifting hers.

With an excited smile, Max took his place beside her, hand in hand. Along the beach, like a series of ocean swells, the guards were rising to their feet.

The clutches erupted with dozens of tiny creatures; their outsized flippers propelled them towards shore. Angel squealed as several hatchlings crawled over her bare feet. The turtle company fanned out over the sand, a slow-moving reptilian carpet scampering into the surf. Soon she would follow into the Great Mother's arms.

"I love you," she said softly, leaning into Max.

He wrapped her in his warm embrace. "I love you, Angel."

Moments before the telephone rang, Angel struggled against an unseen, suffocating presence, familiar and terrifying, which shackled her to a deep sleep. All at once she sat up and cried out her daughter's name.

"Faith!"

Max startled beside her. "What is it?"

Angel grabbed the ringing phone. "What's wrong, Kiddo?"

"Mom!" Faith said. "He won't let me leave the apartment."

"Who?"

"My stupid father. He went out for a drink, he's always drunk. He keeps ranting about you and a sailboat."

"Are you okay?"

"I'm not great."

"What's going on, Faith? Tell me."

She broke into hard sobs, her words muddled. "Tied to a chair…I knocked it over, on my side…crawled to the phone."

"Good heavens." Angel shot to her feet. "Where are you?"

"Shit. He's back."

Angel recognized the unmistakable terror of Santiago's curse. "*Gonjo.*" She winced at the old familiar sound of a slap, then her poor daughter's wounded cry. The line went dead.

"That bastard," Angel said, slamming down the receiver. "I never should have let her go." She threw her suitcase on the bed and began tossing clothes into it. "Tilly said it would be unexpected. Good Lord!"

Max strode to the door. "I'll meet you in front with the car."

"You're coming with me?"

"Naturally."

FORGET ME NOT

Does the Song of the Sea end at the shore
or in the hearts of those who listen to it?
—Kahlil Gibran

KEY WEST, FLORIDA

SUMMER 1985

The headlights on the Valentine Mobile carved a path along Highway Seventy-Five. Dark storm clouds blotted the night sky. Each bump in the road rattled the items in the picnic basket, which he had prepared in no time. An occasional car whizzed past, puncturing the net of worried silence that had fallen around Max and Angel.

Angel tugged a sweater round her shoulders to ward off the swarm of memories that descended upon her like a cloud of blood-sucking mosquitoes. Eighteen years ago she had escaped with her baby in the opposite direction on the old pockmarked two-lane road, Alligator Alley. Neither the endless monotony of the flat landscape, with its craggy otherworldly swampland, nor her overwhelming dread, had changed much.

"I stopped writing to Tilly soon after Faith's second birthday," Angel said, as if they had been deep in conversation. "I remember watching her blow out the candles and realizing that Santiago and I would never be together. We'd never be a happy family. I don't know why I nursed that silly dream for so long."

"Time is a stranger to the heart," Max said.

"I wanted to believe I'd done the right thing by leaving. Each time I heard from Tilly, I struggled with my decision. Then one day after Faith started asking about her father I packed away Tilly's letters and never wrote again. It wasn't a conscious decision, more like sleepwalking. My dreams were so much sweeter than real life. I think I've only just woken up, with you."

He tenderly touched her arm. "Sometimes dreams can save us, no?"

"Maybe, for awhile. But now I think real life is better. I'd rather feel something, even pain, than be stuck in the past."

As they passed a large roadside sign—*The Last Chance For An Air Boat Ride!*—a clap of lightning cleaved the skies, loosening fat raindrops that pounded the car roof. Max turned on the windshield wipers, which fought a losing battle against the downpour.

"Perhaps we never forget the past," he said, staring ahead at the slippery road.

"Or maybe," Angel said, "The past never lets go of us. Like the Sailors' Valentine you gave me, I'm sure it belonged to my grandmother. I left it with Tilly when I moved here. Somehow it made its way back to me."

"Is that so?"

"I doubt she would have sold it. Where did you find it?"

"In your home town, as a matter of fact." He wiped the perspiration from his forehead with the back of his hand. "An antique store, I don't recall the name. The work I found quaint; the message, however, I hoped to share with someone special. How can I explain the odd feeling I had when I came upon this Valentine?"

"I know exactly what you mean," she said.

A terrible foreboding slipped around her, like a boa squeezing an alligator to death. Her sputtering cough competed with the noisy rainstorm. As she sipped from a thermos, she calmed the raging fear within by doubling down on the bargain she'd made with her supernatural pals: As soon as she found Faith—*she must be alive and well*—she would devote herself to whichever spiritual force won her raggedy old soul. *I promise.*

* * * * *

Dear Faith,

I wish I had a prettier ending. I hope you finally understand.

Love,

Mom

A SONG FOR A BUCCANEER

KEY WEST, FLORIDA

MAY 14, 1968

A loud crash in Tilly's courtyard woke me in the middle of the night. I feared Santiago had returned, but a familiar stream of Spanish announced your grandfather, the Captain, three sheets to the wind. The neighbor to the left, a teak restorer, shouted for quiet, as I hurried to the door.

In the pearly moonlight, the Captain's shadowy movements appeared surreal, his melancholy expression almost clownish. He picked himself up from the rubble of clay pots, scattering dirt and gardenias. For the first time I noticed a shiny bald spot, which lent him a fragility and reminded me of you.

Poor Papi, cuckolded by the very same man who had cut off his cojones.

He begged me to listen. "*Hija, escucháme.*"

We hadn't spoken since the hateful night he'd kicked me out, yet I felt nothing but love for him. "What is it, Papi?"

He swore that that bastard Santiago might hurt us. "*Te lo juro, ese hijo de puta Santiago les hicierá daño. I saw it in the Tarpon Moon.*"

Though I didn't believe in the old ways, a chill ran up my spine. If a school of silver-scaled tarpon ran towards the September full moon at low tide, Yemayá was pleased, and it would be a good year. Some fishermen, like the Captain, believed the Great Lady's moonlit waves foretold other aspects of the future as well.

He staggered closer, kicking a clay shard that skittered into a neighbor's door. A light came on; a man threated to call the cops. Despite his animosity for your father, the Captain professed his love for you.

"*Por Dios, yo amo mi nieta.*"

"Come see her, Papi. *Se llama Faith.*"

Instead, he turned away, rocking like a ship in the doldrums, until he set his course and shouldered his way to the street. As I began to follow him, I stubbed my foot on a package.

"Papi?" He slipped between the stark shadows.

I ripped off the newsprint covering, surprised to find a Sailors' Valentine, dulled with age. Under a flock of seagulls, a schooner sailed over a poignant message: *Forget Me Not.* A short handwritten note was taped to the back:

Querida Angel,

This belonged to your grandmother Willow. She loved Yemayá like I do. Don't forget who you are—no olvides quien eres.

Con amor,

Papi

I read it over and over again, my mind buzzing with questions that had no answers. Sounds of Tilly moving about inside distracted me. I found her at her worktable, deep in concentration, her eyelids lazy as a sleeping lizard. Strange energy percolated in the room.

Her fingers glided over three small piles of assorted shells, deftly arranging each into a sweeping arc. For a moment she swayed in the numinous light, delicate as a feather, despite her bulk. Her hands hovered over the table, from one arc to the next, as if pulsing to tidal rhythms locked within the shells. She selected a handful, seemingly at random, from each group, gathering them into a separate pile. Swirling the shells into a tight coil, she stopped at some secret signal.

"What is it, Tilly?"

She continued staring at—or you might say, into—the shells. "Just the ebb and flow of life, Kiddo. That's all there is to it."

"Is it Santiago?"

"There's nothing you can do now." She looked at me, her glassy gaze coming into focus. "Get some rest, you're gonna need it."

No point pressing her—she would wrestle the devil rather than reveal her secrets.

I slipped back into bed, tossing and turning, until sleep won me over. As the cheery light of dawn poked its head through the curtains, the telephone rang. Here it comes, I thought. You woke, too, and latched onto my breast with surprising strength.

Tilly soon appeared in the bedroom doorway, dressed to leave. "I'm sorry as hell, Kiddo. Your mother called. The Captain's hurt bad."

"What?"

"Plowed the Chevy into a tree last night. He's in the hospital." A knock at the door prompted her to add, "Carlos's daughter Anna will stay with Faith. Hospital germs are no picnic for an infant."

Had she seen disaster in the shells? How else to explain her preparations?

"You knew? Why didn't you tell me? I could have stopped him."

"Could anyone have stopped you from running off with Santiago? Your father's accident was set in motion years ago—just like the triggers that made you leave home. Hell, your parents and their parents laid that trap long before you were born. We're all lost at sea, Angel. If you're lucky you'll come to understand who you are. Mighty few do. Till then, all you can do is make the kindest choice possible when it's your turn at the wheel." She took a deep breath. "It's your turn now. Hurry, Carlos is waiting."

With trepidation, I turned you over to Anna's care. No one said a word as I squeezed into the cab of the pickup truck. Carlos gunned the engine and we traveled north on the oversea bridges towards Marathon, like a tireless insect climbing the rolling tongue of a great watery serpent. The plaintive sounds of Cuban Son on the radio echoed my desperation. Pressing my forehead to the window, I watched the great fireball rise over the Atlantic and prayed to the Sea Goddess. *Save, him, please.*

A nurse at Fishermen's Hospital directed us to intensive care. Down a sterile corridor, I flew past anxious faces and white coats. The powerful stench of decay touched the air. Ahead, I spied Mother, who appeared shrunken under the harsh lights. As soon as she noted my arrival, she slipped past, ignoring me. I had nothing to say to her.

I was ill-prepared for the sight of the Captain, stiff and beached like an old piece of driftwood. His skin was white, like the sheets and walls and bandages—not the sparkling white of bubbling surf or billowing sails, but a dull plastic color unkissed by the sun. Tubes, dripping bags, pumps, and electronic monitors grappled him to the land of the living, while the shadow of the valley of death edged close.

I asked Tilly for salt packets and a glass of water. The Captain's eyes flickered open at the sound of my voice.

I whispered in his ear. "I love you, Papi."

Tilly brought me what I needed and I dampened his parched lips with salt water as I softly sang the buccaneer's love song.

"Ven, ven, mi amor. Tu eres mío, todo para mi. No luches mas. Ven aquí."

And for one thrilling moment I witnessed once more the exhilarated spark of a fisherman who spies a great fish leap into the air. The Captain was sailing homeward.

The Sea Goddess rose before him, bedecked in celebration of his homecoming. Her emerald scales glistened with sunlight; strings of precious pearls enlaced her crown of shells. The siren's eerie, irresistible song filled the room as she swept him into her cold embrace, until finally, with a sigh, he sank into the watery depths of eternity.

For some time I stood by his side, lost in a daze of hurt. It felt wrong to leave him among strangers, but my breasts ached with milk; you needed me—you were all I had now. I only hoped Mother would agree to a burial at sea.

It was late afternoon when Carlos drove Tilly and me home, the radio silent, their whispering lost in the soft, warm wind rushing through the windows. How foreign the world seemed without the Captain. Perhaps one day I'd see him leap high over wind-swept waves, daring any cocky sea dog to catch him.

As we crossed the last bridge into Key West, Tilly cried out. "Hurry, Carlos!"

I felt danger approaching. "What is it?"

She stared ahead, tight-lipped. Carlos wrung speed out of the old truck. Moments later, we saw Anna running to meet us at the curb.

"*Dios mío!* The father, he took the baby!"

My baby kidnapped? Breast milk oozed onto my blouse, panic knifed through me.

"I'll kill the bastard!" Tilly smashed her fist against the dashboard. "Angel, where would he take her?"

"I don't know."

"Think!"

I flashed on the Captain's drunken warning as the truth hit me. "Oh, God, Santiago's taking Faith to Cuba."

Tilly pushed me out of the cab. "Carlos, gather some men, meet us at the marina."

She bustled into her apartment, moving faster than a cockroach in a dirty kitchen. I ran to telephone Santiago, my fingers shaking with every turn of the dial. Each unanswered ring was a slap in the face. I slammed down the receiver and tried again, because I had to do something.

Tilly huffed past with a bulging suitcase and my canvas tote. "Time to go."

I followed her out the door, too distraught to ask about the luggage. We careened towards Garrison Bight in her rusty old pink Cadillac, with Tilly bent over the fur-covered wheel as if she could plow down time.

My mind raced with maddening possibilities that even now I can't bear to recount. And, as I pictured your father absconding with you, I recalled his misbegotten plan to smuggle in a communist newspaper.

"He has a friend with a sailboat, a smuggler, Enrique."

She gave me a worried look. "What kind of sailboat?" And crashed her front bumper into the parking lot wall.

We spilled out of the caddy, neither of us commenting on the wreck. Carlos waited by *La Libertad* with half a dozen sailors who had come to avenge one of their own. The Captain would have been pleased to see he wasn't forgotten.

I saw Mother, her eyes blank like sunlight, hand Carlos the floatable key bob. If she spoke one word to me, I'd start wailing, so I stayed in Tilly's wake.

She called out to Carlos. "Do you know a smuggler named Enrique?"

I recalled something else. "His sail is red, like the communists!"

A middle-aged Cuban with a straw fedora winced. "An old sailboat. *Pequeño*."

"How small?" When he didn't answer, I was left to imagine the worst.

Tilly shouted at the men. "Let's get a move on."

I looked to see Mother's reaction, but she was gone.

Just like countless times in the past, I climbed on board, carrying with me now an awareness of how life can turn dark in an instant. Poor Tilly, green at the gills, plunked down in a fishing chair, holding the armrests tight.

I understood then how little seawater ran in her veins, how hard-won her battle was to leave behind a shell-less past.

I placed a bucket between her feet. "Keep your eyes on the horizon. I'm going forward."

"Stay, it's dangerous." She tried to stop me, but she doubled over, retching, and we hadn't even left the dock. Her witchy ways couldn't help her now.

The engines fired, echoed by a second vessel and yet another. While our small flotilla filed into the channel under overcast skies, I moved hand over fist along the railing to reach the bow. My sea legs were rusty, my heart weak with fear. I edged onto the slippery pulpit as we entered a nasty chop. The whistling wind drowned out all but the heavy drone of diesel engines and the rhythmic slap of metal on water. We plunged over foam-crested waves into yawning hollows, their tongues lashing me with cold wet spray.

Oh, God, the sea was vast, my child so small.

Steadying myself against the rail, my sneakers planted hip-wide, I scanned the horizon, back and forth. The unforgiving sea was to our advantage against a flimsy craft, though your peril terrified me. I figured Santiago had gained a three-hour advantage, maybe more. There was a slim chance the Coast Guard might intercept his vessel at the legal limit. Or run into it. Once we motored into international waters, the Cubans might shoot—at the sailboat or at us. Each scenario added to my terror. Time warped with excruciating slowness, pressing each into my mind.

The coastline recedes from sight as we push into the deep blue cradle of the sea. Dull sky meets dark sea in a seamless, impenetrable sheet of gray. Our engines churn ahead, though headway is illusive in this endless bowl.

We have been underway for over two hours; at this pace we'll reach Cuba in ten hours, by dawn. I glance back at the solemn crew; all eyes scout the bleak field. Our intrepid armada fans across the ocean, its lights like fallen stars wavering in the gloom.

With the pounding of the ship, my knees bend; wet clothes stick to gooseflesh; fear chokes my breath. Shivering, I strain to see in the coming darkness. Generations of experience percolate in my blood: I'm ready for a fight. I will either save my child or die the way of a buccaneer.

Tears roll down my checks, as I beg Yemayá, *dentro*, like Papi taught me. *Show me the way.* Into the relentless wind, I sing at the top of my lungs.

"*Ven, ven, mi amor. Tu eres mío. El mio. No luches mas, ven aquí.*"

Over and over again, like a warrior on a rampage, I repeat the cry of my Ancestors, until my fears abate. I surrender to the will of the Great Mother, when the answer appears: the mermaid goddess sails into view, a bejeweled trident in her hand, iridescent locks tumbling over her naked torso. With simple clarity she speaks to me in a high-pitched eerie voice. *Have Faith.*

With regret, I recall Tilly's admonition to finish my Sailors' Valentine. Would I be chasing Santiago on the high seas if I had turned that corner? I vow to Yemayá: *If you will keep my baby from your watery arms, I'll craft as many Valentines in your honor as I can.*

A pair of bottlenose dolphins appears; their sleek torpedo shapes roll on the surf on either side of the prow, as if pulling us to our destination. I wave to the captain, pointing frantically as the pod veers east. He changes course with the blast of the horn and our fellow ships follow.

The dolphins leap high and dive into the darkness. I wait for them to reappear, knowing they are gone. A cold hand grips my heart. Is it a false sign? My eyes burn from the strain as I scour the rolling surface.

At last, in the distance, I spy a shadowy shape rise and fall among the waves. My heart beats as fast as a hummingbird's wings at orange blossom time. It's a sail. A red sail.

I point towards it, shouting over the wind. Again, the roar of the ship's horn rips through the air and we continue as the crow flies. In no time, our mighty trio surrounds the small craft, forcing the captain, a weathered old Cuban, to lower his sail. We pull abeam, our engines shift to neutral, as one of our crew tosses a rope to the old man.

He looks bewildered to be caught in our net. "*¿Qué pasa?*"

It's a ruse; my heart detects my child's unmistakable scent.

"He's got my baby. She's here!"

A tall wiry fisherman scrambles over the bow towards me; Tilly has instructed him to hold me back.

From the flybridge, Carlos tells the fugitive captain we're looking for my kidnapped child. "*Buscamos un bebé secuestrada.*"

The old man shrugs, pretending to know nothing. "*No sé nada.*"

"*¡Váya!*" Carlos orders one of our men on board.

Santiago appears from under a tarp, holding you. "I'm taking my daughter to Cuba. Viva Fidel!"

I scream. "No!"

Deadly tension braces the company; no one moves. A strong wave could knock you from his grasp and send you flying into the dark blue abyss.

Santiago's fearful eyes dart from one ship to the next. Then he fixes his hatred on me as he raises you above his head.

"She belongs to Cuba or no one."

A glorious streak of shimmering light breaks through the matted haze, awaking a blue marlin. The beast shoots high into the air, a mere five yards away, and lands with a shuddering splash.

The Captain? *I like to think so.*

While the others stare in amazement, Tilly heaves her bulk over the gunwale and snatches you from your father's grasp. Two men swarm past her like worker bees after the queen and pin him down.

Tilly gingerly hands you to Carlos, their hands stretched between the two boats. Slipping and sliding, I make my way to the cockpit. At last I hold you in my arms, your unique softness like a limb reattached.

Our engines rev, the old fisherman throws off the line. *La Libertad* turns about, our escorts in tow. I cradle you to my breast in the Captain's fishing chair, my feet braced on the stern, my heart full of gratitude.

As we pull away, Santiago's angry threats fly on the wind. "I'll get her back, you'll see." I'm as good as dead to him. "*Estás muerta, princessa.*"

Sooner or later, he will punish me. Like the Almighty, his is a vengeful love. Tilly and I never debated whether or not I should leave town; it was the only option. We stopped at Howard Johnson's to satisfy the ravenous hunger a windy sea outing can bring, before Carlos drove us to Miami. It might have been an ordinary shopping trip, except for my packed bags, the knot in my gut, and the sad sighs my dear friend heaved beside me. I stared out the window, memorizing every bit, wondering how we would survive. Some transplants never did.

Tilly squeezed my hand. "Home is wherever your child is, believe me."

"Do you have children? I never asked."

"It doesn't matter anymore."

How would I manage without this angel of mercy?

"Come with us."

Her voice trembled. "I thought about it. A second chance, that's what you've been to me. Faith, too, I love her like my own. Oh, hell, I'm too old to start over, and well…" To my amazement, a rosy blush crept over her cheeks as she jerked her head towards Carlos. "I've got good reason to stay put."

"What am I going to do?"

"Are you kidding me? You saltwater folks are survivors." That faraway witchy look stole over her. "You'll be back. I can't say when, but I guarantee it."

For once, her predictions offered little solace. I thought of Jesus entering the wilderness for forty days and forty nights. Had he felt this lonely? But then, the Holy Spirit had accompanied him, while I felt as empty as a discarded clamshell.

As I brushed a lock of shiny black hair from your sweet face, I decided you would grow up free of the past and the overwhelming fear for your soul. Never would you suffer as I had, not if I could help it.

At last, we entered the final stretch of highway into the mainland. A traffic sign read: *Gator Crossing.* Conchs, too, I thought.

A wall of white noon light bleached the sky above the downtown Greyhound bus terminal. Carlos carried my things, as he and Tilly walked behind us, already receding into the past. Bums sprawled on benches with too much skin exposed; the smell of urine replaced the briny sea air. An exciting crossroads to many, to me, the station felt like the end of the road.

Inside, I scanned a large board offering destinations and hope. *Pick a city. Freedom waits.* Each option presented a different life. Which was the right choice? The responsibility was daunting; my courage faltered.

Tilly sidled up beside me. "It's like Shell Talk, Kiddo. Listen and the answer will come."

At the top of the board, a light blinked for the next departure to Fort Myers Sanibel Island. She pointed to a pastel-colored poster of beachcombers in the stooped position of shelling on pristine sand. Underneath, it read: *Sanibel Island, The Shell Capital Of The World. Forty minutes from Fort Myers.*

She seemed so certain. "Isn't that what you want?"

I recalled my promise to continue the tradition of Sailors' Valentines. Yet my newfound determination to escape the past pointed in another direction. At that moment, floundering like a fish on land, I found purchase in the familiar.

"I guess so."

"Better hurry." Tears streamed down her flushed face. Underneath her mock scowl, I felt her love. "You take care of that baby and yourself, too, or you'll answer to me."

"I'm going to miss you, Tilly."

"Me too, like hell." She thrust a thick envelope from Howard Johnson's into my purse. "Severance pay."

I tried to refuse it. "Oh. I can't."

"You better."

"I'll send it back, soon as I can."

"Never mind, you paid me plenty." She closed us in her hefty arms and kissed the back of your head. Too quickly, she released us.

Carlos tipped his hat with a blessing. "*Vaya con Dios.*"

I kissed his cheek. "*Gracias.*"

He smiled as he wrapped his arm around my friend, who looked petite and happy beside him.

I lifted my bag and carried you down a tiled hallway. Your moist cheek lay in the hollow of my neck, your monkey grip clinging to the straps of my sundress. What an imposter—I had no right to be a mother. How would I ever care for us?

Swallowed up in the noisy interior, I wished I'd taken Willow's Valentine, *Forget Me Not*. In time I forgot about it, as well as my promise to remember who I was. Now you know our story, Faith. Please, don't forget who you are. *No olvides quien eres.*

* * * * *

KEY WEST, FLORIDA

SUMMER 1985

As the Valentine Mobile passed mile marker thirty-eight point seven on the Overseas Highway, dawn stretched soft pink arms across the ocean. Angel leaned forward in her seat like a rider in the saddle urging speed from her mount, while Max kept a steady pace.

"Bahia Honda," she said, wistfully. She looked to the West Hump, imagining the day her mother had sighted a sailfish. "The Captain proposed to my mother here, or so I like to think."

"I remember." He gave her a quick, happy smile. "Perhaps it is not the moment or perhaps there is none better. *Ach!* I do not know about such things. Will you marry me, Angel?

"Max."

"Yes?"

"No."

"No, then?" he said, sadly.

"No," she said. "I just meant, oh, heavens, I don't know what I meant." As tickled as she was at the prospect of being his wife, Angel reminded herself that she had little to offer. A fact she must soon confess.

"Forgive me," Max said. "It is not the time. Allow me another chance, when your daughter is safe." At her worried look, he added, "All will be well, I promise."

"We should go straight to his apartment," she said.

"Do you know where?"

"If I know Santiago, he's right where I left him. He never did anything he said. I don't know why I believed it would be any different now."

“And if he is not there?”

Her shoulders slumped. “Then we go to the police.”

By the time they drove onto Stock Island, the sun was in a hurry to light the sky. On either side of Roosevelt Boulevard lay the wide expanse of the Gulf of Mexico and the Atlantic Ocean, separated by a concrete road.

“Turn here,” Angel said, as they reached College Road.

As they wove past the community college, a dingy, gray concrete apartment building came into view. Angel gasped. Her former love nest.

“There it is,” she said, through a fit of coughing.

As soon as Max parked on the road, she began to bolt. He held her arm.

“Angel. You must allow me to take care of this.”

She had always taken care of herself and now this trustworthy man was at her side. “Okay,” she said. “But I’m coming with you.”

He took her hand as they walked to the entrance, where they found a row of mailboxes.

“It’s number one-oh-three,” she whispered.

The occupant’s name was rubbed out, the metal box locked.

She tugged at his hand. “Let’s go to his door.”

Instead, he pulled her forward. “First, we investigate.”

She hardly recognized his hardened demeanor. His accent had thickened, perhaps as it had been in the war of his youth.

A middle-aged Latino man swept past them as they rounded the corner of the building. Max pinned Angel against the wall as he faced off with the stranger.

“It’s not him,” she hissed.

The stranger mumbled in Spanish as he continued ahead. Max stepped away, releasing her. Maybe he could handle this. Finally, a real savior.

The parking lot was crammed with old cars. Near the end wall sat a dusty pick-up truck with a cargo bed full of building debris and a cheap plastic bilingual sign: *Faith Construction — Construcción de fe*. As they came closer, they saw the Red Bug tucked on the other side.

"Let's go," Angel said with a note of triumph.

Again, Max stayed her hand. "No."

Angel stared out the car window at Santiago's apartment, impervious to the fluffy white clouds threading the blue sky or the stark sunlight soaking into the glossy green grass. She twisted to look out the back of the car then scanned the perimeter of the building as she had done, over and over, for two hours.

"Can't we just knock on the door?" she asked, repeating the question she'd put to Max many times.

And he gave a fresh version of the same answer. "With the element of surprise, we gain an advantage. If we knock on the door, who is to say he will open it? Or use Faith as a wedge against you? Better, you see, to separate them."

"I guess he has to come out some time."

He rested his hand on her shoulder. "Exactly what I am saying, *Schatzi.*"

"But Faith…"

"He may threaten, but after all, she is his daughter. He is not a monster."

"He can be."

"Perhaps," Max said. "However, he wants something from you and, as long as he has Faith, he has a hold on you. You must trust me."

She recalled Santiago's spiteful threat to her on that awful day at sea. She was a dead woman. Well, he would soon be right about that. At least, Faith must understand the extreme measures Angel had taken to hide from her father.

Angel felt his presence right before the apartment door banged shut. She ducked down in the seat, her heart slamming. Peering over the window's edge, she saw a down-at-the-heels version of the young man she had once loved. A beer belly strained Santiago's scruffy tan shirt and camouflage pants. No more the idealistic revolutionary, his bushy beard, now flecked with gray, and lined face suggested defeat. With a slight stoop, he pounded the ground in his lace-up boots to a hostile rhythm only he could hear.

"It's him," she whispered.

"Stay here," Max said, jumping out.

Angel watched him hurry across the lawn, aware that the vicious predator outmatched her well-intentioned shopkeeper. What did she have to fear now that death held her in its crosshairs? She sprinted after Max and, as she rounded the corner into the parking lot, saw Santiago square off with him.

"You talking to me, man?" he said, his voice slurred with drink.

His sightline shifted to Angel with an electric jolt of anger. A sick smile slid over his face. When Max looked over his shoulder at her, Santiago clocked him cold. Her would-be hero tumbled to the ground.

"Max," she cried, running to his side.

Blood trickled from his mouth onto the pavement. Dazed and hurt, he tried to wave Angel away as she bent over him. His eyes darted up, wide with fear, as a strong hand gripped her throat.

Santiago hauled her to her feet, slamming her against his truck. She heard the window crack. A searing pain tore across her head. For a moment, the world turned bright red. He pinned her against the hot metal, her feet dangling above ground, his cock hard against her thigh.

"*Hola, princessa.*" Pressing his hot, sweaty face close, Santiago smothered her with a wet kiss. "Miss me?"

"Let me go!" she said, and here came the sharp stinging slap—just like old times.

"You don't tell me what to do. You fucking that guy?"

Another slap, harder this time. Angel tasted bitter blood and the wilting urge to appease the angry master. But she was no longer a confused girl cowering in the name of love; she was a mother full of fury. She spit in his face.

"You bastard."

Santiago flinched. Neither did he expect the swift kick she landed in his groin. Cupping his crotch, he doubled over, moaning. She grabbed a plank of wood from the truck, and as she lifted it in the air, he looked up to meet her vengeance.

Whack! Angel brought the board down on his head and he crumpled into a silent heap. Blood pounded in her temples, as she dug into his pants pocket for his keys. From where he lay, he grabbed her wrist, bending it until she feared the bones would snap. She cried out, clawing at him in vain with her free hand.

Sudden release landed her on her ass. Smeared with blood and dirt, Max stood over them, one shoe pinning Santiago's hand.

"Go, get Faith," he said.

She seized the keys and ran.

From the modest hotel balcony, Angel watched the young children on the beach below chase the receding waves, running once more in retreat. Their electric squeals punctured the lazy air. The ocean swirled at their ankles—a cool, salty blessing from Yemayá.

At last Angel unwrapped the desperate hope she had carried for days: her daughter was safe. The nurse at the clinic had given her a clean bill of health. Faith had a chance to start her life anew. Would she take it?

The dynamic duo, Jesus and his cohort Lucifer, had kept their part of the bargain. Now what did they expect of Angel? The details of the next great adventure would come soon enough, but here and now, what about Max? The thought of him made her heart swell. Like the sea, life was rolling away from her, even as it came barreling ahead.

"Mom?" Faith called from inside.

Angel stubbed out her cigarette, waving away the smell. As she stepped into the room, she met the reproach in her daughter's eyes.

"You're awake," Angel said, hoping to change the subject.

"You promised to quit," Faith said, propping herself up with pillows.

"And I will. Now that you're okay."

"I feel gross." She gulped down a glass of water.

Angel pulled a chair close to the bed while Faith picked at a hole in the bedspread that sprouted white stuffing. The rope burns on her wrists would heal but what about the heartbreak? Like mother, like daughter, would Faith hold onto loss and longing for decades?

The quiet hum of the air conditioning and the soft crash of waves filled the silence between them. Then Faith said, "Wayne's a jerk. We had a huge fight. That Southern chick showed up at his place and I freaked out. Can you believe he took her side? He was drunk, as usual. I packed my bags and split for Key West."

"You know," Angel said. "My father was a lot like yours, though they'd both hate the comparison. And I saw similar traits in Wayne. The

Captain used to say all men are bastards. It isn't true, Kiddo; there are good men, too."

"Wayne's nothing like the Captain." At her mother's inquiring look, she said, "I read your story. You're a good writer, Mom." Her approval erased her previous rejection of Angel's "stories." "When can I meet him?" Faith added.

Angel hesitated. "You didn't read the end?"

"My stupid boyfriend—ex-boyfriend—ripped them up."

"Well," she said, recalling the timely appearance of a blue marlin that saved the sea rescue. "The Captain died right after you were born."

"Oh." Faith tugged at the bedspread again. "What about your mother?"

"I wish I knew what happened to her."

"I bet I could find her."

"I bet you could, Kiddo. Speaking of which, there's still time to register for college."

Faith's eyes welled with tears. Rubbing a tuft of cotton between her fingers, she began in a quiet voice, "You know, Dad was really happy to see me. When I met him at that shitty little apartment, we just looked at each other. I swear it was like we already knew each other." She shook her head in disbelief as she flicked a wound ball of cotton onto the floor. "Like, how I fidget? He does the same thing. Isn't that weird?"

Angel nodded, willing her to go on.

"I didn't even have to say who I was," Faith continued. "He hugged me. He said he knew he'd see me one day. It felt good, you know, the hug, somehow normal. I'd imagined meeting him so many times that it wasn't strange or uncomfortable." She shivered and pulled up the blanket around her shoulders.

"He took me to a fish place for dinner and asked a ton of questions—about my childhood, school, my plans for the future. He asked if I was saved and insisted we go to church together. I would have, too; I was just happy to be with him."

She fell quiet, and when she began a moment later, her voice cracked. "Things was good for awhile. Then he stopped asking about me and only wanted to know about you— ridiculous, stupid questions like what you wore, how much money your books made, if you were dating anyone. At first I thought it would bring us closer, but whenever we talked about you he just got mean and angry.

"Then, two days ago, he wasn't there. I waited for hours, sitting on his doorstep like some desperate kid. It was dark when he finally showed up, roaring drunk and pissed off at the whole world, ranting about his boss and pissed as hell at you. He seemed like a different person, you know?"

"I'm so sorry," Angel said.

Faith had been holding in the pain, maybe for years; at last the tears fell in small streaks down her soft cheeks. She struggled to get the words out. "I tried to leave. He caught me, tied me to the chair. I couldn't believe it. He told me he'd let me go when you showed up. 'A trade,' he called it." Through fits of sobs came the big hurt. "He said I was a mistake, that you never wanted me."

"Oh, honey, that's a bald-faced lie." Angel shot to her side and rocked her in her arms. "A lie he invented to make up for his failure. You were—you *are*—the best thing that ever happened to me, Faith Rose Valdes del Corazón."

"It's a cool name," Faith said, as she dried her tears on her sleeve.

"It'll look cool in your byline, too."

Faith tucked her chin down. "I'm sorry about the money, Mom. I'll pay you back, I promise."

"Don't worry," Angel swallowed hard, wondering how long she could hide the truth. "I have a book or two left in me. I mean, who ya gonna call?"

"Ghostbusters." The eager light of ambition, extinguished for months, lit Faith's face once more. "I'll go to community college," she went on with new determination, "Get a part-time job. I can save money living at home. In a year or two, I could transfer to UT."

"Good idea," Angel said. It might not be the dream, but it was an exciting new beginning, a change in course that would send the ghosts to sea.

A tap on the door jolted Angel from a light nap. *Santiago?* As she took in the hotel room, and saw Faith sleeping peacefully, she exhaled. They were safe. Angel hurried to find Max outside, a wide bandage above a swollen black-and-blue eye. Stepping into the hallway, she fell into his comforting embrace.

"Oh, Max."

"*Schatzi*," he said.

She liked the team they had become in crisis. "How can I ever thank you?"

"I'm here for you, always."

Always, but not forever.

She tilted her head, searching his expression. She should tell him now; she owed him the truth. Hadn't he proven his loyalty and love? And then he kissed her, and she couldn't interrupt it with sorrow. How many meaningful moments were there left to share?

"What happened?" she said at last.

Max led her to a railing that overlooked a shaded courtyard dotted with fuzzy ferns. The thick humidity gave the stucco walls a slightly moist sheen. A pair of middle-aged, sunburned men, wearing cargo shorts and flip-flops, passed underneath, hand in hand.

"I called the police from a neighbor's apartment, an older woman who bandaged me," Max said. "She had experienced several unpleasant incidents with Valdes and insisted I wait there. Obviously, I could not hold him as prisoner."

"Thank heavens you didn't try."

"*Ach!*" He shook his head in dismay. "If only I could have."

Her brow knitted with worry. "Tell me."

"Perhaps twenty minutes later, Deputy Sheriff Gonzalez arrived with a young colleague whose name I cannot recall. Their guns and stoic expressions—I confess I was nervous."

He paused to wipe his brow with a linen handkerchief. "The sheriff banged on his apartment door, but no one answered. It fell open, in fact. Everywhere, quite a mess. 'Somebody left in a hurry,' Gonzalez said." Max stared down at the tile floor, his voice heavy. "The truck was also gone. I'm sorry to say Valdes escaped."

"Oh, no," Angel said.

"My dear, you want a final ending, but life does not always comply. You needn't worry, I will protect you."

"What about Faith?" Angel said in a small voice.

"I don't believe he will hurt her. Already he had the chance, no? Perhaps he is gone for good. Deputy Gonzalez will search the island. They will notify Tampa, in case he appears there."

Angel studied the profusion of plants below. Ripe on her tongue was the realization that, once she was gone, Santiago's motive to retaliate would also disappear. If she wasn't going to waste precious time on fruitless medical treatments, she sure wasn't going to spend another minute worrying about her ex.

“You’re right,” she said. “It’s like a sunken ship, gone forever.”

Max turned her to him, his smile and touch like cool salve. “You see, my beautiful mermaid, you are free.”

“Free and happy.” She buried her face in his shoulder, for comfort and to hide unspoken thoughts.

An incandescent white sheen permeated the afternoon, its heat heavy on Angel’s shoulders. She carried a package of snacks and items from the drug store, as she treaded a purple carpet of bell-shaped Jacaranda flowers on the sidewalk. Here, along the passageways of her youth, painful memories collected around her. Like fish caught in a net, they were flapping for attention, but she ignored them.

Glancing at her watch, she made a detour past the hotel. *One last look, for old times’ sake.*

Soon she reached her destination. The Tropical Arms Apartment House now sported a coat of mint paint with white trim, an unsuccessful effort to ward off its weariness. To her surprise, the wind chimes still hung in front of Tilly’s old door. As a gentle wind stirred their delicate notes, she ached to see her old friend. Perhaps they would meet again, in heaven or hell, along with the Captain, too.

As she turned to leave, she heard an unmistakable voice. “Angelica?”

Had she imagined it? She hesitated, fixed on the hypnotic mosaic of blue sky and green foliage.

Again, came the call. “Is that you, Angelica?”

It was her mother, no doubt about it. She stood two doors down, mere yards away, yet eighteen years of silence barred Angel’s way. Santiago hadn’t changed, why expect that Mother had?

Tilly answered the question, as clearly as if she'd stood on the lawn. *We're all lost at sea, Kiddo. All you can do is make the kindest choice possible when it's your turn at the wheel.* Her old friend's reminder pushed Angel across the lawn.

"Mother."

"Goodness," Mary said, wiping her hands on a faded housedress. "I'm so happy to see you."

On closer inspection, Angel saw the change in her. Though time had weathered her skin and robbed her bones of vitality, her eyes shone bright and the beaming smile belonged to a vibrant woman.

"I had no idea you were here," Angel said. She noted the nameplate that read Mary Porreca. Had shame led her to drop her married name?

"Can you stay awhile?" her mother asked.

"A short visit, yes."

Angel followed her inside. The sun angled low, catching the dance of dust motes and wrapping the old wooden furniture, a scaled-down version of their former life, in a warm glow.

"Shall we have tea?" Mary said.

Angel nodded, trailing her to the tiny kitchen. A mixing bowl full of flour beside a bunch of overripe bananas recalled the childhood pleasure of banana bread.

Mary lit the stove. "How long are you in town?"

"Not long."

A ceramic teapot painted with frolicking, half-naked mermaids caught Angel's eye. In the past, her mother never would have allowed such heathen images. She smiled at Angel's curious appraisal.

"It reminds me of your grandmother Willow," she said, busily preparing tea and cookies. "She was a mermaid, or so she thought. After all, if you think something is true, then it must be true for you."

“I’m not sure what you mean.” Personal belief, not scripture, now ruled Mother?

“Along the way, I came to understand how our beliefs determine the future. Shall we sit down?”

She led Angel to the old oak dining table, which was too big for the room, and somehow humbled and softened like its owner. Mary sat ramrod straight as ever, looking elegant rather than severe. The old, familiar ritual—lace place mats, an embroidered cozy, the citrusy aroma of Earl Grey—set Angel at ease, despite a gulf of hurt.

Not knowing where to begin, she offered a safe statement. “You look good.”

“Thank you,” Mary said. “I feel good. And how are you?”

“Fine,” Angel said, studying the blue and white Willowware dishes. “I followed Faith here. She came to look for her father. I never told her his name or yours until now.”

Full of remorse, she waited to be reprimanded, only to receive warm sympathy.

“It must have been difficult for her to approach him,” Mary said. “Was he receptive?”

“At first, though he used her to seek vengeance on me. She’s heartbroken.”

“That’s a pity. A young girl needs a family’s support. I’m sorry you didn’t have mine, Angelica.”

And just like that, her simple apology lifted the tired weight from Angel’s heart. Unable to form a response, she offered a small smile.

The tangy aroma of the tea seeped into the air as Mary poured. The tilt of her wrist, the angle of her chin, the precision had not changed. Mother and daughter placed their left hands in their laps as they brought the delicate cups to their lips, the same way Faith had mirrored this habit over the years.

"You'll like your granddaughter," Angel said. "She's a lot like you."

"Is that a fact?"

"Smart as a whip. Disciplined, too, but stubborn as a shark on the scent."

As her words hung in the silence between them, Angel fought the impulse to soften her description. If she couldn't speak her mind, a reunion meant nothing.

Mary crumbled a cookie on her plate and sighed. "I'm sure you've been a good parent. I've enjoyed following your impressive career and must tell you how much I love Stella the Starfish."

It was the first time Angel could remember her mother giving her any praise. The joy that lifted her spirits took her by surprise.

"Thank you," she said in a girlish voice.

"Your grandmother Willow was not of this world—a dreamer, lost to her imagination and visions. Lord knows you reminded me of her. I feared for you, I truly did. Now I can see I was harder on you than necessary. I couldn't bear to lose you the way I'd lost her." As soft tears began to rain down her lined face, she placed her hand over Angel's. "I hope we can start over."

"Me, too," Angel said.

A mischievous glint came into Mary's eyes. "Come, I want to show you something."

She led her down the hallway. As they came near a bedroom door, Angel recognized the intimate whisper of the sea. *Ven, ven, mi amor.* Here was the source of the change in her mother—a workshop of Sailors' Valentines.

"Tilly?"

"Tilly Kemble, what would I have done without her? When I fell from grace, I wanted to die, like your father. I thought he took the easy way out. As if a sinner like me had any right to judge."

Mary picked up a conical Ladder Horn from the worktable, rubbing it between her fingers, as she went on. "I hadn't realized Tilly lived here. Lord, she was a noisy neighbor. On Sundays, when I cried the most, she shouted at my door in that brassy voice. 'Mrs. Corazón, you can't hide forever. You got a lot of living to do.' A year passed before I let her in. I guess I'd run out of tears. She bullied me into shell work and we fought like cats and dogs until, gradually, I began to listen."

She pointed to a Sailors' Valentine hung in the center of the wall. The handiwork lacked fluidity and nuance but carried a message full of feeling: *Forgive Me.*

"My first effort," she said. "Tilly said it proved I had seawater in my veins, no matter what I said."

"What happened to her?" Angel asked.

"She and Carlos were on an overnight fishing trip when a powerful storm hit. They never came back. At least they were together. The locals held a party in the courtyard then paraded down Duval to Mallory Square to watch the sunset. Tilly would have approved. I think she was an angel sent to earth."

"A sweet bully with angel wings." Angel dreaded bringing up the subject, but she had to know. "And the Captain, what happened?"

"The fishermen buried him at sea." A familiar sternness crept into her voice. "Angelica, don't blame yourself for the past. We're all little children struggling to find peace with God."

Angel's old defenses flared. *Please, not another sermon.*

"Your father had his path, I had mine, and you have yours," Mary continued. "I used to think there was only one way. How silly. God is big enough to love each of us, no matter how we worship."

She tapped the edge of a Valentine-in-progress, its delicate artistry equal to any prized work. It depicted a mermaid goddess shimmering on the horizon, over an azure sea in which the embedded message read: *Come Home.*

"I started this three months ago," she said. "The process never ceases to amaze me. Sometimes I feel like I'm touching heaven."

"Maybe you are." Angel laughed out loud, imitating their old friend. "'Heck, I never said it was easy, but it's the best game in town.'"

Mary chuckled. "That was Tilly. Does Faith know shell work?"

"Not yet."

"Then we'll have to teach her, won't we?"

"I'm counting on it."

It was almost noon, the time of day when every corner of the sky surrendered to the sun's embrace. The ocean below waited like a lover, open and wanting, its sequined waves dancing in the bright light. Max parked in the lot at Rest Beach and gave Angel an expectant look.

"What is it?" she said.

"You promised," he said.

"Really?" But he looked intent, so she laughed. "All right."

Hand in hand, she led him away from the picnic area, where her family and friends were gathering. Soon, the sweltering heat gave way beneath the fluffy green fringe of a grove of Casuarina pines.

"I think it was here," Angel said, coming to a stop in a sandy clearing.

"Are you sure?" Max said. "It will count for nothing if you are off. Look again."

"It was such a long time ago."

"Surely, for me, one small thing you can remember."

She circled around, holding out her arms, looking for something to spark her memory. A glint of sunshine slanted through the trees. She blinked in a daze, overwhelmed by deep impressions her teenage body had made: Santiago on their first date, his taut strong body reclining with ease, the halo of smoke, the magnetic stare with which he had pulled her to him. How young she had been; how irresistible he was.

"Yes, here," Angel said. "I had my first kiss."

"Very well." Max kissed her harder than usual, then whispered in her ear. "A new map of memories we shall make, yes?"

"I hope so." She was on the verge of revealing her illness, when he produced a handful of old letters tied with red and white baker's twine. "What's that?"

"I intended to tell you many times and…" His face colored, the German accent thickened. "You arrived at Maeapple's party like a goddess in your orange dress and me, an old shopkeeper. But your name was Rose, not Corazón, though the eyes fit her description, 'bewitching green, like the ocean on a sunny day,' and you had a daughter named Faith."

"Whose description?" Angel said, though a knowing feeling suggested the answer.

"Please," he said, holding up a hand. "After the party, I searched my old correspondence to confirm my suspicion. No, not suspicion. Who was I to question your story? The war had taught me that secrets could save a life." He tapped the packet in his hand. "*Mein Gott*, a fire went through me when I knew it was you. For many years I nurtured a ridiculous romantic fantasy. I would find Angel del Corazón and share the love of shells and perhaps more." He shrugged. "Time passed and I forgot this beautiful dream until you walked into my store."

He thrust the packet at her. "Perhaps this will explain."

An envelope addressed to Max was stapled to the front of each letter. Flipping through the stack, Angel noted an address in Miami, where she recalled he had lived. The postmarks ran from 1972 through 1979. As soon as she saw the familiar scrawl on Howard Johnson's stationery, she knew who had written to him.

August 15, 1972

Hello there Max,

It's always good to see you at the Shell Show. Thanks for the tip. I added brown to the acrylic mix and my frames look like classy antiques!

I've enclosed a photo of Angel del Corazón, the girl we discussed who lives on Sanibel Island with her child, Faith. If you happen to cross paths, I hope you'll remember your promise to give her a helping hand. I might as well tell you, the shells say you will meet one day, and Shell Talk is never wrong! Drop me a line when you run into her, will you?

See you next year. Can you believe I sold two Valentines? You know, I wish I had them back!

Your Friend In Shells,

Tilly Kemble

The yellowed Polaroid confirmed how young Angel had been. Tilly stood beside her in front of the restaurant with a mischievous grin. Golden sunlight lit their faces, their bond clear as the day.

Max spoke softly, "My last letter was marked *return to sender*. I placed several calls and was sad to learn she passed away. I hope you do not think less of me."

Angel caressed his face. "How could I?" There was no escaping the truth. "Max, when we go home, I'll need serious medical treatment."

A look of surprise, then realization, filled his face, as if his concerns were confirmed.

"Yes, of course, *Schatzi.* Whatever you need."

"I'm afraid I can't promise you anything," she said. "Even if I'd like to."

"Don't worry, I am here for you."

"I'm not worried." It was a perfect day and she intended to treasure it. "Come, let's join the others."

As they retraced their path, Angel studied the beads of sunlight twinkling on the sea like diamonds on a jeweler's velvet cloth. A light breeze rustled the palm fronds, carrying an echo of the buccaneer's song. *Ven, ven, mi amor.* She had a fight on her hands, but if the Captain could wrest salvation from the sea, *mano á mano*, so could she.

"Did you know?" Max said. "Mrs. Kemble said your shell work was the best she ever had seen."

"Really?" Angel said. "I was only a beginner. I wish I had completed a Sailors' Valentine."

"Shall we make one together?"

"Yes, I'd like that. As many as we can."

Made in the USA
Columbia, SC
02 March 2022

57075327R00174